TRUE TARGET

An Urban Assassin Novel

by Austin S. Camacho

Cover Designed by: GinnefineArt.com

ISBN: 979-8988533351 - PAPERBACK
ISBN: 978-1940758930 - EPUB

Published by:
Audecyn Books, LLC
Upper Marlboro, MD USA

TRUE TARGET
An Urban Assassin Novel

Chapter 1

"Housekeeping!"

The knock was insistent, but the voice reflected the boredom Gomez expected.

"Yeah, hang on a sec." He gulped down half the bottle of cheap red wine, rolled off the bed and landed lightly on his bare feet. Two steps later he flipped the security chain aside and opened the door.

The woman's facial expression was as bored as her voice had advertised, but otherwise this was a nice surprise. Dark skin and a face that was pretty enough but not too pretty under the long dreadlocks. Her eyes were even darker than her skin. He liked her mouth, with no lipstick. Maybe not too much up top but with her holding an armload of towels he couldn't really tell anyway.

As she brushed past him, he couldn't miss the natural swivel. Even under the stupid maid's smock he could see she had a prize-winning ass. She went straight to the bathroom to dump the towels. He pushed the door closed and stood in front of it, smiling.

When she came out, she stopped as if expecting something. She was staring straight at his bare chest. He knew it wasn't just because it was at her eye level. Yes, she was maybe five foot five or six, but her eyes would go there anyway because not many Hispanic guys have hair there. Then, as expected, her eyes traced down his chiseled abs to the top of his jeans.

"Did you need something?" she asked in a lilting Jamaican accent. "You know they don't supply shampoo or conditioner and that stuff here."

"The girl yesterday came in smoking a joint," he said. "I scored from her, and I was thinking maybe you got some to replace what I smoked up."

The maid played with the top button of her smock and favored him with half a smile. "I don't got no ganja, but I think I can offer you some other services. If you got the cash."

Gomez had been holed up in that dump for nearly two weeks. He was ready for some fun. "I just might be interested if I like the merchandise."

The maid kicked off her sensible shoes, turned to rest one palm on the bed and, now in profile, poked her derriere out. Her left hand gripped her smock and began to slowly slide it up her body until the hem just reached the bottom of her enticing curves. Gomez liked the trim, athletic legs, the thighs just thick enough. He imagined them wrapped around his waist.

"Yeah, I can definitely cover the price of some of that."

The bed squeaked as she placed both palms and one knee on it. "Well, then, let's not waste too much time, eh?"

Gomez moved to the bed. As he also got one knee on the tattered spread, she raised one finger in front of his face.

"First, I got to see the cash please."

Of course. In his experience it was always pay before play. He leaned forward to pull his wallet from his left hip pocket. He figured her for a fifty-dollar girl and he would sweat his money's worth out of her before noon. Her smile never dimmed. Her small teeth were perfect, her eyes bright with anticipation.

The swift blow to the throat startled him. The web of flesh between her thumb and forefinger was hard enough to make his tongue stick out. Her other hand's stiffened fingertips thrust into his solar plexus, pushing the breath out of him.

He was stunned but only for a second. They had tapped Gomez to kill that boy two weeks ago because he had been on the streets all his life and handled business for his gang smoothly for nearly a decade. No black bitch was going to take him down by surprise.

His right cross was lightning and would have taken her head off if she hadn't ducked under it. She slapped the back of his arm, pushing him further forward and slipped behind him. Her wiry left arm whipped around his throat. Her right slid under his right arm, the hand coming up to grip the back of his head. Her left leg wrapped his waist. Her right leg rose to clamp his right arm down.

"It's a little different when it's not a nine-year old, ain't it?" she whispered. "Guess nobody ever taught you rule number one."

Desperate to free himself, Gomez reached up with his left to grab a handful of braided hair. The dreadlocks pulled free in his hand. Then he pushed up to his feet and with the last of his energy snapped his body backward, smashing the girl against the wall. She grunted but clung to him tightly.

The classic choke hold was not designed to cut off breathing. The pressure was actually on the sides of the neck, stopping the blood flow to and from the brain. With the jugular vein and carotid artery clamped down, unconsciousness comes fast. His knees hit the tile floor hard, but Gomez was barely conscious of it. The last thing he was aware of was a hand slapping the wall from the other side, and a harsh voice screaming, "Hey! Keep it down in there."

Sometimes Skye wondered if the pay was worth the experience. Not the fight, the fight was nothing. But holding this sweaty pig, even breathing in this room that smelled of years of cigarettes, it was enough to turn her stomach. And if this casual, heartless murderer had to hide out, and was too stupid to leave town, why in God's name did he stay here? No refrigerator, no microwave, not even a hair dryer. No shampoo or conditioner in the bathroom. She could only imagine what Motels One through Five had been like.

But this was the job, and she needed to get to it. First, she inserted nose plugs soaked in chloral hydrate to keep Gomez asleep. After that, well, each one was different. Sometimes you wanted the world to know it was a mob hit. In that case, an ice pick to the medulla oblongata was good. Death by natural causes? To do that right, she'd do something tricky, like using a tiny .50 gauge needle to inject adenosine into the semilunar fold on the inside of the eye. In this case, certain people should know it was a hit, but not right away. There should be questions, enough to prompt a police investigation.

Skye pulled a syringe from the pocket of her maid's smock and pushed a shot of the barbiturate lorazepam into Gomez's neck. She pocketed the needle and pressed two fingers against Gomez's neck, feeling for a pulse until she could tell that his heart had given up. Then she gripped him under his shoulders and dragged him into the bathroom. The tub had a huge hair ball left over from when it was last cleaned, and there was a bit of standing water. No matter. She closed the stopper and turned the water on full force, both hot and cold.

While the tub filled, she faced another ugly part of the job. It wasn't just touching this slimy beast. She had to reach down and unzip his jeans. Then she reached under his ankles to grip the denim and heaved to pull the jeans off him. Next came the nasty boxers. Finally, she gripped him under his armpits and wrestled the corpse into the filling tub.

While water rose around the dead body, she fetched the wine bottle and stood it beside the tub. She pulled the dead man's right arm so that it hung over the side, not far from the bottle. She shut off the water, stepped back to survey the tableau and shrugged her shoulders.

At first blush, maybe suicide. A low-level thug nobody cares about drinks some drugged wine and relaxes in the tub and just floats away. Of course, depending on how long it took someone to notice he was here, there would be questions of whether there was enough lorazepam in his system to be fatal. Eventually someone would notice the bruises, subtle signs of a struggle. The medical examiner, if they were any good, would take another look and find the needle mark in his neck. They'd test the wine and find no drugs there. More questions, and by then too much time would have passed for finding forensic evidence in the room.

Then word would reach those who knew this slug that someone had taken action. And then the right people would start to get nervous.

Skye straightened her wig and brushed off her smock before she stepped out of the room and locked the door behind her. She was pleased with her work, and certain her client would be too.

Chapter 2

The woman stepping into the lobby of the JW Marriott Hotel bore little resemblance to the maid who had killed a man the day before beyond having the same height and weight. Professionally applied makeup softened and slightly lightened her complexion. Four-inch Louboutin heels and blonde hair piled high on her head made her appear a good deal taller. The simple black dress clung to her exaggerated form but implied understated elegance when paired with the Coach clutch purse and rope of pearls around her neck. A casual observer would probably dismiss her as a high-class call girl.

Despite the JW Marriott's Pennsylvania Avenue address she had had to walk around to the entrance on 14th street to enter the lobby. She strode across the polished parquet floor beneath the row of huge, phallic shaped chandeliers, ignoring the staff and other guests. She walked up the wide staircase from the dimly lit lobby to the much brighter gallery. As she rose to the floor level, she locked eyes with the man standing by the elevator. He was her height, with a ruddy complexion, neatly trimmed beard and salt-and-pepper hair. He pushed the button and by the time she reached him he was holding the doors open for her.

On their way up he asked, "Well, Skye, am I sufficiently dressed down? I found these slacks at Walmart and this corduroy jacket at Target. No one would suspect me of being a man of wealth, am I right?"

The doors slid apart and they moved down the hall toward his suite. She shook her head, but in a kind way.

"You've been an international shipping mogul for too long, Milo."

"Mogul?" Milo said. "Where'd you get a word like that?"

"From your bio online," Skye said. "The same one that called you reclusive, and said you kept your family out of the public eye. The point is, you might fool a lot of men, but no woman would fail to spot you as a man of wealth and power. In fact, a smart woman would instantly spot you for what you really are: a rich man trying not to look rich."

"I don't understand," Milo said, swiping his card to let them into the room. She stepped in, looking around. For such an expensive hotel, the room seemed very average. All black and white and silver with no more space than average and stock hotel paintings. It did have a magnificent view of city hall and the National Mall.

"You promised a snack," Skye said.

Milo pointed to a side table. Skye's face lit up as she moved toward the plate holding four crab cake sliders sitting beside a silver bowl piled high with thick cut fries. An opened bottle of wine stood by in a chafing dish.

"Why women?"

"A man might look at your jacket or pants," Skye said, sliding a well-padded chair up to the table and selecting a bun filled with crab cake. "When a smart woman looks at a man, the first thing she notices are his shoes and his watch. A man who cares about himself doesn't wear cheap shoes and he doesn't let them get run down. And there you stand in seven- hundred-dollar Ferragamo loafers." She took a big bite out of her slider, her smile widening even as she chewed.

"So I guess I need to ditch the Patek Philippe for a Timex."

"Yeah, that too," Skye said, pouring herself a glass of wine. "And on top of that, you smell of Clive Christian. Middle class men have never even heard of that cologne."

Milo settled onto the sitting room sofa. "Well, is the food at least to your liking?"

Skye nodded, filling the second glass with wine and examining the bottle's label. "It's all right. This New Zealand Sauvignon Blanc hits the spot too. But you can really make me smile if you tell me the funds transfer is done."

Milo sat forward. "Wait. Have you dispatched the first assignment already?"

Skye finished her slider before answering. "Crossed the first name off your list."

"Well then," Milo pulled out his phone and tapped some keys. "There. Thirty thousand just jumped into the account you gave me."

"Just the beginning," Skye said, standing to hand Milo his glass, then staring out the wide window at what some believe to be the halls of power. "Each of the five names will pay better than the one before, right?"

"As promised," Milo said. "And as I said, each will be more challenging to get to. But if you complete this commission, you will be half a million dollars richer."

"Don't worry. Like I told you the day we met, there's nobody that can't be got at. If the motive and the money are right."

"I owe it to my son," Milo told his glass before swallowing half its contents. Then, after staring at the glass for another moment he said, "After cancer took his mother, he was all I had. I couldn't strike out at that killer. But these killers, I can make them pay."

Skye returned to her seat and allowed what she considered to be a respectful amount of silence. Then she finished her wine, stood and smoothed her dress. After a breath, she rested her hand on his arm.

"Milo, trust and believe you will get the revenge you deserve on all the men involved with your son's death. I'll check in with you again when I get to the next rung on that ladder."

Milo's head snapped up as if he had been jolted out of a trance. "Wait. Why don't we take in a show? We can have a real dinner someplace nice. I don't have many friends here…"

"Sorry to disappoint," Skye said, moving toward the door. "But I got shit to do."

Chapter 3

Jayla Johnson unlocked her office door but hesitated just a moment before walking in. It was more than an hour after her usual office hours and even psychotherapists needed their personal time. *Especially psychotherapists*, she thought with a smirk. But some clients had special needs and sometimes you had to accommodate them. Besides, once in a while a client appeared whose mind might allow their doctor to add substantially to the profession's knowledge base.

Jayla walked through her waiting room without turning on a light. These offices on Connecticut Avenue were equipped with motion sensor lights, but she had disabled them. Not that it bothered her. She just took a dozen steps straight forward and pushed the door to her private office open. Even in darkness she could picture it clearly. To her left a comfortable chaise lounge. To her right, her desk. Ahead of her stood the padded armchair where she sat during some client sessions. A low antique table took up the space between the end of the chaise lounge and the armchair. The art deco lamp on the table was a twin to the one on her desk. She moved through the darkness, leaving her purse on the desk and picking up a pre-positioned notebook and pen on her way to her seat.

"Good evening, Doctor," said a voice out of the darkness. "Good dinner?"

"Hello, Skye. I just went to Ocean Prime down on G Street. Nice blackened snapper. Shall I just record our conversation tonight, or can we have the lights?"

"Lights will be okay this time."

Jayla had long since given up trying to figure out how Skye got into her office undetected. And in fact, it no longer mattered. Jayla was just glad she kept coming to her regularly scheduled appointments. When Skye first contacted her, she offered an odd incentive for accepting her as a patient. She said she was a unique patient, someone who could be the path to the Award for Research in Psychiatry, the prize they used to call the Hofheimer Prize. Winners are recognized for a contribution or a body of work that has a major impact on the field. Surely the inner workings of this particular mind would qualify. It was an interesting thought, but that impulse faded quickly. Jayla's focus shifted to finding a way to help this unique patient. Still, just the fact that she had chosen this incentive approach to get counseling revealed a great deal about her.

She reached to click on the light on the table and opened the notebook, already labeled "Skye Maddox." Jayla knew her office was one of very few places on earth that Skye's true name was recorded. Thinking of how significant that was, she nodded to her client. "You're looking well today. Tranquil. Are you on an assignment?"

Jayla had seen Skye in a variety of disguises over the past several weeks and was gratified when she was greeted by what she believed to be the real Skye. Her skin tone betrayed her Jamaican or perhaps Haitian heritage. Her black hair lay in tight cornrows, not hidden under a wig. In jeans and a denim jacket over a tight tee shirt, there was clearly no padding this time. Skye was small breasted but broad shouldered for a woman of medium height, with a narrow waist atop substantial hips and thick thighs. Combat boots seemed to be her natural style. More interesting was that she wore no jewelry, not even earrings.

Jayla's most important observation was that Skye appeared to be relaxed, leaning back against the chaise with knees apart and feet flat on the beige carpet. Skye's smile always made her look as if she was holding some fascinating secret, but it was no less genuine. That smile was all the response she offered to Jayla's query, so the therapist changed it. "… or have you just completed a job?"

This time Skye responded with a slow nod.

"Easy or challenging?" Jayla asked. "And by that I mean both physically and emotionally."

Skye poked out her lower lip and shrugged.

Jayla sighed. "Now Skye, you know I can't help if you won't talk to me. That is why you're here, right? For us to get to the root of your socialization issues?"

Skye leaned forward. "Don't get it twisted," she said, and there was a sharp edge to her voice. "I come here because I need somebody to talk to, and I pay you to be that somebody. You want me here not to help me but because of the awards and praise you'll get when you publish the results of psychoanalyzing a professional assassin. It's a nice trade-off, but we are not friends. And I am not crazy."

After five long seconds of silence, Jayla said, "You're wrong. I do want to help you. But if you're not going to talk there's no reason for us to be here, especially after office hours. Unlike you, I have a life."

Jayla closed her notebook with a loud clapping sound, praying that Skye could not see the fear behind her practiced cool exterior. She had learned a lot counseling violent criminals in prison, but she knew that if even half of what Skye had told her was true, then she was certainly the most dangerous person with whom she had ever shared a room.

When Jayla stood, Skye raised a palm to stop her. "Yes. Yes, all right. I just finished an assignment, but it was part of a larger contract so I'm feeling like both the situations you mentioned. I'm on the job, and I just took a player off the board."

Jayla jotted in her notebook. She always collected the euphemisms Skye used for her profession. "So tell me about this latest assignment. How do you feel about this player you've taken off the board? Was it, in your mind, a just action?"

"You always want to go there," Skye said, shaking her head. "What did I tell you? The first rule of the assassin's doctrine. The target has got to deserve it."

"Oh, yes," Jayla said with a half-smile. "Your job, while criminal, does have rules."

"I misspoke earlier," Skye said, sliding a slim dagger out of her boot. "It's not a job. It's a profession. All professions have their rules. For doctors, rule number one is 'do no harm', right? For an assassin, it's that the target has got to deserve it." Skye began to absently flip the dagger in the air, catching it by its tip each time. "In this case, this bastard kidnapped my client's son. I don't know how they got him. My client kept his family totally under the radar. But once he got the ransom demand, the client agreed to pay, and the ransom money was in transit but not fast enough to suit the kidnappers. They killed the boy, I think just to make a point. Just to be snotty. The action took place overseas and no way the police would ever have gotten close to the killer."

Jayla nodded. "I think I understand. So, you were hired to…"

"Correct the balance," Skye said, standing. "I was asked to start with the son of a bitch who actually did the deed."

"So, a bullet through the head from across the street?"

"Oh, no," Skye said, holding her smile as she paced the carpet without making a sound. The little knife continued to fly, get caught, and fly again. "This was up close and personal. With my hands. He was this big, Latin dude. MS-13 you know."

"That's a gang, right?"

"Wow. Where the hell do you live?" Skye asked. "Yeah, it's a gang. About the most dangerous gang there is. And this was one of their baddest boys. Full of all that macho shit. You can bet his last thought was that a girl had kicked his ass."

Jayla doubted that was his last thought but there was no benefit to saying so. Besides, Skye's casual knife play made her nervous. "So, you were taking society's revenge? Or getting vengeance for your client?"

"I was earning my pay," Skye said. "One down, four to go."

"This client gave you a list of people for you to kill?"

Skye stopped for a moment, parking one side of her butt on Jayla's desk. "This was really different. I met this man in a little bistro while I was in Paris. He had reached me through the usual cutouts and I sent the message back that I was taking some vacation time."

"After that domestic abuse issue last month," Jayla said, flipping pages back.

"Yeah, the wife beater." Skye's eyes drifted away almost wistfully, Jayla thought. "Four of her friends put the cash together to go my fee. They'll never find that dick. But anyway, when I said I was on vacation he asked if he could come to me. So we had lunch in this little café and he explained the whole kidnap scenario. But he knew the killer was part of a syndicate here in The District. He had already spent a fortune doing the research to find out who were the shot callers."

"He found the person who ordered the kidnapping?" Jayla asked. "If he could do that, why not just go to the police?"

Skye stifled a chuckle, balancing the knife with its tip on her forefinger. "Please. These people are connected. And besides, he turned out to be Romanian, and they have their own way of doing things. He didn't want to see them in a cell. He wanted to see them in the ground. Do you blame him? Wouldn't you want the same thing?"

Jayla chose not to answer those questions. "So, he hired you to kill the murderer and his boss?"

"I'll eliminate his boss alright," Skye said. "And his boss, and his boss, and his, the top man. Honestly," Skye flipped the knife up, caught it by the handle and pointed it at her therapist. "Doesn't this all make you just a little happy? Really?"

"That you have four more murders planned? Why should this please me?"

Skye was pacing again and stopped right in front of Jayla. "Look, these guys are big league. I'm about to pull the plug on a team of animals responsible for any number of murders and kidnappings, and who knows what else. No telling how many innocent people I might be saving."

"If you succeed," Jayla said.

Skye waved a hand at her. "Well, if I don't get them all I'll be dead and according to our contract, you then get to publish all this psychobabble about the crazed assassin and win the shrink Nobel prize or whatever. So, win-win for you."

Jayla put down her sharpened number two pencil. "Skye, don't say that. I don't want you to…"

"Don't, Doc. Let's keep it real, okay? Besides, I think my time's about up for this session and, anyway, I'm feeling pretty good tonight. Besides, I've got to get on the trail of the next target. Now, this fool I just dispatched was brought up on some pretty obvious drug charges just before he kidnapped the boy. Charged, and let out on the street pretty fast. I've got to find out who the judge was that let this murderer go."

Jayla swallowed hard. "Oh, my. Is he your next target? A sitting judge?"

Skye released one harsh laugh as she caught the knife and slid it back into her boot. "Oh, it's different when I'm not going after a felon, is that it? Well, as it happens, it's not the judge. But I've seen the evidence, and I figure the only way a judge would let this boy back on the street is if he got paid off by somebody. So, I need him to tell me who. That should get me to the next rung up the ladder."

"Wait, I thought your client gave you a list of targets."

"It ain't quite that easy," Skye said. "He only had the name of the actual killer. The hands-on guy. The mission is to get his boss, and his, and on up to the top man. Not sure how my client knows how many steps that is, but he does."

Jayla released a sigh. "I see. Well, if you know the felon's name, the… you called him the hands-on guy? If you have his name and the crime he was accused of it should be pretty easy to find out who sat for his case."

"Really?" Skye asked, leaning in close to Jayla's face. "Could you let me know by tomorrow?"

"Wait, me?"

"Well I want to get back to my vacation," Skye said. "And you wouldn't want me threatening a series of judges until I got to the right one, would you?"

By ten o'clock the RHO Martial Arts Academy was dark and still. Skye had waited until half past ten to go inside with the man she called her tech consultant, Noah Miller. As a rule, Noah would ply his trade in the Library of Congress where the wi-fi signal had exceptional strength. But Noah didn't like to work in the same place too often, so he didn't protest when Skye asked him to check some details for her while she worked out. Aside from sparring areas and a large room for group martial arts lessons, the academy boasted a well outfitted weight room. Skye paid well to have that space to herself three evenings per week.

She knew this environment would suit Noah well. The lighting was dim, the temperature was cool, and silence reigned. He sat cross-legged in front of a weight bench, on which he had set up his laptop. Directly ahead of him, Skye lay on a similar bench, pressing a bar she doubted Noah could move at all. He was a short man, soft in the middle with thinning, wispy hair and a strong nose that curved down like an eagle's beak. She focused on the sound of his fingers tapping his keyboard and pushed herself toward muscle failure.

"So you were just giving the shrink a hard time, eh?' Noah asked, not looking up from his monitor screen.

"Yeah, I like to pull her tail," Skye said, raising the bar one more time and lowering it on its stand. "I figured you'd have the judge's name by the time we met here tonight."

"Yeah, that was the easy part," Noah said. "It's all on the public record. Digging into his finances has been a bit more challenging. There's a lot going on overseas but so far I can't see any income sources that look even a little shady. Are you sure this guy's on the take?"

"Got to be," Skye said. "Are you looking at his spending patterns?" In a soft gray sweat suit she moved like a ghost to a pulley machine and started pulling down a bar to work her back muscles. She knew that skill and speed would always win the day in a real fight but backing them up with unexpected strength made her work easier.

Noah had fallen silent while she worked her back, making Skye think she had prodded him down a new line of inquiry. She was just beginning to break a sweat when she moved to the dumbbell rack and selected the right weights for her arm work.

"Hey, do you actually study here?" Noah asked. "You do karate or kung fu or something?"

The question seemed rather random to her. She nodded as she started a set of seated curls. "Actually I have worked with the instructors here," she said between breaths. "But not the arts you mentioned. That fancy stuff don't really teach you how to fight. That's why boxers regularly mop the floor with karate and kung fu experts."

"Really?" Noah said, not looking up. "You're a boxer?"

"Well, Thai kickboxing," Skye said, panting with her exertions. "Brazilian Jiu-Jitsu. Mixed martial arts. Stuff that trains you to get hit and keep going. Maybe you ought to…"

"Got him!" Noah shouted, interrupting. "So damned obvious, but you know, pretty damn slick."

"What did you find?" Skye asked. She slouched forward on the bench. Her sweatshirt ballooned forward and for a moment she could smell her own perspiration. Crap! But nothing a shower wouldn't cure.

"Spending a lot more than he earns, but the money doesn't go through any bank account attached to him. It's all stuff charged to a credit card. A black card with no limit. He buys, but somebody else is paying off the balance. Nothing the IRS would ever catch."

"That does sound pretty slick," Skye said, raising weights overhead to work her shoulders. "Can you trace the card back to the source of the money? Can you find out who's paying the bills?"

"Maybe. Could take a long time to work my way into that info. A lot faster if I had the card itself in my hand. I can decrypt the metadata."

Skye sat, and stretched forward to grip her feet. "Oh, well then, just relax," she said, lowering her head to her knees. "You give me this boy's address and I'll just go relieve him of that card."

Chapter 4

Sometimes events in dreams are more vivid than they were in real life. In the dream Skye could feel how close the walls were in that little apartment she grew up in. She could feel the linoleum under her knees and smell last night's fried chicken dinner. Her little brother's hands were so soft between her own. Tyrone was no gangster. He just lived there. Until he didn't.

In her dream she could feel the life draining out of Tyrone's body, chased out by the heroin in his veins like the drugs thought they needed the space. They wouldn't share his body with his soul. Drugs were here, so the soul had to go.

With Daddy gone and Mama permanently drunk, it was up to the twelve-year-old girl to find the rusty piece Tyrone carried to feel grown. Then she had to find the boy who sold that poison to her big brother and got him to commit slow suicide by injection. The gun felt cold and smooth in her hand, just like Tyrone's hand had by the time she let it go.

Then, without warning, her mind crossed over into this reality. Deep brown eyes scanned the room for a second before she moved. Once she knew she was secure, she threw off the comforter, a deeper blue than the walls, and bounded out of bed. Her bedside clock read 10:47. She scurried naked into the bathroom. She had a full day ahead and she needed to get it going. It was judgement day for a judge.

After a blazing hot shower she scrubbed her teeth, combed out her hair, and moisturized her face, all with cheap, store brand products. She pulled on a white terrycloth robe and padded into the galley kitchen. She decided on a big breakfast, which started with three strips of bacon. When they were crisp she poured out the excess grease and added diced onions and green peppers to the pan. She added two beaten eggs to the pan and covered it all with shredded cheese. As soon as it was solid she slid the omelet onto a plate. She carried that and a cup of coffee to the island where she took all her meals, perched on a high stool, her bare feet swinging free. While she ate she stared out the window of her Georgetown rental although her view was only of the leafy, narrow street and the similar brick house across the street.

After breakfast Skye immediately washed and put away her dishes. Then she went into her second bedroom, which served as her workshop. Her eyes scanned the pegboard wall that displayed a variety of tools of her trade. After a few seconds she selected a small handgun. Then she opened the closet that was jammed full of a wide variety of clothing. In her mind the clothes in her real bedroom made up her real wardrobe. The things in this room were costumes. The clothes were simply tools of her trade, what she wore to be whoever she needed to be to go wherever she needed to go without getting a second glance.

After selecting the right outfit, she returned to the kitchen, refilled her cup and snuggled into the deep, plush easy chair in the living room. Often this was time she spent with the *Washington Post,* but today she curled up with plans of the house that Judge Jacob Goldsmith built for his family. Like so many Washington DC professionals, he had chosen to live in Arlington, Virginia, just across the Potomac from The District. Skye had spent much of the last week there, within binocular distance of the Goldsmith home, observing and taking notes. If anyone had asked her she would have explained the eleventh law of assassins: own the geography.

She'd be walking into that house later that day but for now she enjoyed the aroma of fresh coffee with hazelnut creamer and let the chair caress her. May as well be comfortable while she could.

The aging Aerostar van passed the Washington Golf and Country club, pulled off N. Glebe Road, and in short order, drove into the long driveway of a palatial French country home. It was wide enough that by parking at the far-left side they avoided blocking the two garage doors. The five uniformed women rolled out of the vehicle bringing the tools of their trade: vacuum cleaners, cloths, spray bottles of cleaner, dusters, brooms and mops. The team moved in single file down the long path around the house to the mahogany front door. All were short and stocky. All were Latin and moved with singular focus. They wanted to get in, get it done and get out. Time was money to them.

The team lead unlocked the door and held it open as her team filed in.

Skye stood in the doorway of the house next door to Judge Goldsmith's home, watching the cleaning team carry all the cleaning gear one would normally expect to find in a home anyway. She had developed the skills for breaking and entering, but this was so much easier and less risky. She was dressed like the team that had filed into the house, and now hurried to slip through the door behind them.

Skye knew the house was almost always vacant during the day. She had studied the floor plan, the five bedrooms, six baths, gourmet kitchen and the rest of the space the residents could not begin to keep up with themselves, even if they wanted to. And she knew that once every week, a half dozen women let themselves in and dispersed through the house to clean it. These women were assigned to the job, chosen from a large pool of workers. They were not a team, per se, and hardly knew one another. They would hardly notice another uniformed cleaning woman over in another room.

Skye had offered one woman twice her normal day rate to stay home that day and was quite sure the woman cared not at all why someone would want to take her place. So, while the five serious cleaning women attended to the French oak floors and the kitchen's Calacatta Marble, Skye moved to the basement door, took a moment to spray WD-40 on the three pins that held the door in place, and slipped downstairs.

Past the exercise room but before the media room she found the laundry. Skye wondered how often Judge Goldsmith, his wife or his adult daughter came down here. It didn't matter. Even if they did show up, she'd be invisible. To accommodate the duct work and hoses the washer and dryer already stood more than a foot out from the wall. She worked the washer forward another couple of inches, then slid the dryer forward so they were again even. She peeled off her uniform after emptying her pockets and dropped it behind the washer. Now in black tights and turtleneck top she climbed over the washer. From the top of the dryer she grabbed all that she had brought with her: two granola bars, a bottle of water and a Smith & Wesson Model 442 revolver. The lightweight .38 special was just over six inches long with its hammer enclosed in the frame so it wouldn't get caught on her clothes. Of course, there were disadvantages to using a double action revolver like this one but when dealing with amateurs she didn't worry about them.

Skye had read of military snipers lying still under camouflage for an entire day or sometimes two in order to take out a target. In fact, that had been part of her training.

She was relaxed on her back, not quite asleep but letting her mind wander away.

There was an odd note of irony to this moment. In the first fifteen years of her life Skye had never been inside a house like this one. Until then she and everyone she knew personally lived in an apartment, and those apartments were all flats. The idea of going upstairs or downstairs in your own home was foreign to her, something you saw on television or in the movies. And the idea of having a washer and dryer in your home seemed ludicrous. The basement was that dark, nasty place where they kept the furnace and you didn't go down there unless you were hiding from somebody. She, like all her schoolmates, hauled her clothes to a laundromat once a week and hoped she had enough quarters to get everything dry after it was washed. Otherwise she had to unfold that wooded frame at home to hang her clothes on.

All of that meant that before her senior year, she could not have imagined being where she was at that moment. Yet, she never thought of herself as poor. She was normal, average. The rest of the world was rich.

After an hour or so she heard the cleaning crew lock up, leaving the house totally still. After two hours, hearing no one in the basement, she slowly chewed one of the granola bars. Two hours after that she had the second one. After two more hours she brought her mind back into focus, stretched, and rose up into the darkness.

Holding her gun close to her waist she slipped through the basement, a shadow among shadows, and eased up the stairs toward the light glowing under the door. When she heard the television, she smiled. She knew the layout of the first floor and was certain that everyone there would be faced away from her.

Without a sound she pushed the door open five inches, just enough for her to ease through. A few steps got her to the second stairway, and she mounted those carpeted steps choking back any haste that tried to push up from her stomach. Her mind churned through everything that could go wrong; a family member moving unexpectedly, a guest, a new pet she didn't know about. She had a catalog of planned responses to any of these eventualities, but none of them came to pass and seconds later she stood at the door to the judge's private study. His personal schedule was so consistent that she could be confident of what she would find inside.

Taking a deep breath, Skye turned the knob, stepped inside and closed the door behind herself, her pistol pointed at the desk across the room and the man behind it.

"Good evening, Judge Goldsmith. Hold that pose. A scream is suicide and murders your family."

Chapter 5

Jacob Goldsmith's face and hands were pale to the point of being pasty. His pink scalp reflected the ceiling light except where it was covered by the half circle of gray rings that wrapped his head from one ear around the back to the other. His sloping shoulders and protruding stomach marked him as a man accustomed to affluence. Still in his black bespoke suit, his top shirt button was open with his tie pulled down three inches. Thick, gray brows arched over penetrating eyes that stared over the top of reading glasses and bored into Skye's face. She knew exactly what he was looking for and let him see her sincerity.

In that first crucial moment Goldsmith had stood, not to his full five feet and seven inches, but supported by his left hand on his desk. Was his right hand poised to hit the intercom? Or pull a weapon from a drawer? No matter. Skye knew he had to be good at quickly evaluating people and in that moment, he judged her correctly. His brows relaxed. He breathed, showing no fear, and spoke in a slow, measured tone.

"My family?"

Skye stepped forward toward the love seat set to the right of his desk, against the windows. "Safe and unaware of me."

Goldsmith's shoulders lowered an inch. "Who…?"

"Who I am and how I got here ain't important right now, so put those questions out of your mind. What is important is how easy you can end this conversation without anybody getting hurt. In fact, there's no reason for anyone to ever know we had this conversation."

"Alright." Goldsmith sat back down. "Why are you here? What can I do for you?"

"I'm here because you're a crooked judge," Skye said, standing on the loveseat cushions and perching on its back. "Somebody is paying you to influence courtroom outcomes. I need to reach that individual."

Dampness broke out on Goldsmith's forehead. To his credit he managed to chuckle even though Skye could smell his fear. It mixed with smoke from the cigar smoldering in an ashtray beside the intercom and the result almost turned her stomach. "Seriously? This myth of the crooked judge is just that. Juries determine the results in court. We judges simply maintain order."

Skye grinned wide. "Oh, your honor, that really is good. But the truth is, you can tip anything but a total slam dunk in the direction of your choice. Sort of like a basketball ref, you decide which fouls to call. By being tough on the prosecution and easy on the defense attorney you can point the jury in a certain direction. To continue the sports analogy, what you do is the equivalent of shaving points."

"Do you have an interest in a particular case?" Goldsmith asked, rubbing his sweaty palms down his thighs.

"I have an interest in Juan Gomez being acquitted when charged with the murder of Eric Williams, a murder he most surely committed."

"You're here for revenge?"

"No, moron, I'm here for the connection. And that starts with the money."

"You want money?" Goldsmith's eyes widened as if he suddenly saw the path to safety. He pulled a fat wallet out of his hip pocket and tossed it to Skye. "Here. And if you let me get to my safe…"

Skye slapped the wallet aside with her left hand. "Stop being stupid. I'm here for a particular credit card and I'm pretty sure you don't keep it in your wallet. Probably not in your safe either because I'm betting your wife goes in there."

Like most lawyers, Goldsmith had a good poker face. But like most liars, he couldn't keep his eyes from wandering toward the object of concern. And like most professional psychics, Skye had trained herself to watch for the tells a desperate man showed.

"Most likely it's in your desk."

Goldsmith swallowed hard. "You don't know what you're getting into. You don't want to piss these people off."

"No, Judge," Skye said, hopping to her feet and moving closer to him. "I want to kill them. Now, do you hand me the card? Or do I blow off one of your kneecaps and then you hand me the card?"

The phone rang, cutting through the tension in the room. Judge Goldsmith jumped like he had touched a live wire. The landline on his desk sounded a second time before Skye said, "You probably ought to take that."

As Goldsmith reached for the receiver, Skye moved in close. She put a hand on his shoulder, like a close friend would, and gently pressed the muzzle of her pistol against his ribs. He looked into her eyes as he pressed the phone to his ear. She gave him a comforting smile and winked, making sure she was close enough to hear both sides of the conversation. She hated that his clothes smelled of cigar smoke.

"Judge Goldsmith?" a man's voice asked through the phone. When the judge grunted acknowledgement, he continued. "It's Anderson. Mr. Hetman asked me to call. He didn't want you to be caught off guard. A police investigator is about to visit you. He's on a fishing expedition, no evidence of any kind just groundless suspicions about some of your work. Mr. Hetman says he doesn't know anything and wants to make sure you don't do anything to upset that situation."

Goldsmith bared his teeth as if he had forgotten Skye was there. "What the hell, Brandon? Really? Look, you tell your boss I'm not an idiot. I know how to play this game. He's got nothing to worry about."

"Okay," the caller said. "He just wanted you to be aware, so you'll be prepared."

"He just wanted me to know that he knows I'll be talking to some cops," Goldsmith said. "Let him know he can trust me. Now get lost."

Goldsmith came short of slamming the phone down, but not by much. It made Skye chuckle.

"You take orders from that guy? A dude who calls himself the Hitman?"

"Not Hitman," Goldsmith said. "Hetman. That's his name. Or at least the one he uses."

"Yeah, well he sounds like a dick. Better give me that credit card before the cops get here."

Goldsmith grunted and pulled open the second drawer on the right of his desk. Then he reached under the desk and pressed a button. A hidden compartment at the back of the drawer popped open. Goldsmith reached in and retrieved a black credit card and handed it to Skye.

"Half of me hopes you catch up to this asshole," he said.

"Really?" Skye said, slipping the card into the top of her bra. "What, the half that don't like money? Well, don't worry, I'll catch up to him, so you might want to get used to living within your means."

"Maybe so," Goldsmith said. "But if I get the picture, it's all good. You've got no reason to kill me now. And I kind of know how this business works with you types. Right now Hetman is the man, and you work for somebody who wants to be the man. Either Hetman will eliminate your boss, or your boss will eliminate him. Either way, I'll be here to render a service to the winner."

Skye might have corrected the judge but a soft rap at the office door got her attention. A female voice borrowed from the Hamptons said, "Jacob? Honey? There's a policeman here to see you." Then after a short pause, "Excuse me. A police detective."

Skye raced across the room and slid a window open. "Ask him in, Jake. I'll wait outside. But don't mention me to the cop, okay? That would be bad for your family down the line."

Chapter 6

Orson Rissik nodded politely to Mrs. Goldsmith, stepped into the judge's office and locked the door behind himself. He maintained a passive expression as he scanned the room, taking in every detail for later consumption. Then he walked over and extended a hand.

"Jacob Goldsmith? I'm Orson Rissik, Fairfax County Police Department."

Goldsmith shook hands, then settled slowly into his seat. "You're a detective?"

"Yes sir, in our Major Crimes Bureau. Was just hoping to chat with you for a moment."

Goldsmith looked up and licked his lips. "I'm not sure what I can do for you that we couldn't have talked about during normal business hours."

Rissik walked over toward the loveseat, not looking at Goldsmith. Again he wondered why people found him so intimidating. He was average in height and weight and wore a conservative blue suit that probably cost a quarter of anything in the judge's closet. He spoke in a calm voice he thought might actually be soothing. But when he questioned people, he could always feel their discomfort.

"Well, it's hard to get on your calendar during the workday," Rissik said, turning to face Goldsmith. "And I was in the area on my way home."

"Speaking of which, you're a little out of your jurisdiction aren't you, detective?" He leaned forward and swelled up, looking like so many judges Rissik had seen on the bench in a courtroom.

"Arlington County Police are granting me a courtesy since I'm working on a case that falls into both counties."

"Really?" the judge said. "And what case is that?"

"I'm investigating the murder of a man who stood in your court recently, one Juan Gomez."

The blood rushed out of Goldsmith's face leaving a ghostly pallor. "Gomez? Gomez is dead? How?"

"Death by misadventure," Rissik said with a smirk. "Maybe he got careless in the bathtub after too much drinking. Maybe drugs. But because of his history and record I haven't taken murder off the table. In any case his death is part of a larger racketeering case I'm working on."

"I see," Goldsmith said. "Not sure how I can help you, though. I've heard nothing of this man since he walked out of my courtroom."

Rissik stepped closer, hands in his pockets, and focused on reading the judge's eyes. "Yes, reports are that a lot of people are surprised he did that. The prosecution had a pretty strong case. That's none of my business, of course, but I can see how a man like Gomez, accused of murder and all, might attract enemies. I just dropped by to ask if you had any insight as to who might have wanted Gomez dead."

"Sorry," Goldsmith said, shaking his head. "The victim's family believed Gomez guilty but seemed to accept the court's ruling. And Gomez had many gang affiliations and was reputedly a figure in the local underworld. But did he have enemies ready to commit murder? Honestly, detective, I do not know."

But you know something, don't you? Rissik thought. Aloud he said, "I'd appreciate it if you'd give it some thought and see if anything comes to you. If you were contacted by anyone during the trial who seemed to have an interest in Gomez being convicted or acquitted, that would be a big help."

Goldsmith nodded, the picture of the cooperative citizen. "I'll consult my notes when I get back to my chambers tomorrow and see if anything springs to mind."

"That would be helpful," Rissik said, moving toward the door. "Anything you could share would keep me from bothering you again. Thank you for your time, Judge. I'll see myself out."

Orson Rissik closed the door behind himself and jogged down the stairs. He waved to the family gathered around the television and stepped out into the night air. His little Honda Civic seemed out of place in the shadow of this monster house. Rissik thumbed his fob to unlock it, walking across a driveway that was nearly as wide as his was long.

This night he was really working on his own time. He stopped at Goldsmith's home in order to make eye contact with the judge and put him on notice that Gomez's murder would not be overlooked. Rissik's first look at the court records convinced him that things had not gone as they should have, and a deeper dive into the judge's career raised suspicions that he knew he could not prove. But that was okay, the judge was not his target. Rissik was hoping to make a connection that helped reveal a larger conspiracy, and if Gomez turned out to have been killed by some underworld character that would justify rattling a few more cages.

Opening his car door Rissik looked up at the huge edifice that Judge Jacob Goldsmith called home and wondered how many times his own modest condominium would fit inside it. Oh, well, if money had been the point he wouldn't have chosen law enforcement.

He had just settled into the seat, started his car and put it into reverse when he felt the steel tube pressed against the back of his neck. A woman's voice behind him sounded bored or maybe impatient.

"Almost seventy years of TV shows and movies, and people still don't look in their back seat when they get in their car."

Chapter 7

Rissik backed down the driveway and moved onto the road. When he stopped at a red light, he let out a long breath he didn't know he was holding. He looked into the rearview mirror and saw the top half of a black woman's face.

"No mask," he said in a calm, controlled voice. "That's generally a bad sign."

"I get that," the woman said. "Usually, felons cover their faces unless they plan on eliminating you as a witness."

"On the other hand, if you wanted to kill me you could have done it when I first got in my car and been long gone before anybody even knew I was dead. Which prompts the question, what do you want?"

"You're smart for a cop. Very promising. Both hands on the wheel, please."

Rissik pulled away from the light and by reflex aimed for the nearest highway, I-395.

"Not the highway," the woman said, as if it were just a suggestion. "Why don't you get on Arlington Boulevard."

"So, are you here for information?" Rissik asked. "Or to threaten me?"

"I'm here to talk."

"Okay," Rissik said. "I'm Detective Orson Rissik, Fairfax County Police Department. And you are…"

A chuckle from the back seat. "Brains and balls. This could be fun. Since you asked, you can call me Skye."

"All right, Skye," Rissik said, flowing with the sparse traffic. "Where are we going?"

"Let's just head for your office."

"That's a bit of a drive," Rissik said. "You want to ride all the way to Fairfax?"

"Yeah, I know. You're not Arlington County, but you stopped to question Goldsmith. That's pretty interesting."

"You had the judge's office bugged?" Rissik asked. He noticed there was no scent in the car. What woman doesn't wear any kind of cologne or perfume?

"No, I was hanging outside the window. Heard you ask about Juan Gomez."

She had no accent he could pin down. In fact, no accent at all. "Friend of yours?" Rissik asked. "You looking for revenge? I'm afraid I don't know who killed him, and I don't think Judge Goldsmith does either."

Streetlights strobed past, illuminating the inside of the car as they flashed by. In the half-second flashes of light Rissik thought he saw a smirk on the face of the woman in his rearview mirror.

"No, he doesn't. It was me. I took Gomez off the board."

Rissik felt a chill roll up his spine at this calm confirmation that the woman behind him was a killer. "May I ask why?"

"He was guilty but not convicted."

Rissik nodded. "Can't really argue with that analysis. So, is Goldsmith next? Are you here to confirm that he's on the take and is responsible for Gomez's freedom?" Arlington Boulevard widened to three lanes and cars began to fly past them as Rissik held to the forty-five miles-per-hour speed limit.

"On the take, yes," Skye said from the shadows, "but he's not on my list. I want the man he takes orders from. On the phone he said a name. Hetman. I suspect he's the ultimate target. Since we're sharing our intel, you got anything on him?"

"Oh, are we sharing our intel now?" Rissik asked.

Skye pressed her gun barrel harder into the back of his neck. "Did you miss that? My friend here thinks you agreed to tell me all you know. He's not mistaken, is he? Now, what do you know about this Hetman fellow?"

"Maybe I've heard the name. You going to kill him too?"

"For sure."

"Can't help you. Don't know who he is, or where he is."

Skye pressed the barrel a little harder against the detective's neck. "Are you sure?"

Rissik nodded again, fighting the urge to tense up. "This is not a situation in which I would lie. I've heard the name, but he's a blank to us."

"Okay, what do you know about this guy?"

Rissik took another deep breath. "Look, I know you're a professional and all that, but there's a lot of potholes out here and accidents do happen. Is it absolutely necessary for you to keep that gun on my spine?"

"Yes," Skye said. "Take it as an expression of respect. You're a dangerous man."

"Don't know why you'd say that," Rissik said. "I don't feel particularly dangerous right now."

"Later." Skye added the slightest bit of extra pressure against the Rissik's seventh vertebrae. "Now about Hetman."

The light ahead turned yellow. The car on Rissik's left shot through it. Rissik slowed to a stop just as the light turned red. He fought the temptation to turn and face his captor.

"I've got scattered bits of data on this mystery man. Nothing that would hold up in court yet but I'm slowly connecting the dots."

"Excellent," Skye said. "How about we go take a look at what you've got on him. Then I leave you alone, and we both go about our business."

Rissik gripped the wheel tighter. "I won't take you to the evidence locker. There's stuff there that…"

"Not an issue, Detective," Skye said. "I don't need weapons, and I got no use for drugs. I just want to read your notes. Now I think your service weapon is on your right hip. Can you hand it to me please?"

At the Fairfax County government complex Rissik parked in his habitual parking space, deep in a cluster of vehicles that let him know exactly how many people were on duty. He also knew that almost all were out of the building on calls or on patrols. The handful of men in the building were handling administrative duties while they waited for trouble to call. They had no way of knowing that trouble was making a house call that night. As he put his car into park the pressure against his neck disappeared and the woman behind him spoke again in hushed tones.

"I want to lay out the scenario because I think you're a rational man and I can explain things to you. Am I right?"

"A rational man? I think I am."

"Good. So, to be clear. I believe that at this time of night you can get me into and out of this building without encountering anyone else. I am not here wanting to hurt anyone. I want whatever information you got that will help me do my job, which ought to make your job easier too. I don't spook or shoot at shadows. You are safe as long as you stay cool. Now, if you alert anyone to my presence in any way, if anyone tries to hurt, capture or detain me, there will be a bloodbath. That would piss me off, and trust and believe I will kill everybody I see on my way out of here. And that will be on you, Detective Rissik. Is all that clear?"

"Crystal. I comply, no one gets hurt."

"Just so," Skye said. "Let's get into your office."

The trip into the building was trouble free. Rissik led Skye around to the side of the building, to a private entrance reserved for law enforcement. He tapped the lock's five buttons in a certain order. Once inside that door he had to hold an access card against a panel to open an inner door.

Skye followed Rissik at a safe distance, just out of his reach, holding her small pistol close to her side. The tiled halls were silent except for the hum of the air conditioner which evidently worked just as hard whether there was anyone inside or not. They moved like they belonged there never pausing until they reached Rissik's office door. He entered first, flipping on a light switch. Skye followed, locking the door behind herself before even looking around.

They stood in a large communal outer office. They walked past a receptionist's desk to one of four office doors. A small sign on the wall next to the door said "Rissik" in block letters.

Rissik's office was pretty much what Skye expected for a civil servant at his level. It felt small but very clean and brightly lit. His desk dominated the long wall, facing in. There was a neat little coffee service set up to the left of the office. A row of three steel filing cabinets stood to the right, each drawer labeled. His desk was almost too orderly for a workplace. Every sheet of paper lay in one of the neat stacks, or in an OUT box, or one marked Hold. His IN box was empty. She assumed this was always the case at the end of his work day. Three framed citations clung to the walls left and right of the desk. A wheeled office chair was tucked in at the center of the desk. Behind it hung the only other picture of any kind in the room. It was a poster of a pelican trying to eat a frog. His head already in the bird's mouth, the frog had reached out and wrapped a hand around the pelican's throat, preventing it from swallowing him. A caption under the picture said, "Never Give Up".

"I bet you always get your man, eh detective?"

"So far," Rissik said.

"Well then, glad I'm a woman. You got handcuffs in here?"

Rissik reached behind his waistband and produced the shiny stainless-steel bracelets. Skye took them from him and waved him into his own chair. There she locked his right wrist securely to the arm rest. Up close she picked up the smell of pipe tobacco on his cheap blue suit. She imagined him poring over clues with a pipe in his mouth like a modern-day Sherlock Holmes wannabe.

"I know these won't hold you long when you decide to be out of them," Skye said, "but I'm confident I'll see you trying to get free in enough time to kill you before you kill me, so let's not play that game, okay? Now, I figure you for a pretty old-school guy. Are there really folders and such in that cabinet over there?"

Rissik sighed and nodded. "You want the center file cabinet, starting with the second drawer down. Would it be too much to ask that you leave things as you find them?"

Skye grinned and slid her pistol into a squeeze pocket on her right thigh. When she pulled the drawer open her grin dropped. The files were both numbered and labeled clearly. The labels were typed and color coded. She pulled open the third drawer and saw that the color coding continued. Some of the labels referred to numbers on other folders and it required only seconds for her to see the connections between them.

"No, detective," she said in a solemn tone. "It would not be too much to ask." She pulled the file labeled Hetman, then selected five others that were referenced on its label and laid them on Rissik's desk. She pulled a chair to the desk and sat facing him. Three minutes passed in stony silence while she carefully turned pages. Some were photographs, some documents, but most were handwritten notes. Actually, hand printed, in block letters. The lettering was so neat and precise that a casual observer might think their creator had found a way to type in pencil.

"You're what they call an anachronism I think," Skye said.

"Anachronism, huh. Well check out the big brain on the hit woman."

"Yeah, you're a relic, but I got to respect it," Skye said. "This is the kind of obsessive attention to detail that gets things done."

After a moment, Rissik said, "Thank you, I guess."

Skye began spreading the folders around the desk. "I see the connection to this file on MS-13," she said, "And to this one on the Chinese Triad. These people do not play well together. Or do they?"

"People seem to do stuff for this guy," Rissik said. "It's spelled out in that folder on your left, with the red label."

Skye read for a moment more. Rissik said, "You act more like a spy than a murderer. I'm surprised you're not photographing pages with a little camera."

"I'll remember what I need to know," Skye replied, then looked up to make eye contact. "And it's assassin, not murderer."

"I'm sure your victims are no less dead."

"You've pulled together some interesting shit here, detective. Is all this going where I think it's going?"

Rissik closed his eyes as if considering if he wanted to continue. Finally he said, "No one wants to believe it, but these clues tell a story that seems to imply that this guy Hetman is building a new crime cartel based in The District. In fact, I've heard that's what they're calling it. The Cartel."

Her eyes flipped from one file to another. "You saying he's pulling together members of MS-13 and the Triad?"

"And the Jewish Mafia, the Yakuza, the Irish mob and the Albanian Mafia."

"A super group," Skye said. "But it won't happen. Can't happen. Them guys are competitors. That would be like…"

"Like Sprint and T-Mobile teaming up," Rissik said.

Skye opened her mouth to speak, then reconsidered. These organizations may have all started as local national gangs but now they were like any other multi-national corporation. They'd sit down with anybody if there was enough money on the table.

"Okay, let's say you're on the right track. How long has he been at this?"

"Maybe a year," Rissik said. "Or at least, that's what I think. The man's a shadow, works through cutouts from what I can see, leaving no footprint. He's working like a terrorist only there's no ideology except maybe the love of money."

"So you got no pictures, no location, nothing on this guy. Hetman can't be his real name."

Rissik rolled his eyes. "It's not a name at all. It's a word. It's an allegory."

"Allegory?" Skye said, grinning. "Check out the big brain on the detective."

"It's what writers call a character that represents something else," Rissik went on. "A symbol for something else."

Skye settled her elbows on the desk, hands palms up. "You can't think you can handle this. Eliot Ness couldn't handle this. Ain't it best for this guy to get dead?"

"Well, I don't think you can get to this man," Rissik said. "And of course, I don't condone murder, even if the victim is a murderer."

Skye looked down, scanned a few more lines, then put her finger on the page she was reading to hold her place. "You, detective, are in the business of maintaining law and order, right? Don't you want order in our society?"

"That's rhetorical, right?"

Skye leaned forward, looking deep into Rissik's eyes, daring him to look away. "To quote Robert B. Baer, If the death of one member of that society reduces violence or moves history in the right direction it is an acceptable social bargain."

Rissik held her gaze for few seconds, then released a puff of air and shook his head with an ironic smile. "Some Eastern philosopher?"

"Actually, he was a CIA operative and kind of a subject matter expert on killers."

The next twenty minutes passed in relative silence as Skye worked her way through the information Rissik had collected about this theoretical new local crime lord. Twice she stopped to ask questions, but otherwise she searched for useful details, continually surprised at Rissik's ability. Most detectives develop their gifts of observation and deduction on a tactical level. What Rissik did, to Skye's mind, was intelligence analysis. Most of the raw data was in plain sight. It was the connections Rissik made that impressed her.

When she was finished Skye closed all the folders and carried them back to the file cabinet, careful to put them back where they were when she started.

"You have saved me a lot of digging," Skye said, moving back to Rissik's chair. "It looks like this guy Levin, is the money man, making the payoffs for Chen. That unlikely pair seems to handle the bulk of the kidnapping, murder and extortion, but you don't have any hard evidence to nail them with. Have you talked to him, yet?"

"Levin?" Rissik asked. "The guy who travels in an armored car with two bodyguards? No, I don't think so. He's a hard man to interview."

"Your notes say he's suspected of running a secret, high-end brothel in the District," Skye said. "It shouldn't be that hard to get to see a guy in such a social business." As she spoke, Skye slipped Rissik's gun out of her pocket and set it on one corner of his desk.

"Good luck with that," Rissik said. "Maybe when you see the competition, you'll rethink your profession and, who knows, maybe gather some evidence that will help me pull this guy off the street without a bloodbath."

Skye chuckled. "You're a riot, detective. Listen, I'm heading out now. I figure I'll go out the way we came in. I didn't see a touch pad on the inside but do I need that card to get out without setting off an alarm?"

Rissik nodded. Skye held her left hand out. Rissik fished the card out and flipped it at her on edge like a playing card. Skye snatched it out of the air.

"So that's that. I'll leave this on the floor just inside the door. Pretty sure you've got the key to those cuffs in your pocket, so you'll be free in a minute. But give me five before you come out, okay? I'd hate to waste any ammo in your direction."

As Skye moved toward the door Rissik said, "I have only your word that you've committed any crime except of course kidnapping a law enforcement officer. But if I ever see you again, you know I'll pull you in for this, right?"

This time Skye's chuckle was louder. At the door she turned and managed to regain a straight face. She slid her own pistol out of a pocket and pointed it in Rissik's direction, somehow not being threatening at all.

"By the way, it's your eyes. That's why people are nervous around you. You've got dangerous eyes. Let's hope we don't meet again."

Chapter 8

Midnight on the edge of downtown in the most powerful city on earth. This was where the bright energy of the nation's capital bumped up against the darkness of the crumbling inner city. On one side of this line, late night government workers were finally shutting down. On the other, night people were just getting into the work best done in the shadows.

Skye strutted down 12th Street NW and turned right to head west on M Street. For the next block she would be walking in front of the DC Convention Center. That's what they call it, although it's really just an eight-story red brick Comfort Inn with delusions of grandeur.

She now wore a poorly tended "Goldilocks" wig, tightly-wound curls cascading down onto the fur jacket that embraced her shoulders. As she passed from one shadow to the next, the few precious drops of light glinted off her red vinyl shorts and matching knee-high boots.

She was dressed to attract attention and that much was successful. By the time she reached Thomas Circle and headed north two cars had already pulled over and hailed her. Luckily she was never out of sight of a real street walker, and so was able to simply explain that their specific kink was not her specialty, but the lady over there would be happy to fulfill their wishes.

On her way up Vermont Avenue a police cruiser shot past as she was passing the Plaza. Good. She did not want to attract the attention of the District 3 police, although she was prepared to pay them off if necessary, to stay on the street. She hoped she didn't have to circle these two blocks for long before she got the right person's attention.

She was just beginning to feel the night's chill when she took the right on N Street. Here it was darker still but she smiled when the white Eldorado pulled to the curb up ahead of her. There aren't too many of those on the road anymore. Her smile grew when the driver got out of the car alone. He was tall and thin, in a fur coat that went all the way down to his white shoes. What she could see of his face was burnished ebony. He might even be handsome, but no black man should wear a hat with that big a brim. He was a throwback parody of a pimp. And he was waiting for her at the corner.

Skye made her walk even more exaggerated, like Beyonce in that old video where he's got her acting so crazy right now. As she approached him, she eyed him up and down as if she had no idea who he was or why he was there. With one long stride he stepped in front of her, blocking her path down the sidewalk.

"Yo, bitch," he said in a low growl. "Where the fuck you think you going?"

Skye looked up at him, showing a slight touch of fear. "What's up, daddy? Just getting back to 12th Street. The 1100 block is where all the action is, right? Sister's got to make a living."

"Who set you out here?" the man demanded.

Skye took a step back. "I'm out here on my own. Don't need no man to take my money when it's my ass getting sold. I…." Now she let fear overwhelm her face. "I didn't mean to piss nobody off."

"This here's my territory, whore," he said. His big right hand snapped out and clamped onto her left upper arm. Exactly as she had expected. Instead of pulling away, she stepped close in to him, her right hand slapping up into his crotch and clamping hard. In one quick movement she swept her left hand back to slap the wig off her head. Then a short blade dropped out of her left sleeve and this she pressed up against his neck.

"You called Slickback," Skye whispered, "and you been in this game too long. You know who I am?"

His eyes grew wide with recognition and his mouth dropped open to reveal his gold tooth. "Oh, shit. You that bitch Skye. Look, I don't know what them bitches told you but I'm good to my girls."

"Not here for you, Slick," she said. "Just want to talk. But let's get out of the middle of the street."

Twisting Slickback's genitals, Skye guided him into the alley between two big condominium buildings. With his back against the rough bricks, Skye released her grip on him. The knife stayed pressed against his neck and now her right hand pressed a gun barrel into his ribs. He might twist or muscle free of one threat, but not both. Not that it mattered. What really held the pimp in place was Skye's reputation.

"Who you after?" Slickback asked, "and what you want from me?"

"Only two things I want from you," Skye said, "and who ain't your business. It's where. I'm looking for a whore house."

"I work street walkers," he said. "When you got a house, you asking for raids."

"Yeah, I know," Skye said. "You kind of old school. But I think you know all the players in this town. The place I'm looking for would be upscale. And it doubles as a casino so Johns can lose some money while they waiting their turn. You know the place I'm talking about?"

The pimp swallowed hard, his breathing speeding up and his eyes darting left and right. "You ever heard of a Chinese mob called the Triad?"

"Yeah," Skye said. "What about them?"

"They running the cathouse you talking about. A couple of my girls went to them cause they pay good and you indoors all the time. And I ain't gone after them cause I don't need that kind of trouble. These guys don't dance. Especially this boy called Chen."

"Chen?" Skye lowered her knife, but kept the pistol at her side pointed at Slickback's heart. "Is he the H-N-I-C? Head Nigga In Charge?"

"Yeah," Slickback said, pulling his oversized brim down as if it could conceal him from the man he was talking about. "I heard he liked to play with hatchets."

"That's an old-school Triad thing," Skye said. "That's where the term hatchet man came from. Chinese assassins who used a hatchet or a cleaver to do the job."

Slickback's face twisted into an expression of disgust. "Damn, a switchblade do the job fine with a lot less mess. But anyway one of my girls who went over to them came back a while ago. She say this Chen checked how well the girls was doing. She was there when one bitch got pulled in for not bringing in enough cash. A couple of his boys held her still. Then he comes up, looks her right in the eye, and then wham! He slams this hatchet down and takes off one of her fingers. That's when this other bitch decided to come back. She was good, but a week later she stopped coming home. Turned up folded in half in a garbage can."

"And I'm betting you didn't do shit about it," Skye said.

The shadows seemed to darken around Slickback's face. His eyes narrowed and his voice lowered. "I ain't fucking with that kind of crazy. Nobody with a lick of sense should. This boy's some kind of nut case."

"Not your issue, is it?" Skye said. "You just tell me where this place is and how I get in."

"I'm down with that. But you said two things."

"Oh, yeah," Skye said, stepping back a pace and lowering her pistol. "You don't tell nobody about tonight, like this little conversation never happened. You feel me?"

"Shit, who I'm gone tell? I ain't never met no bitch called Skye. And I sure as hell hope I don't never meet her again."

Chapter 9

Crystal City isn't really a city, or even a town. Nor is it a neighborhood the way most people would define one. It's a strip of Arlington, Virginia, less than a mile and a half long pressed against the Washington National Airport. A few people do live there in high rise apartments and overpriced townhouses, but it is primarily populated by office space, expensive hotels and a wide variety of shops and businesses. One such business, Earth Treks, was Skye's morning destination. They opened at six o'clock, but thanks to the Metro rail schedule, Skye couldn't get there before seven.

Earth Treks was an urban climbing center, filled with colorful, faceted walls set with hand and footholds for scaling. As the man at the desk welcomed Skye, she guessed he was prepared for their usual banter.

"What's up, Benny? Or should I ask who's up?"

"Nobody's in the air yet, ma'am," he replied. "As usual, you're our first climber. Go get changed and I'll belay you myself today."

"Aw, man, can't I just fucking climb? Me and the walls is good friends by now."

He shook his head. "You bouldering today? That you can do without a rope."

"Pointless," Skye said, waving the idea away with one hand. "The bouldering wall's only seventeen feet, right? Not even worth my time."

Skye was already in her black leotards and tights so, once in the locker room she had only to hang her denim jacket and swap her running shoes for climbing shoes. Then she slid her phone into an elastic pouch on her upper arm and pulled on her headset with the mic. This workout would also be a business meeting.

Out on the floor she pulled on her harness and pulled the rope through the front pulley. Benny checked the knots, although there was no need. Then he stepped behind Skye and gripped the safety rope that looped around a ceiling pulley.

"Aren't you going to chalk your hands?" Benny asked.

"That ain't real life. Climbing," she called, and leaped onto the wall. Hand and foot holds were easy to find on the first half of the wall so she scurried up fairly quickly. Ten feet off the ground she tapped her phone and listened to it ring twice.

"Noah? You there?"

"I'm here, Skye. Too damned early, but I'm here."

"Okay, well what you got for me?" Handholds were moving farther apart. She had to stretch to get her right hand around a small outcropping and swung free for a moment before her left hand was secure.

"You knew this was impossible, right?"

"Didn't find Chen?" No way upward except to push with both feet and leap up. Left hand held, right hand slipped loose but after one short swing she was secure again. Now her arms were just starting to tremble and she had to work to drag air into her lungs.

"Way too common a name," Noah said. "Hey, what's with all the panting? You having sex while we're talking?"

"You jealous? What about Brandon Anderson? Anything?" Now the route she had chosen leaned out a bit. She clenched her teeth, scanning for the next hand hold.

"I can give you the dope on a dozen Brandon Andersons just in the DMV. Can you give me anything to narrow it down?"

Skye reached again and for a long fifteen seconds only her hands held her to the wall. When the wall returned to vertical she paused for a moment, feet pressed tight to give her forearms a bit of respite.

"Skye?"

"Yeah, I'm here," she said, blinking to clear perspiration from her eyes. "What about the mystery whore house?"

From below Benny shouted, "It's not a race." *The hell it ain't,* Skye thought. *I'm just racing against me.*

"Ahhh, the Twilight Club," Noah said. "This has got to be the place. On M Street. In the middle of an otherwise residential street. Don't know how they got a license, and frankly, don't know why either. The place has never shown a profit, according to the city records, but it keeps on being there."

"Great," Skye said. She was inching upward now, her face almost touching the wall. That tiny section of wall was all she could see, and all she wanted to see right then. "Text me the address."

"Done. But you sound like crap. Maybe you need to take it easy for a while."

Almost out of breath, Skye murmured, "No time to relax, Noah. I'll talk to you later, okay? Out."

Legs shaking, arms quivering, stomach cramping, she reached forward one more time and her knuckles bumped the padded ceiling. Good. She was pretty sure she had beaten her previous time for this path. Uncle Alex would be proud of her. She remembered the sweat soaked month she spent under his tutelage in Yosemite National Park. That was real climbing, where mistakes could be deadly, but he had taught her how to navigate the toughest rock face. At the time she could not imagine the practical application of this particular skill, but it certainly sharpened her focus, strengthened her grip, and gave her new understanding of the nature of fear and how to control it.

"You going to stay up there?" Benny called up.

Smartass! "On belay!" she called in return. Rappelling was the easiest part of this sport. She'd rest up on the ground for a few minutes and do one more climb before getting back on the train. She wanted to change before her appointment, and the new outfit might raise Jayla's eyebrows.

Chapter 10

"That's a different outfit, even for you," Jayla said. "Big night tonight?"

"You like it?" Skye asked, bouncing to her feet. "I'm working tonight, and I want to look special." The ankle length dress was a soft yellow chiffon with a plunging neckline and angel sleeves that flared out below her elbows. Silver hoop earrings matched the silver four-inch spiked heel stilettos and silver starburst-shaped buckle of the black leather belt that cinched her waist. When she raised her arms and spun, the dress flared out exposing her strong, smooth legs up past her knees.

"Not your usual work clothes I'm sure," Jayla said. "Fairly revealing I'd say." What Jayla did observe, and make a note of, was the look of anticipatory joy on Skye's face. The woman loved her work, and Jayla had seen this energy and happiness bursting out of her client before on the days she expected to end some man's life. It seemed more evident when there would be an element of danger attached to the job.

Skye started strutting across the office as if on a model's runway. "It's funny. A couple nights ago I was dressed like a whore. Tonight I'll be stepping into the lion's den, and I want them all to be relaxed. It helps if it's obvious I don't have anything hidden about my body. And this outfit makes frisking me pretty easy, unless they want to check my panties and my bra. In which case it would be fun *and* easy."

"The lion's den?"

Skye turned at the end of the room, flipping her shoulder-length auburn hair. "Tonight's assignment runs an underground gambling den that's really a fancy whore house. Whenever he's out and about he's surrounded by bodyguards and he travels in an armored car. So, the easiest thing is to go in there and extinguish him. Besides, putting him down on his home grounds will shake up his boss, who is after all the next target."

"You're not simply excited by the thrill of the hunt, are you?" Jayla asked. "The risk is part of it for you. Yes?"

Skye dropped onto the chaise lounge and sat examining her nails – also painted silver. "I think you're starting to get it. It's like gymnastics. Sure, you get credit for perfect execution, but the level of difficulty matters too. Look," Skye's eyes shifted to Jayla's. "Any asshole can kill somebody. Look at these terrorist bombers. Killing is easy. Killing and getting away with it, that's the challenge. It's getting away that shows what you got."

Jayla nodded and jotted in her little notebook. "So this is a game to you? Or more like a sport, to stick to your analogy."

"Yeah. Maybe. Kind of." Skye stared harder at her fingernails, watching the lamp's light glint off them. "I don't know. I just know I take pride in my work. Not just what I do but how I do it."

"I do get your reference to gymnastics," Jayla said. "You're saying your… profession… is about personal accomplishment. You're working to perfect your craft. But your work is of necessity anonymous. So, who are the judges? Other killers? Me?"

Skye's brows furrowed as if she had never thought this far before. Jayla feared for a moment that she had pushed too far. But then Skye's face eased into a half smile. She looked up and waved a finger at her therapist.

"The police. The cops are the judges. If I do what I do just right, the cops are left scratching their heads, or maybe even in awe of how the thing got done. I can tell by the way the investigation is done how much respect they got for me. Which sort of leads into what I wanted to tell you about."

Jayla just managed to stifle a gasp. In nearly three years of therapy, Skye had almost never actually wanted to tell her anything. Jayla leaned back in her chair, working to cover her surprise. "What's going on? Nothing related to the actual job I assume."

"Well, kind of," Skye said with a smirk. "I met a guy. A guy who surprised me. A cop."

Jayla leaned forward, her head tilted to one side, but stayed quiet. She could tell that her patient was fishing for a response. Jayla figured silence would prompt more spontaneous sharing.

After a few seconds of silence, Skye said, "Yeah, I met this Virginia detective, well, snatched him actually, to get some intel about the people I'm going after. Of course, he was all, 'I won't support a killer' and shit but, the thing is, he actually talked to me. I mean talked to me in an intelligent manner. We had conversation."

"Was that a unique experience?"

"Are you kidding? This guy wasn't an idiot and he didn't have that one track "I'm gonna get you and make you pay" attitude. This was a guy I could actually respect. I ain't never met a cop at any level that I could respect. Ever."

"I see. You can respect him. Even though he's the opposition?"

"Oh, God," Skye said through a laugh. "And here I thought you were getting it. This is the guy who can judge my work, who can truly see if an assassination was a ten or an eight point five. The guys surrounding the target, the guys I'll be in the middle of later tonight, they're the opposition."

On M Street there are blocks of row houses that good people drive past every day. One of them has been converted into a little-known tavern. Over-priced drinks, uncomfortable seating and a lack of convenient parking has kept it off the list of popular nightspots in The District. Just after midnight Skye marched up the brown sandstone steps and through the ornate glass and wood door. Past the inner door she turned left and joined the two bulky men sitting at the bar. Lighting was dim but the room-length mirror behind the bar gave everyone a clear view of the entire narrow room. The music, the kind of dance music DJs play at the American Legion, was just a little too loud. No one she could see was smoking, but the smell of cigar smoke was oppressive. At the end of the bar, the bartender was chatting with one of the men sitting there. He was tall, his face and hands like polished ebony. When his conversation reached a lull he wandered over to Skye.

"What'll you have?" the bartender asked, not wasting a smile on her.

With her brightest smile and her full Haitian accent, Skye said, "M'dear I got no use for the cheap rail liquor you have up here. I'm looking for some action, some real action, and I understand this is the place to find that."

The bartender stood taller and locked eyes with her. He was the gatekeeper, and this was his initial evaluation. Skye held her smile. He'd see that the diamonds in her necklace were real and the bracelet on her left wrist was genuine platinum. She took a step back, so if he looked down he'd be able to see the Louboutin heels on her feet.

"Ma'am, I really don't know what you're talking about."

She reached forward slowly, to gently slide the nails of her left hand down the bartender's cheek. "Now don't be bullshitting me, Captain. I been doing good work for the man, making good bank, and me boy Brandon told me this was the place. Brandon Anderson. Do you maybe know that name?"

"You saying you're here to meet Brandon tonight?"

Skye continued to show her teeth, but it was no longer a smile. "No, asshole, I'm just throwing his name around to get a discount on these shitty drinks. Now are you going to show me to the tables, or do I need to tell Brandon you didn't recognize his name?"

The bartender pulled back, feeling increased pressure from the tips of the nails. He waved one of the muscular men over to him.

"Danny boy. Take the lady in."

This one had a longshoreman feel, big rough hands and a nose that had been broken a couple of times. Thin, straight brown strands hung to his bushy eyebrows. He looked her up and down, muttered "follow me," and turned around. Skye trailed him to the back of the room. When he pushed into the ladies' room, she glanced back at the bartender in surprise, then shrugged and went in. On their left stood two sinks. On the right, two stalls. Straight ahead, a full-length mirror hung on the wall. Her guide walked to it, then turned again.

"Arms up."

"Seriously?" Skye said. "Look at this dress, Captain. What the hell could I be hiding under here?"

"Arms up," he repeated.

"Oh, you just want to be feeling a girl up." With a frustrated sigh Skye did as she was asked. Danny boy patted her down, very professionally, then asked for her purse which he upended in a sink. Lipstick, compact, eyebrow pencil, and a money clip. He counted the seven bills, all 100s, glanced at the credit card, and loaded everything back into the little clutch.

"Is all this really necessary just to gamble a little?" Skye asked.

Danny Boy grimaced but did not respond. Instead he pulled the right edge of the mirror which swung open like a door. He stepped past the mirror into the tunnel behind it, turning his broad shoulders just a bit to get through. Skye followed him down a long passage. Christmas tree sized lights lined the floor on either side, reminding Skye of runway lights. The tunnel was long enough that Skye was certain they had passed through the building next door into a third. It led to what looked like a dead end, but Danny Boy knocked three times, then pushed the wall and a panel swung out emitting a burst of brightness.

They stepped into a broad, high-ceilinged room filled with laughing women and smiling, well-dressed men. Danny Boy nodded to the matching muscle man on this side of the portal, then returned to the tunnel. The guard on this side pushed the panel-door closed and returned to arms crossed thousand-yard-stare mode.

Skye drank it all in. The floor was polished hardwood, the walls painted dollar bill green. To her left she found a comfortable lounge area. That is, it was defined by a comfortable deeper green carpet, and outfitted with several comfortable looking chairs and loveseats, about half of which were occupied by a diverse collection of comfortable looking women. They all appeared to be eagerly awaiting company.

To her right an impressive casino set up eagerly awaited the less adventurous visitors. Skye walked past two craps tables and could see three blackjack tables and a roulette wheel across the room. This was going to be fun. She strutted to the cashier's window and pulled out the borrowed black card.

"Good evening. Let's start with ten thousand in chips. I'm feeling lucky tonight."

Armed with chips, Skye scanned the room to choose her game. She wasn't quite settled into her seat at the roulette table when a woman in fishnet stockings asked what she was drinking.

"Do you have ginger beer in this place?" Skye asked. "Of course you do. Let me have a Moscow mule, darling." Then she dropped a thousand dollars on black. The top-heavy redheaded croupier spun the wheel and tossed the ball. It bounced, rolled and settled into a black slot.

"Yes! A good start to the night," Skye said. She held her winnings, pushing the same thousand over onto the red. Another spin while she sipped her cocktail. This time the ball chose a red slot.

"Hey, I'm liking this place. We'll stick with the red, girl," Skye said, just a little too loudly. This time she doubled the bet. The ball was still in play when a thin man with black, slicked-back hair, an olive complexion and an oddly pug nose appeared behind her.

"Good evening," he said. His accent was New Jersey but educated. "I couldn't help but notice you."

"Of course not," Skye said. "I mean, look at me."

He smiled. "Indeed. First time here?"

Skye looked up into his flashing black eyes. "It is indeed. Are you a regular?"

"Martin Levin," he said, offering a hand. "I don't believe I caught your name."

"I don't believe I threw it," Skye said, seizing the hand and shaking it like a man. "You can call me Cloudy." The woman at the wheel announced that Skye had won again, and she squealed in delight. "Damn, I am hot tonight."

"Actually, I'm in management here," Levin said, matching Skye's smile without the enthusiasm. "There was a question in the cashier's cage. May I please see that credit card?"

Well that was fast, Skye thought. She fished the card out of her purse, handed it to Levin, and turned back to the table. This time she pushed three thousand onto the black. "After this I think I'll switch to odds and evens," she told the player beside her.

Behind her, Levin asked, "Where did you get this card?"

Without turning, Skye said, "I thought it came from you."

"Yes," Levin said, "But not to you."

This time the girl announced that red was the winner and raked in Skye's chips. In her peripheral vision Skye could see that she was now flanked by a pair of obvious bouncers. The black guy on her left looked like a heavyweight contender. Skye glimpsed a shoulder holster under his left arm. The white boy on her right could be a WWE grappler. No bulge under his jacket but a slight bump at the back of his waist. His gun would be there.

"I think it best if we discuss this further elsewhere," Levin said. He took a long step back. The other two men took small steps forward.

"I'm having a bit of fun here," Skye said. "Can't we talk later?"

"I really have to insist," Levin said with a slight edge in his voice. The croupier's smile dimmed, and the other players looked at the trouble maker who was slowing the action.

Skye stood slowly, said, "Hold my chips, girl," and followed Levin across the floor to a small room behind the cashier's desk. The room was empty except for four wooden chairs and a small wooden desk. She stood with her arms folded. Levin held up the black card and looked from it to Skye and back again.

"So, how did you come to be holding this particular card?" Levin asked. "And why are you flashing it here? Surely you knew someone would recognize the account."

"Look here, asshole, I'm here because this is where the judge told me I could enjoy some gambling. You need to treat me with a little more respect, you know. I'm Mr. Chen's new Haitian connection. I can supply girls and help clean some of this money, but not if this is the way I'm getting treated. Now give me back my card."

"I don't think so," Levin said, waving the card in her face. "You're saying you know Mr. Chen?"

"Give me back my card, you twit." Skye's eyes smoldered with indignation.

"You know Mr. Chen?"

"I haven't met him, asshole! I work through this Anderson boy. Now give me!" Judging herself in no danger yet, Skye leaned in, slapped Levin hard across the face, and snatched the card out of his hand. The man on her left stifled a chuckle. The one on the right looked away. Good. Neither saw her as a threat.

Levin raised a hand to his face and bared his teeth for a moment before slipping back into his smooth, continental persona.

"So you haven't met him, eh? Maybe it's time you did." Levin stepped out of the room and signaled his men to follow. When Skye didn't move the man on her left gripped her upper arm and pulled her forward. She pretended to resist but moved along with him.

"Brother, you're going to regret putting your hand on me," she said. He didn't even look at her. The little group stopped at a door on the other side of the cashier's cage, totally ignored by the gamblers on the floor. Levin pushed a button and the door revealed itself to be an elevator. Her guards ushered her inside and Levin pressed another button.

They rode up one flight or maybe two. Skye had just a moment to wonder if she had overplayed her hand. Her intent had been to get to Chen, but she didn't think it would happen the same night. Who knew he would be on the premises? And she had visited the city records and studied the blueprints for the building she was told the gambling den was in. But she was now a couple of buildings over and who knew how different the layout might be. Oh, well, she was still an unknown quantity to them, and she knew a bit about them. With luck that would be enough of an advantage to get her out of there alive.

Then the doors slid open and one of the guards pushed her forward into what appeared to be a private lounge. She scanned quickly. Only one small door entered into this room, and Skye would bet it was a bathroom. On the left, a small wet bar like you'd find in someone's finished basement, complete with a bored looking bartender. On the right, three small tables. At one table, two Asian men sat playing cards. At the second, two white girls, drinking and talking. A single light-skinned black man sat at the third table, tapping at a tablet. Two windows graced the wall directly ahead. Of course, row houses only had windows at the front and back.

A leather recliner sat in front of the windows, and the man in it commanded the room. A small table separated him from the tall blonde perched on a lower chair. The blonde stayed focused on the man in the recliner, but he gave Skye his full attention.

He was Chinese, a bit less than six feet tall, with very even teeth and short-cropped black hair. Despite the thousand-dollar black three-piece suit, his pot belly pulled her attention. His eyes were black marbles and when he sat forward, she felt them examining her like an X-ray machine.

No one spoke for five full seconds. Then the man who was clearly in charge asked, "What have you brought me, Levin?"

Levin walked over to the bar. Unasked, the bartender poured him a double scotch. "I thought this might amuse you, Mr. Chen. I found this woman downstairs in the casino. She was gambling on Judge Goldsmith's black card, the one we issued him."

Chen raised one eyebrow. "Indeed. Is he compromised?"

"I haven't had the chance to investigate," Levin said, tipping his glass to swallow half its contents. "But there's more. She tells me she is your new Haitian connection."

Again, Chen said, "Indeed. What is your name, girl?"

Skye yanked her arm free from the man holding it. "I'm known as Cloudy. Cloudy St. James."

Chen smiled, reminding Skye of a Cheshire eyeing a mouse. "This is amusing. Of course, I've never heard of you. And your accent is excellent but not quite true. Who do you work for, girl? And how did you manage to get into my casino?"

"She claimed she had come here to meet your man Brandon," Levin said. He slapped his glass back down on the bar. The bartender immediately refilled it.

The black man sitting alone sat up taller, staring at Skye. Chen turned to him and raised one eyebrow. "You know this woman?"

Brandon shook his head, glancing from Skye to Chen and back again. "I swear I've never seen this girl before in my life. Never heard that name before. No idea what she's talking about boss."

"Now I'm wondering how you came to hear his name, girl," Chen said. He got to his feet and stepped forward, still a dozen feet away. Skye's escorts each wrapped a hand around her upper arms.

"Hey, your friend the judge is maybe a little friendlier than you thought," Skye said. "I needed both a name and the card to get in here, to meet you."

"You came tonight to meet me?" Chen's eyes went up and to his right as if he was considering something. "Well, I don't like indirect approaches. I don't need a connection in Haiti, and for all I know the clumsy local police sent you. I can use more good-looking whores though, and you are an attractive package. You looking for a job, Cloudy?"

Skye didn't respond. She was surveying the territory. The women were clearly not fighters. The one they called Brandon looked like a personal assistant, not a shooter. The two men at the table and maybe the bartender were thugs. The men flanking her were muscle. So the real opposition was five strong.

"Nothing to say, girl?" Chen asked. He reached behind him into a pocket on the right side of the chair and withdrew a miniature axe, like a tomahawk but with a longer blade. "Things not going exactly as you planned? Well I think we'll put you to work anyway. But of course, you must be tested. So, my friends, who wants the Haitian girl?"

Chen started laughing. The girl beside him joined in. The men all grinned except for Brandon who looked a bit uncomfortable. When Skye didn't respond Chen pointed his weapon at her. "Or we could have some fun persuading you to comply."

"So you think one of you is going to get lucky?" Skye asked the room. "Well, in a way you're right." Then she turned to the man on her left, dropped the accent and said in a low tone, "You get to live."

A lot can happen in one second.

Skye stamped down on her left escort's right foot. The silver paper sheath on her heel fell away, allowing the steel spike of the shoe's heel to slice through the man's instep and into the floor. Her left hand was already pulling her star-shaped belt buckle free as she stamped out to her right, dislocating the other man's knee. Her left arm arced out, flipping the buckle forward fast enough that Chen had no chance to move before it sliced deep into his throat. One spike of the star sliced his carotid sending arterial spray into the blonde's face, The blonde's horrified scream was louder than those of the two injured men.

Everyone in the room was frozen in shock for two seconds except Skye. She reached across the black boxer type. Her hand darted under his jacket to grasp his pistol. She spun back quickly, firing twice as she kicked off her shoes. The two men at the table fell before they even knew they were under attack. She ran forward but looking left. The bartender had produced a shotgun from beneath the bar so she put a bullet in his right arm.

Chen had fallen back into his chair, his eyes glassy, staring at nothing. Skye's forward momentum put her left foot on the cushion at Chen's crotch. Her right foot hit the top of the back of the chair and then she was behind him, yanking a window open and slipping through it.

Clinging to the wall in the cool night air, Skye had to admit that she felt pretty good. The rush of adrenaline pumping through her body would not explain the wild grin on her face. If Jayla saw her now, with this light in her eyes and a smile too big to cover, she would be sure Skye was insane. She'd never really get it.

Skye pictured the chaos in the room behind her. They probably thought Chen was untouchable right up to the second his blood sprayed across the room. Skye had not touched the other women in the room but she left three men with bullet wounds and two more otherwise injured. They would all likely recover, but these were injuries one would not soon forget. And that was fine. She wanted the word out that whoever was gunning for Hetman's team was daring, reckless and effective. Some crazy woman with a name no one had heard before or would hear again because she would retire the name Cloudy for a while.

If the survivors had the wits to raise an alarm, they would all assume she would drop to the street. Instead, Skye reached upward. This room at the back of the building was dark so she used the pistol butt to break a hole in the glass. When she heard no sound in response she reached in and unlocked the window. Then raised it just enough to slip inside. Still no sound. It appeared to be an unoccupied bedroom filled with the stale smell of unwashed bedding. Probably just a spare crash room for the hired help, or one of the rooms the hookers took the lower-paying men to. She appreciated the bit of luck sparing her from having to hurt anyone else. She carefully moved past the broken glass and listened at the door. Nothing.

Skye tiptoed into the hall, hating the creaking of the hardwood floors but confident no one on the level below could hear. If this building was like the one two doors over, she would find a window at the end of the hall. A ladder outside it would take her to the roof. In a few minutes she'd be relaxing in her shower and texting her client about payment for assignment number two.

Near the end of the hall a new sound made her freeze in place. It was from the room she was about to pass. Whining? No, more like whimpering. The sound of a child who was all cried out. She thought a little girl, but whoever it was she wasn't moving just lying there half crying. Skye took a couple more steps. The girl presented no danger. Crying at this time of night seemed odd but it had nothing to do with her.

A man's voice in a low tone said, "Jesus, bitch, can't you just shut up?"

He sounded tired, and frustrated. Stuck with babysitter duty maybe. But he hadn't heard Skye pass by. He presented no danger. Still, it had nothing to do with her.

Except.

This crew was known to supplement their income with kidnapping. It was them snatching her client's son that had put her on this job. Shutting them down would probably spare a number of children from this awful experience.

But what about this particular child? No worries, unless the target didn't or couldn't pay the ransom. Then she might join Eric Williams in a premature grave. An ugly business, but again, nothing to do with her.

Skye reached the window at the end of the hall, opened it, but hesitated. From the room she heard, "Shut the fuck up!"

Crap! A deep breath. I don't have time for this.

Then, a slap. Sigh. She turned and moved back toward the door.

Well, it was one more way she could hurt Hetman. In fact, it would really piss him off. It was really good tactics, she told herself.

Holding her pistol forward Skye opened the door and stepped inside. A white girl lay on a bed on her left, under a blanket. Maybe twelve years old. Brown hair in a ponytail, eyes red. On the right, another standard issue thug, his sport coat on the wooden chair he was sitting in, shoulder holster on display. He sprang to his feet but had the good sense to keep his hands forward and in plain sight.

"Who the fuck are you?" he snarled.

"Child protective services," Skye said. She stepped forward swinging her gun backhand to smack the side of the man's head. He collapsed and stayed down. She turned to the girl who, to Skye's surprise, looked more arrogant than frightened. "Do you have a robe and slippers?" Skye asked.

The girl nodded. "Uh-huh. Do you?"

Skye expected the girl to be terrified but saw a bit of herself in this waif. Then she smiled, realizing that she was barefoot and her flimsy dress was hardly appropriate rescue gear. "Mine are home, smartass. Get yours on if you want to get out of here."

In the hall Skye closed the bedroom door and hustled her new charge out the window and up the ladder to the roof. Gripping the child's hand, she pulled her across five connected roofs to the end of the block. On the way, she saw the tears begin. The arrogance of privilege had served as a strong defense, but now the trauma was eroding it. Still, she was doing a pretty good job of sniffing back the fear.

They stopped at the fifth building because it had a functioning iron fire escape. With Skye in the lead they climbed down to the street. Only then did the girl speak again.

"Where are we going?"

"Only another block, kid," Skye said. "There's a car waiting for me there."

Skye pulled her forward down the dimly-lit street. She saw no reason to tell her young charge that the waiting car was an Uber, or that she always rode with the same driver. She paid him enough to get him to wait when she knew she would need a lift. Times, days and locations varied so much that no one would see them as unusual in any way. Still, she used four different Uber accounts just to be on the safe side.

The ground was cold on Skye's feet. She envied the teenager's pink fuzzy slippers, just one thing she had never had as a child. No one would have bothered to kidnap her. No one would have paid to get her back. Now she wore the best names in women's shoes but when she was this girl's age she would have loved to have those slippers.

The black Honda Accord felt like sanctuary as Skye approached it. The driver started the engine when she was half a block away. As she yanked the back door open, the little girl looked up at her.

"Are you a superhero? Like Batgirl or the Black Widow?"

Skye rolled her eyes, pushed the girl into the car and followed. As the car pulled away from the curb a laugh came from the front seat.

"Shut up, Mo,"

"Mo?" the little girl asked.

"Morris," the driver said. "Not Moe. I'm not one of the stooges. Morris, like Morris Day and the Time."

"Who?" the girl asked, and it was Skye's turn to laugh.

"Kid, you is too young to know anybody who plays good music," Morris said. "What's your name?"

"Carla. Carla Evans."

Skye grimaced. She had not even thought to ask the poor girl's name.

"I'm pleased to meet you, Carla. I've got a daughter but she's a little bit older than you. So, Skye, is this your new trainee? She going to be the Robin to your Batman?"

Skye rubbed her feet on the carpet to warm them. Mo thought he was funny, always cracking wise. Skye thought maybe because he looked a little like Chris Rock he figured the gift for humor went with it.

"Actually, it's a bit past Carla's bedtime, Mo, and we need to get her home. Honey why don't you tell the nice man your address?"

By the time they pulled up in front of the four-level townhome out on R Street, Mo had delivered a detailed history of Minneapolis music of the 1980s and after punching buttons on his dashboard managed to play "Jungle Love" and "Color of Success." Of course by then Carla was slumped in the corner of the seat, fast asleep. Mo turned around, saw his smaller passenger, and turned the music down.

"Going to walk her up to the door?"

"That sounds like a bad idea," Skye said. Then she nudged Carla's elbow. "Hey girl. Time to get moving. You're home."

Carla's smile was dazzling. "Come on. Mommy and Daddy are going to love you! And I'm going to tell them all about the bad men who took me away from school and they're going to fix them good. But you can tell them all about how you found me, and I know they'll be so happy…"

"No, honey," Skye said in the softest voice she could manage. "We have to get going and we really need to be kind of anonymous, you know?"

Carla nodded quickly. "Like real superheroes."

"Um, right," Skye said. "Now just run up to the door and ring the bell until they wake up and let you in," Skye said.

"Ok. Thank you for saving me…" Carla allowed time for Skye to fill in a name but when she didn't Carla just said, "anonymous African American lady." Then she leaned forward to give Skye a big hug. Skye threw Morris a startled look and patted the girl's back a couple times with one hand. Carla backed off, smiled, opened the door and scampered up the long lighted boardwalk that led from the street to her front door. She rang the doorbell, then turned and waved. Skye tapped Morris' shoulder, and they pulled away.

"So, do I get to know what that was about?" Mo asked.

Skye curled up on the seat right behind him. "You usually don't want to know any more than you need to about what I'm doing," Skye said.

"You never brought home a kid before."

A light rain began, making the asphalt reflective and kicking the windshield wipers into intermittent action. Skye wished she had brought a sweater or something. The flimsy gown didn't offer the warm coziness she craved, but she didn't want to ask Morris to turn up the heat because then he'd be uncomfortable.

Of course, Morris was right about this night. In the past he had just dropped her off where she was going to work, then picked her up at a designated time and taken her home or to her next destination. He had to suspect she was involved in some sort of clandestine activity, maybe even understanding that it was good security for her comings and goings to be part of an Uber driver's occasional work, as opposed to registering a car herself or even renting one. It helped her stay off the grid and no one looking at all his calls would pick her movements out as anything suspicious. And he was well paid to stay both available and in the dark about her activities. But maybe this was a reasonable exception.

"I won't let anything evil or crooked touch you, Mo," Skye said. "Actually, you just returned a kidnap victim home."

The next few seconds of silence were uncomfortable for her. She remembered those first couple of jobs after Papa was gone. She had considered a military career or time in law enforcement before accepting what she was best suited for. She remembered walking home after making the touch for men who had been friends of Papa's and knew what she could do. Then it had been that rapist in Baltimore, and she had decided to accept the risk of taking an Uber home. Somehow it made the freelance job feel more normal, to have someone ask her those routine "how was your day" type questions.

But now she feared the driver she trusted and relied on might think she was getting him involved with something dangerous. He might want to stop working with her. She would understand, but damn, she had so few people she could trust.

But when Morris finally spoke again it was through his deep laugh that made the whole car vibrate. "Damn. You really are a superhero. The Black Widow, only really black. No, the Green Hornet. That's it. And I'm Kato."

Chapter 11

"So, how did that make you feel?" It was always the pivotal question for Jayla, and the one she knew Skye dreaded the most. But if Jayla was to understand the mind of a hired killer, she needed to understand her emotional reactions to events, especially events that were outside her usual scope.

Jayla had listened with rapt attention to the story of Skye's invasion of the underground casino cum bordello. She noted how casually Skye related her confrontation with a man she believed to be a high-ranking underworld figure and the pride with which she recounted killing a man in cold blood and shooting and maiming several others.

"I find it interesting that you don't just rely on guns," Jayla commented. "Did I understand correctly that you had on shoes with high heels made of steel spikes, sheathed with rubber?"

"Every woman should have them for self-protection," Skye said. "What size are you? I'll get you a pair."

Jayla stepped away from that offer. "I do note how casually you discuss the death you bring, and that it is restricted to your actual target. You continue to show reluctance to kill men you were not hired to kill, even when you know they would kill you if they had the chance."

"It's assassin's law number nine," Skye said, in the tone most people use when speaking to a small child. "Don't shoot everyone in the room. This job, this profession, is about precision. I get hired because my client has a grievance, but it's a grievance against a person, not a group or an organization. That precision of purpose gives me a kind of power. Blindly lashing out is the fastest way to lose that power."

"I see," Jayla said. "But you don't seem reluctant to injure others."

"Whole different thing, Doc," Skye said. "That's self-defense. If somebody is a threat to me, I shut it down. But you don't have to eliminate the person to eliminate the threat. I think professionals appreciate that."

"Got you," Jayla said. "So, what happened next? You went home after that?"

"Well, not exactly," Skye said. From there the narrative became thin and vague. She had "tripped over" a girl the gang had kidnapped, so she picked her up and took her home. And that's when Jayla had asked the key question: "How did that make you feel?"

Skye had screwed up her eyes, clenched her teeth and shaken her head once, hard. It was the expression she made when she thought she had walked into a verbal trap.

"I shouldn't have even told you that," she said, pointing an accusing finger at her therapist. The fingernails were the only thing that was the same since her last visit. Today's wig was short, in a pixie cut. Skye wore black tights and boots with a loose blouse that hung past her hips and a lot of gold: bangle bracelets, dangling earrings and three rings on each hand.

"Why?" Jayla asked, leaning back in her office chair. "Are you embarrassed by it?"

"No," Skye said, snapping to her feet. "It's just… it wasn't a feeling thing, all right? It was one more way I could hurt the cartel, throw them off balance. Stealing from them shows how big a threat I am."

Jayla nodded. "All true. But that's not the reason you did it. Tell me why."

Skye paced away, almost to the door. "It was arrogance. I showed them I had no reason to even hurry getting away. I was saying how stupid they are."

"Again, true but avoidance. Tell me why."

Skye spun back toward Jayla, her voice low but somehow louder. "Look, it was the thing to do. It was what anybody would have done, anybody with a…" She cut herself off and stared at the carpet.

"Yes," Jayla said, leaning forward now. "It was the normal thing. Anyone with a heart would have done the same. Is that right?"

Heavy sigh. "Yes."

"All right," Jayla said with a smile. "And how did that make you feel?"

"Jesus!" Skye threw her hands up, looked to the ceiling, and walked to the other end of the room. "What difference does that make? I did it."

"Yes, you did. And afterward it affected you. How. Did. That. Feel?"

Skye stood at the window, staring out, hands clasped behind her back. For an instant she looked like she might burst into tears, but it passed quickly. Jayla held her breath, sensing a possible breakthrough.

When Skye spoke, it was in a low tone that Jayla could barely hear. "It felt right. It felt good. I was there. Nobody was there for me when I was that age. Nobody. But God damn it, I was there for her."

Jayla was furiously writing in her journal. She already knew that Skye was not a textbook psychopath or even a sociopath, but it had taken her the better part of a year to get this close to understanding what her core state might be.

"So, what happens now?" Jayla asked.

Skye seemed to shake off the previous conversation. She turned and walked slowly toward Jayla wearing her normal confident, arrogant smile. Jayla knew that smile as Skye's first line of defense.

"Well, next I wisely invest the seventy thousand dollars that appeared in my account yesterday."

"Not what I meant," Jayla said.

Skye laughed. "I know. Seriously, next is, I get a line on target number three. I'm thinking the whole operation at Chen's level will go bat shit! When mystery man Hetman sees the threat to his kidnapping income stream he'll move fast. I'm thinking he'll send in the next man up the chain to take over Chen's operation. And when his head pops up so I can see it…"

"No, Skye," Jayla said. "I mean what happens with the little girl. Will you reach out to her? Will you make contact with the parents?"

Skye's brow furrowed. "What? No. Carla's no longer in play, Doc. She's off the board. No reason to think about her anymore."

Chapter 12

Standing at her kitchen island, wrapped in her favorite white terrycloth robe, Skye munched on a toasted bagel with cream cheese and watched a private television broadcast. She was watching the front entrances of the building she had entered to get to the underground casino, the building that actually held the casino, and the building between them.

It was a bright, sunny day and foot traffic on the street was light, but she did not want to miss her quarry's entrance. The notes in front of her, gleaned from Rissik's impressive data gathering, told her she was expecting a Declan Murphy, but she had no idea what he looked like. She could hardly hunt an animal without knowing its appearance and location. If she was right about the state of Chen's operation, she should soon have both.

Skye sipped tea from a big porcelain mug and wondered why the police still sat on stakeouts when it was so easy to plant small cameras in front of the houses across the street. Positioned in trees facing the target doors, the cameras were housed in what looked like failed birds' nests. No one had seen her on the block at 4am. One night after Chen was put down in his own office, these fools still were not watching the street in the twee hours. Amateurs.

Although she tried to focus, her mind kept wandering to the conversation with Jayla the day before. Why did Jayla think the little girl was such a big deal? She was an accidental diversion from the matter at hand. And anyway, it was good for her to be out of the line of fire since Skye figured that building was ground zero for some bad stuff and would see more action soon.

She sat up when a procession of three large black vehicles on her screen drew her attention. First a Bronco came rolling down the narrow street. The Mercedes Benz G-Class behind it looked a lot like a Hummer with delusions of grandeur, holding a six-foot space between itself and the second Bronco. The three urban monsters stopped in the middle of the lane, preventing any other vehicle from passing on either side.

A thug rolled out of each vehicle, all in black suits and sunglasses, like a backup group for the Men in Black. Two rushed to flank the door Skye had entered just two days ago. The third opened the passenger side door of the Mercedes. Skye was ready for a wrestler, the Joker or the male equivalent of Cruella de Vil to step out.

She was not far wrong. Preconceived notions led her to expect a freckled redhead, but instead the man who rose out of the car was a dark-haired, handsome man, easily 6 foot 3. He wore a blue double-breasted pinstripe suit with a dusty-rose tie, tasseled oxblood loafers and a giant pinky ring that looked like black opal embedded with a diamond. He also wore a pasted-on half smile, yet Skye could see the menace behind his GQ appearance. He walked to the door without looking up and down the street. Not that he wasn't careful, but his attitude said, "I got people to do that."

The ten seconds Murphy spent on the street were enough for Skye to decide that this was going to be fun.

Declan Murphy stepped out of the elevator into what he had been told was Chen's operations center. No desk, no bank of computers just a bar and some tables where men sat around too relaxed. The only person he saw who looked alert was the boss' mouthpiece, Anderson, who probably had never held a gun. Chen's right-hand man, Levin, looked more like a waiter than a fighter.

No wonder Chen was dead.

Murphy wandered over to Chen's empty chair. Dried blood stained one side of the chair and the small table that sat beside it.

"Get this out of here," Murphy said to the room. No one moved. He focused on a spot on the wall just below the ceiling and drew a balisong knife out of his right pocket. He flipped the butterfly knife open with a double roll out too fast for the eye to follow.

"Get this out of here." In the silence, one of the men who had been playing cards the night Chen died got up from the table and grabbed the back of the chair. His partner followed and grabbed the front of the chair. They hustled the chair across the floor and into the elevator. *Those two will keep their jobs*, Murphy thought.

"Listen up," Murphy told the room. "I'm not Chen. I'm not here to play games. This is business. You'll learn to treat it like business, or you'll go someplace else." He stepped over to the bar. "I drink Jameson. Black Barrel if you have it." The bartender, his right arm in a sling, reacted as if stung by a cattle prod, grabbing a bottle from behind himself and pouring a double shot into a glass. Murphy took the glass with his left hand, swallowed half the contents and put it back down.

"My understanding is that two days ago a woman walked in here and killed your boss. A woman. A black woman. She put five of ours in the hospital. Two are still there. I can see our bartender was hurt. Who else?"

The two thugs who had held Skye stood from a table and nodded.

"You fellows are big and you're looking like professionals. What happened?"

The black man, whose right foot was bandaged, said, "Won't speak for anybody else, boss. For me, I got careless."

His partner said, "Yeah."

"Well that's honest," Murphy said. "You look okay now. Get yourself a drink."

The white thug nodded and went to the bar. Murphy had wanted to see that he could walk okay. The limp was slight. He was still useful.

"Who brought the girl in here?"

Levin stepped in front of Murphy but stayed ten feet away. "She was in the casino downstairs. She had one of our payoff credit cards and dropped Anderson's name. I knew Mr. Chen would want to know how she came to have the card and that name." He looked to his left, then his right. "These two fellows escorted her up here. She looked harmless."

"The good ones always do," Murphy said. "Did you pat her down?"

Levin quickly pointed at one of the seated men. "That's not my area. Danny Boy checked her out."

Danny Boy looked up, both surprise and worry showing on his face. Murphy pointed at him and waved him over. To his credit, Danny stalked over and stood right in front of Murphy, looking up into his eyes. Murphy smiled at his countryman.

"What happened, Danny Boy? You let an assassin into our casino."

"Sir, I patted her down good," Danny Boy said. "I was looking for the usual weapons. Nobody would have took her shoes. And they tell me she got Mr. Chen with her belt buckle. I ain't never seen nothing like that star thing she got him with."

"Shuriken," Murphy said, draining his drink. "The Japs call them shuriken. You didn't recognize it. A simple mistake."

"Yes sir," Danny said.

"The real mistake was, you couldn't see this woman was dangerous. Chen paid for your mistake." Murphy shook his head and pointed to his right with his knife at the thug at the bar. "He paid for your mistake with a dislocated knee." He pointed with his blade to his left at the tall black thug with his bandaged foot. "He paid for your mistake." Then he swung his arm back, fast, the blade's tip slashing Danny's cheek. "And now you have paid for your mistake. Go get cleaned up."

Danny stifled a groan, pressed a hand against his cheek and turned to the elevator. The blood drained from Levin's face as Murphy turned to him.

"I'm thinking we'll be more careful about bringing people in here in the future, yes?"

"Yes sir. Of course."

"Good," Murphy said. "Now I'll be needing you to be getting some real furniture in here. A decent desk. And I'll be doing a lot of me own computer work. Anderson's not my secretary. And right away I'll be wanting to see the books, all the records from the last quarter. I'm talking about the casino, the whores and the snatches. You're still doing the kidnappings, right?"

"Yes sir," Levin said. "I keep that all in an air-gapped computer at my office. I usually download it to a laptop, or I used to do that to bring here for Mr. Chen's review."

"That'll still work," Murphy said. "Get moving and get it all together, order that furniture, and get back here after lunch. Do you think you can you handle that?"

"Of course," Levin said.

Skye was propped up on elbows and toes coming up on three minutes in the plank position when she saw new activity on her screen. Murphy's cars had moved on a while ago but now Levin appeared at the door, jogging down the steps to the sidewalk. Did he wear a tuxedo every day? He looked in both directions before moving down the street at a serious pace. He looked nervous, jumpy, as if he expected a giant hand to reach out and swat him like an unwanted insect.

She dropped to her knees, attention rivetted to the screen. Had Murphy fired him, or demoted him to some less desirable job? That was not a smile on his face as he walked out of the camera's range. He had been Chen's main man, but now shared the blame for letting Skye get that close to Chen. Maybe Murphy was bringing in his own team. If that guess was right, it could work to Skye's advantage. She needed a good source of inside intel on Murphy and if Levin had fallen out of favor, he was a potential source.

She hadn't spent much time on Levin and wasn't sure how to get to talk to him, but she had an idea where to start. She pulled on a pair of jeans, black boots and a comfortable, light gray cashmere sweater. She ran a brush through her shoulder-length jet-black hair. After pulling a denim jacket over her sweater it was time to hit the street.

She stepped out into a nice, crisp fall day, the sun smiling on the city whose streets were packed with residents, tourists, government officials and a healthy crowd of homeless folks. There were no homeless on the narrow Georgetown streets near her apartment, but the rest were certainly out in force. Like her, a lot of people were taking advantage of the warmth, light breeze and sunshine.

Skye knew her city well despite the year spent away from it. She thought about the series of hotel rooms they had moved in and out of, that little pied-a-terre in Paris where Andre had taught her so much about locks, second story work and making soft entries. The time they bunked with Hendrick in the Netherlands. He had sharpened her marksmanship beyond what Papa was able to show her. The American feeling hotel in Israel where the man Papa called Irv trained her in the martial art called Krav Maga. Each place was more exotic than the last, but none of them lessened her appreciation for The District, this patchwork of disparate neighborhoods she was born into.

Georgetown was across town from her destination that day, over by the Navy Yard. She could have taken the bus or hopped on a train, but it was just too nice out. Being a history buff, Skye knew that the District of Columbia was carved out of the surrounding states originally as a ten mile by ten mile square, and that was before Virginia decided to snatch back a chunk west of the Potomac. What that meant to her was that there was no place in the city that wasn't within walking distance.

She decided to stay on Pennsylvania Avenue, the diagonal bisector of the city. After passing within a block of her usual Trader Joe's, there wasn't much to hold her attention until she was within sight of the White House. The Renwick Gallery loomed on her left and she reminded herself she needed to visit it again soon. Brick and stone, arches and columns, it was an impressive edifice for only two stories. She wondered who had decided it had to actually have the words "Dedicated to Art" carved into the roof on the front. And with a period at the end of that sentence. She found it so much more impressive than the White House, maybe more for what it represented to her.

Then the White House was on her right, standing like a Grande Dame invited to a tea party and staring with disdain at the women who arrived not wearing white dresses, shoes and caps, and the men who failed to wear black ties and tails. Then a right turn and past the Old Ebbitt Grill, whose façade echoed the Renwick Gallery's. The city's oldest bar and restaurant, it is as historic as any of its neighbors yet somehow seems to embrace the present.

Skye loved the architecture along this stretch of the Avenue, past the Navy Memorial, the National Archives and other great buildings. But then came the long wander around the Capital Building. Now she was past the Washington of tourists and politicians, into The District where real people lived and, in her view, where the city just went to shit.

She stopped at one of the row houses just off New Jersey Avenue, stepped down to the basement apartment and rapped on the door. After a reasonable pause she knocked again, knowing that someone would check her out through the tiny peephole before coming to the door. She heard locks being thrown and the door opened a few inches. The black man on the other side wore jeans and a white wifebeater undershirt. His hair was cut as short as it could be without actually shaving his head, and he looked at, through and past Skye at the same time.

"What up, Jimmy?" Skye said. "I'm alone. Just want to talk for a couple. You busy?"

It all played behind Jimmy's eyes: a little fear, a lot of respect, and the memory of Skye breaking into his place but then saving his life in a frantic shootout. Skye knew Jimmy to be for real, an Original Gangsta, and the respect was mutual. After a moment Jimmy swung the door wide and waved her inside.

She followed him into the living room. The air was stale and musty, the lighting dim. The furniture all looked like it had come from the last century except for the flat screen television on a Walmart entertainment center. He settled into a leather recliner. She dropped onto the couch. Jimmy's eyes fell on the Johnny Walker Red bottle on the coffee table and he hopped back up to fetch a second glass.

Skye sat silent until he got back and poured a shot into her glass, then his.

"Thanks brother," Skye said, not reaching for her glass until Jimmy picked his up.

"So what's up?" Jimmy asked. "It's been a minute, eh? I ain't seen you since that day."

"Not here to hassle you," Skye said. "Couple quick questions and I'm out of here."

"Cool. Don't know what I know that could help you."

Skye sipped from her glass. "Looking for a white boy called Levin. Thinks he's a player. You know the streets. Thought you might know where he hangs."

Skye didn't want to lean back, not knowing what tiny creatures shared the apartment with Jimmy and his roommate. So, she sat with elbows on her knees watching Jimmy do the math. His eyes were never more than half open, but she could see he was making connections. A smile crept onto his face, revealing yellowed teeth that matched what should have been the whites of his eyes.

"Chen," he said. "That was you. Damn."

"Yeah, me," she said, taking a drink. "And Levin was his boy. He's not a mark, but I bet he knows shit I want to know."

Jimmy stared at the floor for a moment, then looked up with furrowed brow. "You know that night you busted in here, I thought you was coming for me."

"Nobody wants you gone, Jimmy," Skye said. "At least nobody I know. Even if they did, I'd never take a contract on you. Never. You can take that to the bank."

She didn't notice Jimmy's shoulders were tense until he lowered them and relaxed. He nodded thank you and drained his glass. "I'm just a hustler," he said. "Hope I don't never make that kind of an enemy, but if I do it's good to know I won't be running from you."

"Bet," Skye said. "So, you know Levin?"

Jimmy shook his head and pointed at Skye. "Chen was an asshole. Good riddance. Levin thinks he's all that. Most nights he hangs out at this place called Bar Deco, up in Chinatown. You know it?"

Skye nodded. "Big ass place. Seems like his kind of joint."

When she got to her feet Jimmy said, "Hey you want to hang for a bit? Smuggla be home in a few and he's bringing some smoke that's as good as the chronic from the old days. Then it's 4-20 time. I'll roll a couple Js and we can chill for a bit."

"Thanks, but gonna pass, bro. Got shit to do and not into a social thing today."

Skye popped up out of the Metro station directly beneath the Capital One Arena and crossed the street to the three-story bar and restaurant known as Bar Deco. Living up to its name, the venue was decorated in a way that would have put Jay Gatsby in his comfort zone. Wrought iron chairs with wooden slats for seats and backs, huge multi-pane warehouse windows and pipes in plain sight across the ceiling. It was just dark enough, and the atmosphere was warm and friendly. After going home, grabbing lunch and a shower, and a quick train ride, she was happy to grab a seat at a corner table, order a drink and consider her earlier conversation.

With eyes on the front door, Skye reflected that in truth, she was never into a "social thing." There were times when she felt like dancing, or seeing a show or having a drink, but those activities didn't require companionship. There were times she just wanted to get laid, but willing partners were easy to find. Three reasonable prospects had hit on her in just the three hours she had been in that bar. If she just wanted to talk, well, she paid a woman to listen to her. She had subcontractors, assistants and informants, but nobody she would call a friend. That situation made it easy to stay off the grid and off the law enforcement radar. And it didn't bother her, although sometimes the fact that it didn't bother her kind of bothered her. Jayla seemed to think the situation indicated something being off, but she said the fact that Skye was bothered by the fact that she felt no need of friends was healthy. It was all too hard for her to think about, so she focused on her Moscow Mule and checked the incoming crowd.

When the room started to fill up Skye checked the menu. Ordering dinner would make it easier for her to keep her table. It was bar food, but she was surprised by some of the options. She settled on pan seared tuna with honey wasabi and Kung Pao cauliflower. The patrons seemed to come in waves. First a crowd of business types wandered in. Then a crowd of louder college types and sports fans rushed the bar. It never really got crowded because of the number of people who quickly moved upstairs.

Then Skye spotted a man who looked like a beefy Secret Service agent pushing just a little too aggressively through the door. He looked everywhere except behind him. She judged him a personal security pro. His boss came in behind him. Thin with black, slicked-back hair, and that odd little nose. Levin smiled, but it was a nervous smile. His second bodyguard pushed in behind him, staying close.

The first man chose a table halfway between the windows and the bar. Levin followed him after sharing a few words with his second friend. The volume was rising so she couldn't catch the words but when the bigger man headed for the bar she assumed he had just taken Levin's order. Skye stood up and a white girl who didn't look old enough to drink grabbed her seat. Skye ignored her and walked to the wall, easing around customers as she made her way around the room's perimeter. While she walked, she drew a folding knife from her pocket and opened it one handed. She wanted to interrogate Levin, but he knew her only as a killer. She didn't want him and his bodyguards to react to her as an immediate threat in this now crowded and noisy room. She hoped the environment would work to her advantage.

When she was behind Levin's seated companion, she walked toward them, working her way through the throng of seated revelers, keeping her hands low. She managed to go unnoticed until she was standing right behind the guard. She seemed to stumble, falling against his back like a clumsy drunk. But as one hand landed on his left shoulder the other pressed her knife against his ribs just hard enough for him to feel it. Leaning forward, she whispered, "Don't" against his ear. Looking over the bodyguard she saw the light of recognition in Levin's eyes. She figured he'd be frozen with fear for two good seconds, so she needed to talk fast.

"Tell your friend it's going to get real messy in here if he gives me any shit."

Levin held up both palms and released a long sigh.

"Thank God it's you," he said.

Chapter 13

Levin's reaction was a pleasant surprise. Skye gave him her smirking smile and leaned farther forward over the bodyguard's shoulder.

"You didn't think I was coming for you next?"

Levin returned her smile. "I watched you put Chen down, remember?" Then Levin spoke to his seat mate, whose face reflected rising anger. "You can relax. She hit Chen and shot three other guys before they had a chance to shoot and got away without breaking a sweat." Turning back to Skye he said, "If I was on your list, you'd have killed me right then, not waited to come up on me in a room full of witnesses."

The second bodyguard approached the table, his hands full with three cocktails. The seated guard looked over his shoulder at Skye, said, "Do you mind?" as he glanced down at the blade.

"Oh, sorry, man," Skye said, folding her knife and slipping it back into her pocket. Then to Levin, "You're a smart guy. Let's see how smart. Can you guess why I'm here?"

"I'm just glad you are," Levin said. "Can we talk? These guys are tame, and I'm no threat to the likes of you."

Skye nodded. "As long as your friends don't get too close. Let's move to the roof. May as well bring your drinks. And I need another Moscow Mule."

Levin stared up at the second bodyguard. He rolled his eyes, put down the drinks he was carrying and headed back to the bar.

The building felt even more industrial on the patio up on the roof, although the wood floors held the same tables and chairs as they had inside. Maybe it was the steel girders overhead, or just the view of surrounding taller buildings. Tables lined the railing to maximize the view. Skye and Levin sat facing each other, with the bigger men a couple of tables away.

"So, you were glad to see me," Skye said. "Were you expecting somebody else?"

Levin sipped his three-olive martini. "Can't be sure. But, as you can guess, I got a new boss, guy named Murphy from – big surprise - the Irish mob. He doesn't seem like the forgiving type, and he expressed… disappointment that we let a girl get to Chen in his own office."

"And since you escorted me into the room…"

"Yeah," Levin said. "I wouldn't be surprised if he sent some guys to rough me up, to punish me for my bad judgement. I got to say, you played us pretty well."

Skye nodded thanks. "Well, I'm pretty good at this."

Levin raised his glass to her. "No debate there, girl. Was kind of hoping we could work out a deal where you'd keep me safe. I'm not sure about the loyalty of these boys."

"Well, I don't do that kind of work," Skye said, "but if you can help me with some intel, I'm pretty sure Murphy won't have his new job too long."

"What do you want to know?" Levin stared out at the cityscape, and Skye thought he was already disengaged from his gang. His loyalty died with Chen.

"Well let's start at the beginning Cang," she said. "What's with the kidnapping? It's big business south of the border, but not so much in the U.S."

"Hey, it's a thing for the new boss," Levin said. "I was happy working hookers and gamblers. Crime with no victims, you know? Everybody likes to screw if the girls are clean and willing and don't run their mouths. And everybody likes to gamble, but not everybody wants to go to Maryland or Virginia, or to declare their winnings to the IRS. But the new big boss decided we're in the kidnapping business. And I got to admit it's been paying off handsomely. As it turns out, fewer hassles than prostitution. Fewer moving parts, so to speak."

"Okay, I can see how it can be profitable if you hit the right marks. But why kids? And why kill them, like the boy Eric Williams?"

Levin shrugged his shoulders and sipped his drink. "Kids make people pay, more reliably than wives. If the mark doesn't pay, they die. I mean, that's the deal, right? Funny, I remember that Williams case. The kid seemed very confused, like he didn't get what was going on." He shook his head, evidently lost in the memory for a second. Then his mouth dropped open and he stared at Skye. In his eyes she saw a new awareness, and a new fear.

"Wait," Levin said, putting his glass down. "Is that what this is about? The kids? Listen I was against this kidnapping thing from the get-go. I was…"

"Yeah, yeah, you was just following orders," Skye said. "And you'll keep doing it, cause I don't need you looking suspicious in there. Your problem is Murphy and his boss and the guy at the top of the pile. And trust me, those are problems I plan to solve. I just need to know who the top dog is."

Levin sat back, shooting a furtive glance at his bodyguards who were digging into a huge plate of nachos and not paying any attention to him. "Is that why you spared me, cause you think I know who he is? Well, I hope it don't get me thrown off the roof or something, but I got no idea who this Hetman guy is. Nobody does. Nobody sees him, nobody talks to him. He sends his orders through Anderson. Now, he's seen Hetman and you can tell he's terrified of the guy. In fact, he talked to me one time about getting out the business, you know, getting away from Hetman. But the big boss picked him and won't let him go."

"So you've only heard from Anderson," Skye said, swirling her drink while she thought it through. "I take it you take your orders from him. How do you know he's not Hetman himself, just pretending to be the mouthpiece?"

"Well, I know guys above my pay grade have gotten calls from Hetman when Anderson was in the room. But trust me, if you was to talk to this guy for a couple minutes you wouldn't ask that question. Anderson is good with reports and computers and shit, but he ain't no boss."

Skye emptied her drink. "That's kind of disappointing, Levin. Guess I just need to focus on Murphy for now. You don't look to be any help there. In fact, it wasn't much worth talking to you."

"I can be useful," Levin said. "I know Murphy's comings and goings. I know where all the money is, at least from the gambling, the girls and whoever we grab. Seriously, I am worth talking to. I ain't a waste of time."

Skye folded her arms and stared at Levin. She had never considered wasting time and energy killing this clown. He wasn't on her list. But Murphy, number three on Milo Williams' list, was worth a hundred grand. If Levin had mistaken her for a crusader and saw himself as a possible target, maybe she could use that fear.

"So you know where Murphy's going to be when?" Skye asked. When Levin nodded with enthusiasm she said, "Well then, maybe I'll keep you around. You know where he sleeps?"

"Not really," Levin said, "But I got designated times to meet and report to him. That would tell you when he's going to the office, right? Got that schedule in the car right now."

Skye made a show of thinking it through, giving Levin the side eye a couple times before finally saying, "Yeah, okay. Let's go get that schedule. Then you're free to go until I need more inside info."

Skye didn't like elevators. They're just small rooms with no windows and only one way in and out. If your enemy is standing there when those doors slide apart there's nothing you can do but get dead. She once shoved a sharpened Number 2 Ticonderoga pencil between a man's ribs on the second floor of an office building and left him and his punctured lung behind when she got out on the fourteenth floor. She trotted down the stairs and out of the building, quite sure that no one would even figure out cause of death until the medical examiner spotted the quarter inch hole under his arm.

This day the ride down was uneventful, first to the first floor of Bar Deco, then the second ride to the parking garage beneath. It was brightly lit with narrow aisles between rows of cars and not an empty space in sight. Skye figured there was a game or show going on across the street and all the patrons parked there for it. Bodyguard #1 led the way, followed by Levin, guard #2 and Skye. Their steps echoed off cement floor and walls, and the smell of dampness and exhaust fumes was oppressive. On television these things were always so spacious. In reality, Skye wondered how people drove into and out of these spaces without hitting another car or a support column.

When they reached Levin's Mercedes AMG sedan the lead bodyguard was reaching for the driver's door while, on the other side, his partner stepped past Levin to open the back door. Standing behind Levin, Skye noticed two young men walking between cars toward them. Jeans, Timberland boots and Wal-Mart jackets with ballcaps on backwards.

They weren't talking to each other, which was enough to make the hairs on the back of her neck stand at attention.

No one else noticed them. She was about to say something to… what were their names? Levin hadn't bothered to introduce them. Before she could get past "Hey, um…" one of the approaching men raised his right arm. Hanging at the end of it was an Intratec TEC-9 automatic pistol.

Chapter 14

"Shit!" Skye shouted, swinging right to roll over the car's trunk. Landing on the other side she saw the first three nine-millimeter slugs punch into Levin and heard them ping against the car's body. The guard in front of Levin managed to draw from a side holster before the second shooter put three bullets into him, center mass. He fell forward as Levin slid to the ground. The driver guard returned fire over the roof of the car.

The gunfire echoed through the cement cavern, savaging Skye's ears. She ran in a crouch down the row of cars away from Levin's bleeding body. She guessed Levin was right. His new boss didn't like him. Apparently he decided to fire his finance man and didn't want to bother with the issues of severance pay or confidentiality statements. But neither Murphy nor his gunmen had any reason to suspect Skye would be there.

Looping around behind the shooters she slid a small .32 auto out of the holster at the back of her waistband. She stopped three cars behind them in the same narrow space between cars. Why were they still shooting? Their mark was down. Surely the bodyguards weren't part of the assignment. The shooters could have slipped away easily leaving the driver to explain the mess. But they seemed determined to kill him too.

Amateurs.

Well, she wasn't going to let people shoot at her and walk away, even if they didn't know she was in the kill zone. Two car lengths away, she took her pistol in a two-handed grip and fired once into the back of one shooter's head. He fell against his buddy, who turned in surprise. Wedged between the cars, he had no chance of turning and getting a shot off before Skye fired into his face. Before he hit the ground she was running for the elevator. She holstered her weapon before reaching ground level where she got out and walked calmly through the lobby and out the door to join the milling crowd. No police on scene yet, but there had to be lots of witnesses to the sound of that firefight, so the law would arrive soon. She crossed the street and joined the mob coming out of a Capitols game. This was one time she was inconspicuous in a mostly white crowd. She managed to squeeze into the next train headed west and stood clinging to the center pole as it carried her away from the shootout.

From the smiles and spontaneous chants Skye guessed that the home team had won that night. As the adrenaline washed out of her system she realized that her clothes were sticking to her. Her face was surely glistening with sweat. She wished she could get into a rest room and clean up a little, but somehow City officials never thought to equip the Metro with any such things.

Now what? Four bodies down in a public place. The bodyguard driver had no chance of getting the car out of there. Whether he got himself clear before the police closed off the building depended on how long he waited to be sure there was no more incoming fire. Either way it was a mess. But if he got clear it was a mess with no connection to her. If the police did have him, she couldn't guess what he'd say. Would he even mention the black girl his boss had been chatting with in the bar that evening? Would he guess that she took the other two shooters out? If so, he might leave her out of his narrative recognizing that she saved his life.

When she reached her stop, Skye burst through the door, forcing herself between the more leisurely people getting out. The escalators were clogged so she sprinted up the long flight of stairs to the street. A nice breeze blew the river's scent onto her and she drew it deeply into her lungs. She jogged the few blocks to her apartment and took the stoop stairs without slowing down. She punched the code into her door lock and reflexively checked her surroundings before turning he knob.

She felt itchy as she walked through her front door. Not really, but that was the only way she could describe it. She didn't pause to turn a light on. She left a trail of clothes from the door to the bathroom where she turned the shower on as hot as she could stand it. She scrubbed her face, neck and down her body as if trying to remove a stain. She had not been too close to any of the dead men when the bullets hit them, but she still felt as if there was blood on her.

Wrapped in her heavy terry robe she stared into the bathroom mirror. Her skin glowed from the heat and scrubbing. She was clean and fresh, and smelled of the orchid scented soap. Why did she feel like she wanted another shower? Silly.

Back in the kitchen she started water for tea and picked up her phone. One of the three speed dials yielded her therapist's answering machine.

"Hey, Jayla. It's your girl Skye. Think you can work me in tomorrow? Yeah, I know we never meet twice in the same week, but I had some surprises today and I think I got something you'll want to discuss. Be good for that book you writing. The same stuff only different, you know? Hit me back when you can."

The rest of the night consisted of cleaning her revolver while she sipped peppermint tea and munched crackers and sharp cheddar. It was one of those rare nights when she didn't want to be alone. Alone was her comfort zone now, ever since Papa left for that last consultant job in Beirut. She never found out what had happened, but after that all her decisions were her own. She knew there was no replacing Papa, and actually alone felt good most of the time.

Just once in a while it didn't, but there was no one she really wanted to hang out with, and she wasn't in the mood to get lost in a crowd. Ultimately, she put on some Enigma and spent forty-five minutes doing yoga poses to their ambient electronica sound. Then she just slipped between the sheets, closed her eyes and counted herself down into oblivion.

Chapter 15

Skye began her session with an apology. "Look I didn't mean to take up your lunch hour. Could have waited."

"Don't be silly," Jayla said, picking at her Cobb salad. "I was going to be here anyway, and your voicemail sounded like you might have been in crisis."

Skye waved that away with a hand. "It ain't no crisis. I just thought you'd want it for your notes is all. Was just trying to be nice."

"I see. Well, I appreciate your consideration." Jayla chewed a mouthful of food watching her client closely. One knee was bouncing up and down. Not much, but more of a nervous movement than she had ever seen. "So, I take it something happened that was a little out of the ordinary?"

With one palm up, sounding nonchalant, Skye said, "I took two boys out of the game last night." Her tone said, "no big deal."

Jayla had trained herself not to react to these revelations. "Um-hm. I didn't realize you were so far up the list on this present job. Or was this a new assignment?"

"Neither one. Unscheduled activity. They gunned down a fellow I was walking with. Blew him away and one of his two bodyguards."

Jayla's face dropped. "Wait. Was this the shootout across from the Cap Center last night?"

"Oh, you heard already?"

"Yeah, but it didn't sound like you. Police reports made it sound like a gang thing. Or maybe... did you set it up to look that way? The news reported four dead and one man found on the scene. He said his boss was a businessman and he had no idea who the two dead gang bangers were."

"Nah, it ain't like that." Skye stood and started pacing toward the door. "This dude was a player. You don't get two bodyguards and a bulletproof car unless you know you got enemies, right? But in this case the shooters were probably sent in by his boss. Chen's replacement. Get it?"

"I think so. He worked for the man you… your most recent paid assignment." Jayla stopped to chew again. It gave her time to think. "Are you sorry he's dead?"

That stopped Skye in her tracks, as if she had not even thought of it. "Huh! Well, yeah, I guess so. Sorry he's dead. Sorrier that his new boss ain't. He's my next assignment."

"You were angry at the men you killed for killing your friend."

"No. Not really," Skye said. "Just wish I wasn't there in the line of fire."

"Ahhh. I get it. The two new guys. When they shot at your friend, they were shooting at you too. So you shot back, right?"

"Not really," Skye said, pulling out her boot dagger and flipping it in the air. "I mean yeah, they were shooting in my direction, but they didn't know who I was. I slipped away into the parking garage. Could have kept going, you know, probably should have. But instead, I circled back behind them and put them down."

Jayla nodded, finished her lunch and pushed the bowl aside. "Okay. This other bodyguard was under fire and you saved him. It was an unfair fight and you evened the odds."

Skye closed her eyes and shook her head. "Nah, I didn't care about that guy. Didn't even know him. I think in the moment I was just about… these assholes sent bullets in my direction. Unacceptable, you know?"

"Of course," Jayla said, pulling her pad close and making a few notes. "Guess it felt personal."

"Kind of," Skye said. Then she stopped in front of Jayla's desk and pointed the blade at her. "But I feel weird about this. I don't close a guy's account unless I get paid to do it. Or at least, I shouldn't."

After a short pause, Jayla said, "I don't know, Skye, I think there's more to this. You've killed before in self-defense, or to just end a conflict. But this seems to have affected you differently."

"Maybe," Skye said, continuing her pacing. "These guys weren't marks but they sure wasn't innocent. They was there on business."

"Indeed," Jayla said, smiling at a revelation that had pushed into her brain. "Members of the same club, right? They were like you. Assassins."

"Oh hell no," Skye snapped, spinning to stare Jayla down. "These two were nothing like me. They were there for Levin. Why the hell did they keep shooting after their target was down?"

Jayla pulled back, palms forward in surrender. "Whoa! I didn't mean to offend you. I was just saying that these two men you killed were being paid to kill someone. In my mind that made them professional killers. Maybe not on your level but hired killers nonetheless."

"Well, they was paid to erase this dude." Skye stopped and sat back down on the chaise. "And I interfered with their work."

"So is it possible," Jayla asked, "that shooting those two men felt a little like shooting yourself? Or like, a shadow of you?"

"Nah. Maybe. I guess."

"You are always in control when you approach a target, right?" Jayla said. "They generally don't see you coming. Just like these two killers didn't see you coming. Maybe we've surfaced a fear here."

"Fear?" Skye asked, tipping her head the way a dog does when he wants to understand you better.

Jayla smiled while writing. "Maybe your hidden fear is that you'll die at the hands of another assassin."

"I don't know..."

Jayla tried again. "Maybe you're afraid that, like your own targets, when it's your turn you'll never see it coming."

Skye appeared to be rolling the thought around in her head. Then she snapped to her feet again, her arrogant smile back in place. "Fear. Of course. That's it. Hey, thanks, Jayla! Talking to you always pays off! Now I got to run."

Chapter 16

Milo Williams had sounded thrilled when Skye called to say she was joining him for dinner. She showed up at his room in dreadlocks and short, unvarnished nails, but the jeans, sweatshirt and boots remained. Skye arched an eyebrow at the food cart as she took the same seat she had used before.

"I've ordered us a nice Beef Carpaccio to share," Milo said. He sat quiet while she gathered a bit of the thin sliced raw beef tenderloin, chewed, and favored him with a smile. Then he followed suit. "Indeed," Milo said. "They do it right here. Covered with just the right amount of shaved parmesan cheese and drizzled with olive oil. Now. To what do I owe this visit?"

"That is some good stuff," Skye said. "And I came by cause I wanted you to know I'm taking some action that won't directly lead to the death of one of the men on your list, but it will hurt their organization, which will make them easier to get at. And, as a nice side effect, it will seriously piss them off."

Milo gathered pink roe onto a cracker. "And why in the world would you want to do that?"

"Cause they pissed me off," she said. "I don't like guns pointed in my direction."

"I certainly don't mind anything you do that hurts this organization," Milo said. "But what makes you think you can?"

"Fact is, it came to me all at once," Skye said, sipping her wine. "It's about fear. Gambling, whores, those things are about human wants and needs. But the kidnapping business, that runs on fear. That's why they had to kill your boy. To prove to future targets that the threat was real. By the way," Skye looked up, riveting her host's eyes. "How come you didn't pay the ransom, Milo?"

Milo paused, as if he had not expected the question. His eyes went up and to the right. Then they came back to her, as steady as ever.

"Understand that although I have strong ties with the Washington business community, I don't spend all my time here. When they took my boy I was at home in Romania. When the demands reached me I started gathering the money right away," he said with a sob in his voice. "Not everyone keeps a mountain of cash on hand. And they wanted American dollars. They just didn't give me enough time."

"Yeah these guys are dicks," Skye said. "but like I said, it runs on fear. I pulled a little girl out from under them, but they'll still want to get paid. So I figure they wait a decent amount of time and grab her again."

"I can imagine that," Milo said. "But her parents are very smart, and very rich. She would be very well protected now."

"Yeah, I'm counting on the parents to be smart. They won't want their girl to be in protective custody the rest of her life. So I figure they'll communicate with the kidnappers. The smart play here is to offer to pay the ransom anyway for a promise of protection for the little girl in the future. That would be the smart move. I've got a man watching their…" Skye's phone rang, interrupting her. Her ringtone was "Killer Queen" and she let Freddie Mercury sing a few bars before answering it.

"Hey, Otto! What do you know? Uh-huh. Yeah, would have to be a big-ass withdrawal. Yeah, two hundred K would qualify. Not a bank draft? And it doesn't show up as a deposit anywhere else? Cool, man. That's got to be it. Never mind why I needed to know. Look he could be moving any time so I got to jet."

When she hung up, Milo asked, "So you're taking off now?"

"Sorry, Milo. I need to call an Uber right now."

Little Carla's neighborhood was more impressive in daylight. Yes the homes were crammed together as tightly as the town homes in Skye's neighborhood, but these places all had very imposing facades that told anyone outside that their interiors would be even more breathtaking. Each had a garage, and unlike suburbia, the residents actually kept their cars in them, so there was no problem finding a parking space on the street a little less than a block away. Skye lay sideways on the back seat of Mo's Honda, bobbing her head to the Tank CD in her earbuds, her eyes locked on the front of the Evans home.

Skye was sensitive to the difference between this slice of The District and most of the rest. There were no people on the streets. No pedestrians, no students wandering, no homeless, no kids playing. When these people were not at work they lived their lives inside those comfortable homes. They walked nowhere, and when they got home moved directly into their houses. It seemed unlikely that most of them knew their neighbors' first names or could identify each other's spouses or children. A neighborhood, yes. A community, probably not.

"Not that I mind getting paid for sitting here reading Michelle Obama's book," Mo said, "But you got any idea how long we'll be here? I might want to get something to eat, you know?"

"I won't let you starve, Mo," Skye said. "I got reason to think this thing's going to pop off before the sun goes all the way down. And all you've got to do is follow at a discreet distance. No risk."

"Yeah, except the risk to my blood sugar. You just don't care if…"

"Hush!" Skye snapped, sitting bolt upright. The Evans garage door was rolling up. Five seconds after that process was complete, a bright blue Lexus LC poked its nose timidly out into the gleaming twilight. This was Skye's favorite time of day. This and Dawn. Those few moments every day when the world teetered on the edge of light and dark. The light fought to hold sway while the darkness slowly overwhelmed it. It would happen the same way in reverse in a few hours.

"Nice wheels," Mo said as the Lexus eased cautiously down the driveway and out onto R Street. "This is the guy we're tailing?"

"That's him," Skye said. "Although he don't drive like a man who ought to have them wheels. Let's give him lots of space. Just on the off chance that someone else is interested."

Skye stowed her IPod and Mo cranked up his stereo, pumping out R&B hits from the last century. As they maneuvered down P Street and around the tricky ramp to get onto the Rock Creek Parkway she wondered why Carla's father, Dennis Evans, had bought this car. She had done a basic Google search and learned that he was a mover and shaker in the pharmaceutical industry. Big names in Big Pharma were known for taking big risks with a fearless disregard for the consequences. But this man didn't drive his sporty car like a sports car driver. Was this his midlife crisis car then? Or did it support the image he wanted to project?

Traffic on the Parkway didn't allow for much speed that evening, and Evans tended to stay in the right lane. That made following him easy, and allowed Skye to assure herself that no one else was following him. That part made sense. When the mark was scared enough, you could count on him to go where you sent him without worrying that he'd call the police or do anything else stupid. Skye's judgment was that Evans didn't want revenge or to make a point. He just wanted this business concluded so he could get on with his life.

Mo wanted this business over too.

"You know girl, I love your hourly rate, but you gone have to add a decent dinner to that tonight," Mo said over his shoulder. "I sat with you close to three hours on the street, and we been following this dude for damn near half an hour."

"Dinner for you and the family," Skye said. "At Morton's if your kids like a good steak."

"They more into barbecue."

"Red, Hot and Blue then," she replied, clapping a hand onto his shoulder. "I need to follow this through, brother. I appreciate you."

Soon after they left the highway they were far enough away from any urban center that they could actually see the stars above. Mo backed off a bit more and Skye watched their quarry through a pair of binoculars.

Like much of the South, Maryland is composed more of counties than cities. Often Skye had no idea what town she was in. Where they were right then the streets were two cars wide with a sidewalk only on one side. These well-maintained asphalt tracks were lined with small brick houses that were spaced about a house-width apart. Low chain link fences were the rule, and many of the yards had dogs running in them.

Mo spent a few minutes driving down these small-town streets before Evans turned down an unpaved road, barely two lanes wide. Mo pulled over on the side of the street without the sidewalk.

"What the hell," Skye said. "Dirt roads now?"

"It's a fire road, hon," Mo said. "Probably runs to the interstate. I used to race down them roads. But you know if I turn down that road behind your boy he's going to see my headlights and know for sure we following him. So. You the passenger, Skye. Go or no go?"

"Pull up a few feet and sit tight," Skye said, jumping out the back door. If, on the off chance, Evans was out here to meet somebody she didn't want to drag Mo into this. She crept down the narrow path on foot, sticking to one side, watching the car getting smaller in her sights. Until it stopped getting smaller.

Evans had pulled into a clearing about a hundred yards ahead of her. On the ground she could just make out an "X" made of glow sticks at the center of the open area. The Lexus eased to a stop and a good-sized duffle bag flipped out of the driver's window. As she had expected, not a meet but a dead drop. Evans never got out of the car but moved very slowly after the drop. The Lexus completed the circle of the clearing and headed back out the way it had gone in.

But by then Skye had pushed six feet into the trees and crouched down. She sat, unmoving, as the blue Lexus eased past. As it reached the street she could hear the throaty roar of its engine. It seemed Evans was in a bit more of a hurry to get home. Skye clawed her way back onto the road, pulling leaves and twigs out of her hair. She jogged back to Mo's Honda. He powered down his window when he saw her.

"Evans left a package back there in a clearing," she said. "I'm going to scoot down that trail and retrieve it. Shouldn't be long but just in case, if I'm not back in this car inside of thirty minutes you head home. Got it?"

"Yeah, but I don't like it." Mo said. "This here smells like trouble to me. You want to borrow something? For protection?"

"Mo!" Skye said in mock horror. "Are you strapped? You, a family man?" When he rolled his eyes she said, "Don't worry. Just trust me that I'm ready for whatever might wander down that narrow path."

Skye winked at Mo and headed down the fire road. She was smiling when they parted, but he was not. She thought it was cute that her driver worried about her but that bag was not much more than a hundred yards away and she sure as hell wasn't going to leave it behind. If trouble did come looking for her it would find that she had traded her usual light carry piece for a nine-millimeter Ruger. Not that she thought it would come into use.

If she had guessed right, Evans had offered to pay off the kidnappers and they told him his daughter would be safe if he dropped a big bag of cash where they could pick it up. She figured whoever was supposed to retrieve that payoff had no reason to hurry so they'd give the mark at least a half hour to get clear before they'd come down. He didn't want to meet them, and they sure didn't want him to see any faces.

A minute later Skye was in the clearing, showered by the light of a new risen moon. The cedars and poplars lent the opening a sweet aroma. She knelt beside the duffle bag and pulled the zipper down just far enough to see it was what she expected. A bag of money. Extortion is, after all, a cash business. She pulled the strap over her shoulder and stood.

Then the ground rumbled under her feet, and she heard a vehicle trundling slowly toward her. Shit! Why were they here so soon? Thank God they were driving with headlights off, but that would likely end when they got to the clearing. She stared toward the tree line. The bag was too big to move with quietly. Hissing with frustration she dropped the bag and stepped back into the woods. She drew her weapon, leaned against a tree and froze.

The Land Rover pulled into the clearing, staying four feet from the edge. The lights came on, illuminating the ground in competition with the moon. The combination painted everything an odd blue. The engine kept running, but the driver's door opened, and a stocky man stepped out. His barrel chest supported irrationally broad shoulders. Moonlight danced off a mostly bald head, but he was well supplied in the mustache and beard department. All the hair he had was red. He wore one of those bulky knit sweaters she called fisherman sweaters. It made him look even bigger.

As he lifted the bag by a strap, a voice from inside the vehicle said, "I'm telling you, Ryan, I'm sure I saw something in here when we was coming in."

Skye thought, *I should just let them take the damn bag. I can hurt them some other way later. Rip off a future drop. Smarter not to mess with these Irish Mob boys unless you have to.*

Then Ryan turned back to the vehicle. "You gone crackers, Van. Nobody knows about this drop excepting the mark. And even if somebody did stumble on it, so what? What kind of an idiot would have the stones to rip *us* off?"

Before she knew she would do it, Skye stepped out of the trees, her pistol pointed at Ryan's head. She heard herself say, "This kind of idiot, I guess."

She was committed now. Staying close to the tree line Skye stepped slowly to the side, moving away from the Land Rover. Ryan stared down her barrel with great calm. Clearly not his first time having a gun pointed at him. He shrugged the bag's carry strap off his shoulder and tossed it on the ground about halfway between himself and Skye.

"Really?"

Ryan spread his hands. "It ain't enough money to be worth getting myself shot for."

"You're a smart fellow," Skye said. "What about your friend in the truck? Is he smart too?"

"Can't say," Ryan said. Skye had moved far enough so that Ryan was between her and the vehicle. His face was passive, signaling nothing when he suddenly dodged to his left. Skye mirrored his movement and felt the breeze from a nine-millimeter slug soaring past her ribs and clattering through a few leaves before stopping in a tree trunk.

"Guess not," she said through clenched teeth. She rolled once to her left and came up on one knee, arms steady. Her target stood at the open driver's door. A quick double tap of her own trigger slapped him up against the truck. She watched him slide down the vehicle's body until he was seated on the ground, eyes blank, blood pooling on the ground in front of his crotch.

With a roar like an injured bear, Ryan lunged. Skye was turning her gun back toward him but he drove beneath her outstretched arms. His right shoulder slammed into her solar plexus, stealing her breath. She was swept up in his momentum, carried along on his massive shoulder until her back crashed into a tree that was nearly as wide as her body. The impact rattled her frame. And she was too close to his ruddy face, his muddy brown eyes, his scraggly beard.

"Stupid black bitch," he spat. "Did you think you could just step up and take our money?" She was pinned in place by his body, draped across his shoulder. His left fist looked like a five-pound ham as he wound it back.

Skye slapped her open palms into his ears as hard as she could and saw the pain in his eyes. She hated those eyes. She pressed her thumbs into them. He howled and backed off. She dropped to her feet, but crouching low, scanning quickly for her gun in the moonlight.

Panting, she managed to rasp out, "Who you calling a bitch, Mick?"

In the light from the stark moon above she couldn't see if his face had really reddened but the rest of his expression made her think so. He moved in on her, this time swinging a right cross that might have taken her head off if she had not ducked below it. Then she was in close enough to leap onto his back. Despite the weight difference Skye was pretty sure she could take this guy, hand to hand, if she had to. But this was no opponent to mess around with.

Her left arm looped his neck just long enough for her to slip her knife out of her right boot. The blade was less than three inches long but that was plenty to get the job done. She slammed the knife in twice, then kicked herself away from him. When he spun to face her, fury still burned in his eyes, teeth bared like a wounded animal, but there wasn't much left there to power the anger. His sweater absorbed the dull, almost bluish liquid pouring out of a jugular vein. The bright red spray pumping out of the neighboring cut testified that she had hit a carotid artery as well.

Ryan's right hand fumbled beneath his sweater and managed to pull the .357 Magnum revolver free. It was a pretty, Taurus double action piece, and if it had occurred to him that he might need it to handle this girl a little sooner it would have been a very different fight. As it was he no longer had the coordination to point the gun with any purpose. He dropped to his knees, the gun hanging uselessly at his side. Skye placed a hand on his chest and stared into his face one last time.

"Who's the bitch now, asshole?"

She pulled away and let him fall forward onto his face. She looked up at the uncaring moon for a moment, then walked over and picked up the duffle bag. She hadn't planned on a gun fight but she wasn't worried about it. It was three gun shots fired in the woods more than a hundred yards from civilization. If anyone heard them they would have no clue what direction they came from. She had no idea how long it might be until someone went back there and saw the scene. They would know that a third party had put down these two men, but there was nothing to indicate who. At a stretch someone might identify her smallish boot prints and decide it was a woman. All they would know for sure was that their ranks had thinned by two and the hostage ransom business was getting costly these days.

Chapter 17

The dirt road felt narrower on Skye's walk back to the street. The tall trees on either side seemed to lean in, interlacing their fingers overhead, trying to block out the moonlight. The insects were so loud it became white noise in her ears. She fought the urge to run, not wanting to be winded when she reached the street, but adrenaline was still flooding her heart, pushing her pulse rate up and prompting deeper, faster respiration.

When she reached the asphalt, she paused to look in all directions. With no one in sight she stood for a moment with hands on knees and forced a few deeper breaths before heading for the little Honda. When she was within a few steps of him, Mo powered his window down.

"Damn, girl, what the hell? You okay? What the hell happened?"

"I'm fine, Mo," she said, her relaxed smile bouncing off his frightened sneer.

He popped his door, preparing to get out. "Fine don't get you all bloody like that!"

Skye looked down at her sweatshirt. It looked like she worked in a slaughterhouse. She wondered if her face was equally blood spattered. She stopped him with a palm and broke into a more genuine laugh.

"Relax, brother. None of this is mine."

"You think that makes it okay?" Mo asked, stepping out of the car. "It's a whole lot of somebody's blood. What the hell happened?"

"Hey, I didn't mean to scare you," Skye said. Mo was just her height and she realized that she had never seen him standing before. She tried to calm him with one open palm while her other hand reached for the back door handle.

"Oh, hell no!" Mo snapped. "You ain't getting in my car looking like no ax murderer it." He walked past her to the trunk, popped it open and pulled out a worn towel. He tossed it to Skye. It smelled of grease or oil, so she figured he used it when he worked on his car. Quieted by his stern stare, she began to wipe her face, neck and hands with the towel.

"Hope you got something on underneath that," Mo said. Skye nodded, tossed the towel in the trunk and peeled off her sweatshirt. She left it inside out. He held out a hand and she gave it to him. He rolled the towel around it, tossed the bundle into the truck and slammed it shut. Then he walked past her and returned to the driver's seat. After a moment Skye got into the back seat with the duffle bag.

Mo drove to the next corner, poked at his GPS and turned right. Now on a new deserted rural street he asked, "Home?"

"Yes, please." Skye pulled herself into the corner of the back seat behind the driver and stared at the floor. Mo had looked at her like she was a monster. He had no idea what she did for a living, but he must have assumed… something. He lived on the edge of the violence that was her life, and he had no idea. He knew where she lived. He knew her comings and goings. Right then, he had her DNA and that of her most recent victim in his trunk. Not that she was at all worried about the risk of betrayal. Instead, she felt discomfort that she might be betraying a trusted agent. Then she thought of someone else whose trust might be valuable.

"Hey, sorry Mo, can we go back to the Evans house instead?"

His head snapped up in surprise and she could imagine his brow furrowing, but all he said was "Of course."

Skye moved to the far right side of the back seat, to see as much of Mo's face as possible, and unzipped the duffle bag. While she silently counted, she asked in a soft voice, "Mo? Do you want to know what happened back there?"

"No. Uh-uh." Then Mo made a noise almost like he was pushing a big rock up a hill. "Shit! Yes. I shouldn't want to know. I don't want to want to know. But… yeah."

Skye took a deep breath. This was not at all like talking to Jayla. "Remember the little girl, Carla? Well, she was kidnapped. I kind of stumbled on her the other night in the process of taking care of some other business. I decided to take her home."

"So she wasn't the reason I took you to that place on M Street?"

"No," Skye said. "It was an unexpected opportunity."

"The right thing to do," Mo said with a shrug. "You must have been visiting some bad dudes."

"Yes," Skye said, smiling at the characterization. "Bad dudes who hold kids for money. To keep his daughter from getting grabbed again, Dennis Evans paid the ransom anyway. A quick flip through here it looks like about two hundred large."

Mo stared into the rearview mirror. "Wait. That's the ransom money you got back there?"

"Yes. He paid it. I decided to take it back from them. They didn't want to let it go. It turned into a fight."

"And?"

"I won. They lost. That's what happened back there. Good enough?"

After a short pause Mo said, "Yeah, I'm good." He settled back into his seat and turned the music up just a little. The Commodores, Rick James and Kool and the Gang got them to within two blocks of the Evans house, where Mo parked. Skye leaned forward and placed a wrapped stack of bills on the front passenger seat.

"What's this?"

"I'm taking a ten percent finder's fee," Skye said. "You get half. That's your ten grand."

Mo shook his head. "I don't want nothing to do with that. I get paid to drive. I'm not part of your… your business."

"Mo, I pay you to get me where I need to be, then get me home. But I think Mr. Evans would want to reward you for returning his daughter to him, not to mention his hard-earned money. Please. Call it a start for your daughter's college fund."

After a few seconds of silence, Mo asked, "What now?"

"Now I take this bag to the house. Unless you would rather…"

"Oh hell no!" Mo said, in the tone he might use if he met a ghost. Skye shook her head and laughed softly, then stepped out of the car. She walked under the streetlamps, noticing that in this neighborhood their separate cones of light just touched. The boardwalk-style path to the door was lined with well-tended plants that she figured most other women could probably name. The front of the house was painted white and brightly lit, with waist-high glass panes on either side of the wooden stoop. She pushed the button, prompting three charming chimes to announce her presence. On either side of the hardwood door, two windows the same size as the door revealed the front room to the world. A man walked past the windows on her left before an intercom spoke.

"Can I help you?"

Skye held up the duffle bag. "I got something belongs to you. Just wanted to return it."

She heard only two locks thrown, one a deadbolt. Then the door opened inward. This would be Frank Evans.

Chiseled features with thick, perfectly cut blonde hair. He looked comfortable in his cardigan and deck shoes. Quick blue eyes scanned her up and down as if comparing her to a previous example, or perhaps a memorized description.

"You're her," Evans said. "Please come in. Perhaps we can talk in my office." His smile was nervous, so she tried to keep hers friendly. He led her through what appeared to be a dining area to a flight of stairs. The décor was stark white with black accents and lots of glass. She faced a long galley kitchen appointed with white appliances to match the cabinets. She feared one would have to wear polarized lenses to cook in there. The stairs appeared to float in space, although they were actually wooden blocks held in place by a plate glass banister rising to the second level. They walked down a hall to a spartan room at the back of the house. Evans' office was maybe ten feet wide and nearly twice as deep. On either side of the modern desk sat a green cloth chair reflecting the huge mostly green abstract painting behind the desk. Neither of them sat. Evans stood at the end of his desk, hands on hips, gathering his game face. Skye sat the duffle bag on the desk and took two steps back. She thought he'd be more relaxed if she let him open the conversation.

"You're the woman who returned my daughter to me."

"Yes," she said. "You're welcome."

Evans actually put a hand over his mouth for a moment. "Oh God. I didn't. Thank you, Miss…"

"You can call me Sunny," She said. "I just wanted to talk for a minute, and I thought that would be easier if I returned that package to you. I'm pretty sure nobody's gone ask for it again."

Evans unzipped the bag. "I see. Do you, er… Clearly you're not police or anything like that. Do I give you a reward?"

"I deducted a ten percent finder's fee."

"Oh. Okay. Good. Well then…" Without words he was asking the right question. Skye answered it.

"As you can guess, the people who took your little girl are not my friends. I got her home safe and sound. I guess she told you that story in detail. It would help me a lot if you'd just tell me how they contacted you. How do you communicate with these guys? They had to tell you where to take the cash for the dead drop, right? Phone call? Messenger? What?"

Evans swallowed hard and looked over at the money. "I don't think so," he said in a low voice.

"Excuse you?"

"Look, Miss, I appreciate all you've done, I really do, but I don't want to get any more involved with this."

"Involved?" Skye tilted her head, looking at him in shock. "What the hell?"

"I don't know what's really going on here, but I don't want to be in the middle of some gang war or something. Giving you information might make these guys want to come back and visit us. I just want to be hands off here."

"Seriously?" Skye stepped forward. "You think they just handed me that bag? Think I just talked it out of them? Bitch, I got blood on my face for you."

Evans back away, eyes wide with fear. "I'm sorry. I don't know who you are or what you do, and I don't want to know. I really just want you to leave my house and we never see each other again. I'm taking my family away from this crazy city as fast as I can. I just… I just want to live a normal life, okay?"

Skye showed her teeth the tway a Doberman Pinscher does. She felt her nails digging into her palms. Ungrateful asshole. How easy it would be. She could snap his neck without breaking a sweat. He was nothing. But he wasn't the job and, to be honest, he had not asked her to do any of what she did.

A deep breath. A second. A third. She pulled herself away from the obvious course of action. She saw the terror on Evans' face. He wasn't worth the trouble. She turned and walked away. At the door she turned to stare at him over her shoulder.

"You know what? Everybody wants a normal life. Sometimes a different kind of life comes looking for you. You better learn to be ready when it does."

Skye trotted down the stairs, wondering where in that big house he had hidden his wife and the little girl with the innocent smile. It didn't matter. Mo was only a block away and at least he appreciated what she did. Well, as little as he knew.

Stepping out the door she was thinking maybe she should read Mo in more thoroughly. He had been very good, picking her up and dropping her off never knowing or asking what she did at those locations. But she hardly ever moved the remains after doing her work so if he read the paper closely he might connect locations with deaths. It would be a special kind of man who would mind his own business to that extent.

She was halfway to the street when she heard the soft pop behind her and her body seized up. Her teeth locked, hands became fists, pain shot through her entire body at once and she dropped to her knees.

Despite being disoriented by the attack she recognized the five-second cycle of a stun gun strike. The twin prongs would be in her back but the pain came from everywhere. At the end of the five seconds, she forced herself to turn her face to one side. Her cheek slammed into the wooden path as she fell forward, but her teeth would be okay. They must have been on the ground outside the plate glass that lined the walkway to the door. She heard a vehicle slam to a stop in front of her. Someone shoved a black bag over her head. Zip ties pulled her wrists together at the small of her back.

Hands clamped on each of her arms and an arm wrapped around her legs. Then she was lifted and moving forward. Then she was flying. Arms and back slammed into a steel wall. The sound of a van door sliding closed. Tires squealed and, like that, they had her.

Chapter 18

Skye worked to sit up to make the bumpy ride easier on her arms and shoulders. Zip ties were applied right. Black bag was totally opaque and smelled of detergent. At least they kept their tools clean. This was a good team, three plus a driver at least. She heard no chatter between them, no fidgeting. That spoke of discipline.

Well, if they wanted her dead she would already be there. Was Evans in on this? Unlikely. He wanted to get away from all of it. Could someone have followed them back from the drop point? Not likely without being spotted on those empty country roads. It made more sense that they were watching Evans' house, maybe so they could take swift action if something went wrong with the dead drop. Did they think Evans sent her to recoup his funds? Maybe, but either way they might have recognized her as the woman who retired Chen. Maybe the new boss told them to bring her in like any other kidnap victim. And she had to give them their props. They were good at this.

Skye guessed her ride to be about thirty minutes, almost all on city streets based on the stops for traffic lights. She had managed to spend most of it sitting cross legged. She wondered what they wanted beyond her death. She wondered if her fellow passengers knew who she was. She wondered what Mo did when she didn't return.

The van stopped. The side door slid open again. Strong hands pulled her to her feet and guided her out of the vehicle. Whoever was guiding her now was gentle, even respectful. They climbed a short flight of stairs and went indoors, then down a long hall. Her monitor guided her into a room. She heard the door lock. The grip on her arm disappeared and the bag rose over and off her head.

She stood in the middle of a ten by twelve room furnished only with two wooden chairs, dragged to a corner now. One man leaned against each wall, all white, all muscular. The fellow on her left wore brass knuckles. The one on her right was empty handed. Behind her stood the man with the stun gun. The fellow at the door held a revolver. pointed at her navel. The Ruger SP101 would spit .357 magnum rounds, even if it didn't have the hidden hammer she preferred. If she could get close enough, she could take it from him.

"It would be nice if we can be civilized in here," the man at the door said in a soft Irish accent. "I'm Ian. You?"

"Call me Skye."

Ian's eyes widened just for a second, and he adjusted his stance so as not to be leaning against the door. "You're her. All right. Respect. I'm hoping you will return it."

Skye shrugged. "We all adults here."

"Finn. Free the lass' hands."

The man on her right stepped forward and flipped out a one-handed folder. He stepped behind her, sliced through the zip ties, and returned to his previous place.

"Don't want to be killing you now, but got no real problem with it," the man at the door said. "There's people wanting to talk with you, but they need to be safe. So, step one. What are you carrying?"

Skye nodded at the efficiency. "There's a nine millimeter in a paddle holster at my back. Got a dagger in my boot."

"Thank you," Ian said. "I'll need you to be putting those items on the floor and kicking them over to Finn there." Skye saw no reasonable alternative, so she did as asked.

Finn, a freckle-faced redhead, scooped up her weapons and dropped them into large padded envelope.

"Now step two's going to be a little awkward but I'm thinking after your past actions you'll understand. You're going to have to get naked."

"Excuse you?" Skye's eyes flared. Was this a psychological ploy to break her down?

"I know what you're thinking, girlie but it ain't about embarrassing you or giving the boys a treat. I just know you're a professional. There's no doubt you've got weapons concealed on you, and I'm not so sure searching you would find them all."

"So, what now?" Skye asked. "You expect me to just strip down in front of you?"

"Actually, there's three ways this could go," Ian said. "The boys here could strip you down…"

"Like hell."

"Or Donny can hit you with the Taser again, and then the boys strip you down. Or you can do it yourself. Your call."

Skye did a slow turn around the room, locking eyes with each of the men. They were focused and calm, almost bored. If she went into action and avoided the gun for a few seconds she could probably take a couple of them but no way she'd take all four down. When her eyes returned to Ian's she saw no impatience there. The left corner of his mouth turned up. Not arrogance. Confidence.

"Fine," she finally said. She let her jacket slide off her shoulders and drop to the floor. Pulled her tee shirt over her head. Lifted each foot to slide off her boots, her balance good enough that she didn't need to sit on the floor. After a huff of frustration, she unhooked her belt, unsnapped her jeans and slid them down and off. She stood in white lace, palms up in a half shrug as if to say, "Well?"

"Come now, missy," Ian said. "We both know you could be hiding all sorts of nasty stuff in them B cups."

"Asshole," Skye said almost under hear breath. She reached behind herself and unhooked the clasps, letting her bra fall on the pile at her feet. Then she turned another fiery look on the gunman.

"Kind of late to get modest," he said.

"What? You think I got a gun hid up in my coochie?"

"You can drop them, or Finn can check for me."

Teeth clenched and eyes wide with rage, Skye slid her lace panties to the floor. Her posture was no less proud. "You want to take some pictures now?"

"Turn please."

"Oh, you a ass man, huh?" Skye turned and stared at Donny who, to her surprise, looked a little embarrassed.

"Lift your left foot please," Ian said.

Shit! Skye did as she was asked.

"Now the right."

Again she raised her foot. She held her breath through two seconds of silence.

"Is that a strip of flesh colored tape on the sole?" Ian asked. "You *are* good. Peel that off if you please, darlin'."

Skye reached down and pulled the tape away, flipping it to Ian. He picked it up, separating the thin blade from the tape. It was razor sharp, no more than two inches long, half of that handle.

"You see boys," Ian told the room. "This is why you can't be underestimating your enemies. Finn, hand me the rest. I'm thinking I better go through everything."

While Skye watched, naked, Ian pulled her belt from the jeans and tossed it onto one of the chairs. He felt through the jeans thoroughly then slid them back to Skye.

"My underwear?" she asked.

"You don't need them. Just pull them jeans on. And what's this? Feels like a metal weight sewn into the end of this sleeve. Lead maybe. All the way around, and the tee shirt fits you tight enough that the weight isn't obvious at all when you move. Nice. You see this, boys? You pull the shirt off and squeeze this together and you got a cosh you can swing at somebody's head like an old time sap. Pretty slick. Hey, Finn, go in my room and get me a shirt for the girl to wear. She's less dangerous barefoot but," Ian looked up to meet Skye's eyes, "the girl's got too much class for me to be taking her to meet the big boys topless."

It was another row house in The District. They walked down the hall in the same configuration as they held in the room. Ian led, and Skye knew the stun gun was behind her, too far to lunge at but too close to escape. She walked barefoot in her jeans and a black pullover shirt that was just a little too big. Ian had at least tried to maintain her dignity. If it came to a battle she would kill him last.

The room he led her into was not at all a business office. It was set up like a comfortable living room with white shag carpet and walls painted a warm off-white, the color of natural egg shells. Brandon Anderson stood on one side of the roaring brick fireplace looking like he'd really rather be anyplace else. Murphy stood on the other side of the fireplace and he did not look happy, which confused Skye. It was his world right now, wasn't it?

Ian guided Skye to the deep brown leather love seat. The well-dressed business types on the facing sofa struck her as generic men, one white and one black. Navy blue suits, rep ties, Florsheim shoes. They were two flavors of the same bland dish. They might even go to the same barber.

Ian stood behind the armchair on her left, focused on her, very alert. The rest of his team stationed themselves around the room, but Ian's was the only gun she could see. There was nothing on the coffee table between her and the business types: no glasses, no pen, no ashtray, nothing that could become a weapon. She guessed this was what Ian meant by respect. She caught his eye and nodded acknowledgement.

All eyes were on her. The business types smiled. Silence hung in the air, a silence Skye felt driven to break.

"Okay. What the hell?" She pointed at Murphy. "I know that asshole but who the hell are you?"

The white business type turned to Brandon. "Is this the woman? The same one who made that mess at Chen's place?"

Brandon looked closely. Her hair was different, her makeup gone. But after a couple of seconds he nodded. The man who asked the question kept staring at him until he said, "Yes, sir, that's her."

That brought the man's eyes back to Skye. "My name's Franklin. My friend here is Assistant District Attorney Harris. And you, you are one dangerous lady."

Skye smiled. "Duh! Everybody here knows that shit. So why are we sitting here chatting like we homeys?"

"Because you're a problem," Franklin said. "And I'm a problem solver."

"Wait." Skye blinked and glanced around. "Are you THAT Franklin? The political guy? The one they call a fixer? You work for the mayor, right?"

"No. I work for the people the mayor works for. Only she doesn't know she works for them."

"Uh-huh. And this nigga sitting here with his mouth shut. He here to arrest me? Or just to impress me that you got the DA's office in your pocket?"

"You don't know how deep this hole is that you're in," Harris said. He wanted to be intimidating but Skye wasn't feeling it. She waved him away with a flip of her hand.

"You boys need to work on your act. You ain't spent enough time playing with the real Gs to…"

"Shut up and listen," Franklin snapped. His smile evaporated. He slid to the edge of his seat and pinned Skye with a hard stare. "You are a problem. You're a threat to the natural order of things in my town. We like things to run smoothly."

Skye leaned back and crossed her arms. "Your town. Now that's funny. But I get it. You're pissed cause I took Chen out of the game."

"And Gomez. And the two bangers who hit Levin. And a couple Irish guys on a simple errand to pick up a payment. Because of you we had to do a lot of clean up in a short time. It's not so much what you do but how you do it. You get attention. You cause headlines. You are too damned noisy." Franklin hooked a thumb at Murphy. "This guy's Irish mob. He wants to just put a bullet in your skull and toss you in the Potomac. But I figure nobody who could find Gomez, find Chen, and know enough to be on hand when Levin got popped is working solo. I figure you got backup, an organization. I don't know how much your people know, and I don't want certain information to become public. I figure if you disappear things could get even messier. And I don't like messy."

Skye smiled at the fixer's wrong assumptions. Even with all the facts he came to all the wrong conclusions, and she had no reason to change his views. Instead, she pointed one finger at him and winked. "You a smart man. But if your plan ain't to kill me, what the hell are we talking about?"

Franklin took a deep breath and his smile returned. "There's a neat, tidy way out of this. Behind that chair your friend is sitting in is a nice leather briefcase. Inside it is two hundred fifty thousand dollars. Cash."

Skye turned her head to one side in confusion. "You talking about buying me off?"

"It's very simple. You take the money and you and your friends leave town first thing in the morning. I don't know why you're doing what you're doing. Revenge for some slight, or you're getting paid by some rival gang or you're thinking you can muscle your way in here and take over Hetman's rackets. Don't know, don't care. I'm saying take the cash and go do whatever it is you're doing in Pittsburgh or Cleveland or some other shit town and leave The District in peace."

"You're for real," Skye said. "You really are trying to buy me off."

"That's the offer," Franklin said, "and I'm only making it once. What do you say?"

Skye looked at the assistant DA, glanced at Brandon who looked so out of place in this crowd, and stared up at the ceiling for a moment. Her lips poked out in a thoughtful expression.

"Seriously?" Franklin said. "Get real. What is there to think about?"

When Skye's eyes came back to Franklin, she looked relaxed and a little bored. "Honestly, I was trying to think of a classier way to say kiss my black ass. But nothing good comes to mind."

Franklin's jaw dropped. Ian stifled a snicker. Harris snapped to his feet, fists clenched, his lips twisted into a snarl. "That's it. I'm done. Let Murphy have the bitch."

Franklin stood more slowly as Harris stalked toward the door. Franklin held Skye's eyes for just a second, then disengaged and turned to Murphy. "Guess we do things your way. No mess this time."

Murphy waited until the lawyer and the fixer were out the door before he walked over to stand in front of Skye. When he was a couple feet away, she rose to her full height. She stared up into Murphy's eyes, nine or ten inches above hers. For three long seconds they looked like two boxers in the center of the ring while they listened to the referee's instructions. Then two of Ian's men stepped up to her sides, each grasping an arm. Skye was aware of the pistol on her and the stun gun behind her, but her entire focus was on Murphy. He pulled his butterfly knife from his pocket and flipped it open with a blinding fast double roll.

"I'm glad you didn't take the deal," Murphy said. "You've cost me a lot in a short space of time." He pointed aimlessly to his right with the knife. "Them two gang bangers were just cannon fodder but they were useful and always got the job done." Then he casually moved the knife to point to his left. "But them boys I sent to pick up the ransom money, I brought them over from the old country. I trusted them, and they'll be hard to replace."

Skye interrupted, her eyes on the knife point. "Hey, you know I'm going to kill you, right?" When Murphy smiled, she said, "It's looking like I'm going to have to wait a while for that. But if you touch me with that blade, if you cut me, I'll have to do it right now. And yeah, I know your man there will kill me one second after that. But you will be no less dead."

Murphy was shaking with rage, eyes wide, teeth bared. Skye stood at the center of a pool of calm, waiting to see if Murphy was ready to die.

Murphy finally glared at Ian. "You heard the man. No mess. You and your boys need to make this bitch disappear."

Chapter 19

"It's time," Ian said. Skye opened her eyes and scanned the room. They had taken her there after she stared Murphy down. A simple ten by twelve room but this time with a twin bed and a small dresser. One of the holding rooms for kidnap victims she assumed. She had laid down without undressing and dozed until Ian stood beside her waking her up.

"What time?" she asked.

"Two a.m.," he said. "Let's go, and please stay civil. Donny has you lined up so if I don't get you he will."

Ian walked past her to the opposite wall and waved her toward the door with his gun. Donny backed up to keep a static distance between them, stun gun focused on her the whole time. The four man escort maintained their positions around her as they moved down three flights of stairs. The pistol and Taser were on her at all times. In spite of herself she was impressed that they got her downstairs and into the back seat of a Bronco without giving her any chance of escape. Now she sat between two of her escorts. One kept the Taser pressed against her leg.

Once they were on the road, Skye figured nothing of interest would happen until they arrived at their destination. No one wanted to clean gore out of a vehicle interior. Before long they were on the Beltway. Even in the wee hours there was always traffic. The driver focused on driving. Ian, in the front seat, held his gun on her, never wavering. Skye felt as if they were rolling down a long dark tunnel, or maybe descending into hell.

"I've never been taken for a ride before," she said, "and this is pretty damn boring."

No response.

"Okay, you're Ian, the dude on my left is Finn and Donny's got the Taser jammed in my thigh, which I must say is making me a little nervous. What's the driver's name?"

When the driver said, "Jimmy" he got a stern look from Ian, to which he responded with a shrug.

"Thanks. It's good to know who's got you. So Ian, where we going?"

Silence.

"Oh, come on," she said. "What can it hurt for me to know? It's not like you expect me to be coming back, right?"

After a pause, Ian said, "Okay. We've got a nice remote spot out on the shore of the Chesapeake where we take people like you."

"Did you hear that stupid ass offer the fixer made me? Dumb ass. With my rep, don't you think he should have offered me a job?"

"Above my pay grade," Ian said.

"Right. You work for Murphy, who works for somebody else, who works for this Hetman guy. Who the hell is he, anyway?"

"Don't know, don't care," Ian said.

Skye leaned forward a little. "So how do you know you're getting the real boss' orders?"

"Well, as it happens, that Anderson boy is Hetman's mouthpiece. We all hear direct from the boss through him."

Skye stared at the blackness out the window. "Seems like a dumb choice to send you boys after me. What's that all about?"

All the men chuckled. Ian said, "Franklin laid it out pretty good I thought. You got too close. Slipping in there and getting right up close to Chen and killing him? It was embarrassing."

"Wouldn't have happened if it was us," Finn said.

"Yeah, I guess the Triad boys ain't all I heard," Skye said, leaning back. "Not pros like you guys. Been with Murphy long?"

"Came over from home with him," Ian said. "Then came down from Boston with him for this job. We're kind of big on loyalty."

"Really?" Skye asked. "Then why take orders from a total unknown, a guy you don't even get to meet, a guy who don't respect you enough to talk to you face to face?"

Ian sighed and raised his gun an inch or two. Donny said, "You ask too many damn questions. You know we can kill you any time, right? I mean, we don't have to wait until we get to the shore."

Skye put her face up close to his. "You know if you pop that stun gun on me you'll feel it too since we're touching, right?"

"Wouldn't be the first time," Donny said. "And you'd be still long enough for Ian to put a bullet in your brain."

Skye shook her head. "Damn you guys are good. How the hell did this Hetman guy get in charge over your own mob?"

"You'll have to figure that one out for yourself," Ian said.

Off the beltway their drive transitioned to small roads, then dirt roads for which the Bronco seemed well suited. When they stopped the darkness seemed to close in on them like a big black fist. Donny got out and waved Skye after him. He and Finn both produced pistols and stood side by side. Ian moved in front of her and pulled a Maglite out of his pocket. Donny and Finn also held small flashlights in their left hands. Jimmy got out of the car, also with gun and flashlight in hand.

At some signal Skye didn't catch Ian turned and walked into the woods. Donny and Finn pointed for Skye to follow him. They walked behind her, just close enough. Jimmy stayed back, behind the open driver's door. Maybe the interior light was the beacon the others would follow back to the Bronco.

Skye stayed behind Ian in the cone of light from twin beams behind her, silently cursing the moist, wet ground under her bare feet. Insects, she assumed crickets, clacked loudly all around them and she screwed up her face at the cloying smell of decaying vegetation. Shortly they came within sight of the water. The moon, invisible until now, was a bright reflection off the placid surface of the bay.

Ian turned and held up a hand to stop Skye at just the right distance. He was just out of her reach, but close enough that he could not miss. She heard the two gunmen behind her shift, one to her left and the other to the right, out of Ian's line of fire. He raised his weapon, aiming at her forehead.

Shit just got real, Skye thought.

Lighted by reflected moonlight from his left, he raised one eyebrow. "You've surprised me, girl. I was expecting you to make a break for it. I appreciate you accepting the reality of the situation."

"Thought I'd take one last shot," Skye said. "We could work together. And I can beat whatever money they giving you now."

"I'm afraid I must decline your generous offer," Ian said with a smile. "Now, please turn around. I promise to make this quick and painless."

Skye shook her head. "Nuh-uh. I figure your boys are just a couple of paces behind me and I don't want their ugly mugs to be the last things I see."

Well then," Ian said, "I'm not afraid to look you in the eye and say goodbye."

Ian raised his pistol to arm's length. Skye's left hand snapped out like a striking snake. She could not reach Ian's body but she was just able to wrap her hand around his gun from the top. In the same instant he squeezed the trigger, but nothing happened. Skye saw his brow furrow in surprise as she twisted her hand hard to the left. Her right hand captured the gun wrist. Her left hand released the gun. The cylinder cycled and the pistol roared. Skye heard Donny grunt. Skye leaped, slamming her right shoulder into Ian as another gun fired.

Skye clenched her teeth against a shout as she felt burning lead drive into her left thigh. The impact added to her momentum, driving Ian to the ground with her on top of him. She got her finger inside the trigger guard, turned her head and fired twice a foot to the right of the remaining flashlight. Finn dropped. Ian swung a hard punch into her back. This time Skye did cry out and slammed her right elbow into Ian's temple. That stunned him just long enough for her to free the big magnum from his hand and swing it around against the side of his head. He stopped moving after that.

Skye's ears were ringing from the gunfire, but she was pretty sure the crickets had stopped their noise. She rolled away from Ian and crawled to Donny. Her shot had hit him high on the left side of his chest. He was gone, and she didn't have to check Finn to know he was too. She knew she hit him center mass and no one survives two .357 rounds to the trunk.

"Guys?" It was Jimmy, leaning against the Bronco. Lying in the tall grass she could see his head and shoulders, including his gun pointed in her direction. He probably couldn't see her, but on the other hand she couldn't see enough of him to take a good shot. To have a chance to nail him she'd have to rise up, making herself a perfect target silhouetted in the moonlight. The Ruger SP101 was a big, heavy handgun with a five-shot cylinder. That meant she'd have only two chances to hit Jimmy, and the instant she rose to take the shot, he'd empty his gun at her.

Pain lanced up and down her body, reminding her that she didn't have much time to make a move. If she had one. Jimmy could lose focus and turn away, or get back in the vehicle and drive off, but Skye knew those were idle fantasies. If she waited for either of those possibilities she'd likely bleed out from her wound. Her left leg was already going numb. If she did rise to shoot she'd have to double tap, maximizing her chances of hitting Jimmy. And Ian was only unconscious, so even if she got lucky and managed to put Jimmy down, Ian would probably catch her before she got to the Bronco and away. He'd kill her with one of his dead partners' guns and she had no time to gather them up. It was a no-win situation, but she had to try.

Another pulse of pain racked her body. She took a deep breath. A second. Now or never, she thought, before she was too weak to hold the gun steady.

Just as she rose to her knees there was an unexpected gunshot. The window of the open driver's door shattered. Someone else had taken a shot at Jimmy. The driver spun to his left and returned fire, exposing his right side. Skye had time to aim and fire once before falling forward to the ground. Jimmy fell against the car and slumped to the ground. No sound of movement from that direction. Her one shot had been enough.

The surprise distraction had saved her life, and she wanted to find and thank her savior, but before she moved toward the Bronco, she had one other bit of business to take care of. On hands and knees she lurched back toward Ian. He was sitting up, still disoriented. She waited for him to focus on her. He was staring into the muzzle of his own pistol.

"How the hell…?" he muttered.

"Yeah, these Double Action Only pistols," Skye said. "You can't let nobody grab the gun and jam their fingers in one of the cylinder grooves. If the cylinder don't turn, the gun won't fire."

"And now?"

Skye held Ian's eyes with her own. "Now I keep a promise to myself. You treated me with respect and I said I'd kill you last."

The roar of the pistol blast assaulted her ears, and the recoil turned her wrist more than it should have. But she saw the hole appear between Ian's startled eyes before she dropped to her hands, panting. Dizziness and nausea were competing with pain for her attention. Her left leg was one big ball of hurt, pulsing like the world's biggest toothache.

"Miss? Miss?" The calls were from behind her, near the Bronco. And she knew that voice.

"Here!" she said as loudly as she could, then fell forward. She heard hurried yet tentative footsteps getting closer. Then a murmured "Jesus." He must be close enough to see the bodies. A moment later Brandon Anderson was kneeling beside her.

"Miss? Um, Cloudy, right? Are you okay?"

"Call me Skye," she said, not raising her head off the ground. "And I am most definitely not okay. Shot in the leg. Need you to see how bad it is."

She felt his hands on her. "It's kind of dark, but, damn, you're bleeding bad."

"Them boys all had flashlights. Get one and check it out."

Brandon moved away but was back in seconds. Again she felt one hand on her upper thigh.

"Please tell me the bullet went right through," Skye said.

"Actually, it looks like it just kind of ripped across the back of your leg. Not so much a hole as a, I don't know, like a furrow across the back."

Skye thought it was more luck than she deserved. No arteries cut. But the pain pulsed hard, making thinking a challenge.

"Got to get to the Bronco fast. Can you carry me?"

"I, I don't know," he said. "I don't think so. Not that far." Fear made his voice tremble. She pictured the man she'd seen twice, surrounded by real thugs. He wasn't one of them.

"Never mind," Skye said. "Get that guy's jacket. The boy in front of me with the hole in his head."

Brandon went to the body but stood over it, uncertain. Skye snapped, "He can't hurt you, Anderson, he's fucking dead. Roll him over and pull the jacket off him. I got to protect my leg or I'll be the next dead body out here."

Brandon grabbed the jacket and pulled it to turn Ian over. He muttered "Oh, God" when he saw the back of Ian's head, which was mostly gone. He pulled the jacket off the body.

"Lay it down over here. Right here. Lining up." Skye watched him place the jacket as directed, then she spun so her head was toward the Bronco and rolled over so she was seated on the jacket. She tied the sleeves around her hips as tightly as she could. It was all she could do right then to protect the open wound.

"Now, come grab me under my arms and drag me over to the car. Quick."

Brandon gripped her upper arms from beneath and pulled her across the grass. His hands slipped off her twice before she spoke again.

"Look, grab my arms overhand. Don't worry about touching my tits, just get me over there before I bleed to death." As he gripped her arms again, she reached up to grasp his jacket sleeves. A few steps later they were close enough that when Brandon stopped, she was looking over at the driver's feet.

"All right," Skye said. "Now take a look in the back end. I'm betting they got a good first aid kit." Skye loosened the jacket and rolled over onto her stomach. She felt the world pulling away from her and fought against passing out. She had no idea how much time passed before she heard Brandon's voice again.

"I got it. Now what?"

"You got a knife?" Skye asked.

"A Swiss Army knife."

"That'll do," she said. "You need to cut my jeans away from the wound. Down to my knee, and up past my ass. Then put some antiseptic on the wound. Tape a bandage over it, tight as you can. Then get me in the car. Jesus that hurts like a mother…"

The world floated away again. The ground was more comfortable than she had realized before. Warm and soft. A nap might be nice, and the pain was distant when she slept.

A jolt of pain shocked her awake. She was face down in a car, but not the Bronco. They had hit a deep rut. She reached back and felt a bandage over her bullet wound. She couldn't see much aside from the inside of the door. It was warm in the car and she was covered by a sticky sweat.

"God I hope that's Anderson up there driving," she said.

"Yes, ma'am" he said from the front. "Just trying to get to a real road. Then I'll find the nearest hospital."

"The hell you will," she said. "Give me your phone. I got a doctor who takes care of me and don't ask no questions."

His hand appeared between the front seats and Skye took the phone from him. "Thanks," Skye said. "I take it this is your whip. How'd you end up out there where we were?"

"Followed you."

"What the hell for?" Skye asked.

"Thought maybe I could help you."

While dialing, Skye said, "You took a shot at the driver, huh?"

"Yeah. Had this gun for years but never fired it before. Didn't even come close to that guy."

"Didn't matter, brother," Skye said. "You saved my life. I'm grateful as hell but can't say I understand why you did." Her voice switched as she said into the phone. "Yeah, It's Skye."

The gruff voice in her ear said, "Skye? Bitch, do you know what time it is?"

"Actually, I don't," she said. "What I know is I'm shot and the brother who did some fast first aid had no idea what the hell he was doing. Now I'm going to hand him back his phone. If you want to keep getting that retainer, you'll tell him your address and how to get there."

Then she tossed the phone over Brandon's shoulder to land in his lap. The pain pulsed again. She wanted some water. That would help. She closed her eyes against a wave of nausea. For some reason the boy had saved her. She didn't want to throw up in his car.

Chapter 20

She awoke in a brightly lit white room. She was face down on a narrow bed. An IV tube ran into her left arm. She was still nauseous, and her head felt like it might burst, but she didn't feel pain shooting from her left leg.

"Doc Parris?" Her words sounded sluggish and slurred, even to her.

"Relax Ms. Skye," came the response. "I'm working on it now. The young man is waiting in the next room. Is he a good Samaritan or a friend? How much does he know?"

Skye rose high enough on her elbows to crane her head back to see the doctor, a solid black man who was big but not fat, wearing a white lab coat. His shaved head and salt-and-pepper beard gave the impression that he had somehow dragged the hair on his head down and around to his jaw.

"I'm sorry," Skye said. "Working on it? What it?"

"Your bullet wound," Parris said with a gruff chuckle. "You're all numbed up and I'm putting in the last few stitches. This one will be with you for a while."

Okay, she remembered getting shot. But not getting there. "Young man? Oh, that's got to be Brandon. He's not a friend, but he did help me. He don't know what I do but he's seen me work. You sent him out of the room?"

"You're naked from the waist down," Parris said. Five years in Washington and he still retained his Atlanta accent. "Trying to preserve your modesty."

"Thanks, Doc." Skye put her head down, breathing deeply, trying to clear her head. "But you know, he cut my jeans off me, so he's already seen this fine ass."

Parris stepped back to make it easier for Skye to see him and peeled off latex gloves. "All done. You were lucky. It creased your leg, what they would have called a flesh wound in old movies. A little muscle damage but nothing permanent. It's going to hurt like hell in an hour or so. In a month you'll be moving like normal."

"Thanks! I don't suppose you've got a pair of pants around here I could pull on."

"I don't think you can wear my pants," Parris said, "but I got some scrubs around here you could pull on, just to get you home."

Skye carefully slid her legs off the bed and planted her feet as best she could. Standing with elbows on the bed she was able to face Parris. "As always, Doc, I appreciate your work. Sorry to wake you up like that."

"Not an issue," Parris said. He opened a cabinet drawer, pulled out a set of blue scrubs and tossed the bottoms to Skye. "You're my most reliable patient, at least when it comes to payments. And you whine the least when you get hurt."

Skye wrestled her left leg into the scrub pants with some effort. "In this line of work, you get hurt. Why whine about it? What time's it getting to be?"

"Coming up on six." Parris said. "In the morning."

"Then I got someplace to be," Skye said. Leaning on the bed she managed to balance on her left leg just long enough to get her right leg into the pants. She tied the string and stepped awkwardly toward the door. Parris reached to open it and she stepped slowly out of the exam room into the waiting room, empty but for one. Brandon stood and moved toward Skye but stopped short.

"Good Lord. Sorry to say it, but you look like hell."

Parris laughed hard. Skye smiled. "Yeah, thanks," she said. "You should see the other guys. Wait, you did see the other guys. Now how about getting me out of here. I guess you're on my team now."

"You have a team?" Brandon asked, taking her left arm and acting as a crutch.

"No, not really."

They stepped out of Parris' Capitol Hill home office, not far from Bridge Point Hospital. Brandon helped her ease down onto the passenger seat of his red Camry. She squirmed around, leaning on her right hip while he got behind the wheel.

"Where to?" Brandon asked.

Skye examined her hands in her lap. "I got a lot of questions for you, but most of them will have to wait. Kind of looks like I got to depend on you for a little. Right now I need to finish the business to keep us both safe."

"You can ask me anything," Brandon said. "After seeing what you can do, I really want you to trust me."

"You know where Murphy is right now?"

Startled, Brandon checked his watch. "He'd be home now. Big old place on Massachusetts Ave. In about a half hour he'll head out for breakfast, then go to the office. He keeps a pretty strict schedule."

"I love it when assignments keep to a schedule," Skye said. "If he's in Northwest, we should just about be able to get there before he leaves. Head to his place."

Brandon pulled into crosstown traffic. "Okay, but why are we in such a hurry to see the man who wanted to kill you?"

"Think about it," Skye said, rolling her window half way down. "He probably thinks I'm dead. Too soon to wonder why he hasn't heard from the boys he sent me out with. He's relaxed. It's the best time to catch him with his pants down. You got a gun, right?"

"In the glove compartment," Brandon said. She heard his breathing speed up. "Wait. Are you thinking about doing this right now?"

"No time like the present," Skye said. She pulled the Ruger P95 out of the glove compartment. It looked brand new. She dropped the magazine and pulled the slide back to clear it. A round popped out, which she caught and pushed into the magazine. With one bullet fired, she now had 14 in the magazine. She shoved it back into place and charged the slide again. She knew this gun had a heavy trigger pull, maybe seven pounds. It would do.

Brandon was driving straight up Massachusetts Avenue. Even this early traffic was dense but they were moving steadily. His shoulders were up to his ears and he gripped the wheel as if he feared it might get away from him. His eyes stared straight ahead except for frequent checks of all his mirrors.

Just after they passed Union Station she said, in a low voice, "You really scared." He nodded. "Of me?"

Without taking his eyes off the road, he said, "I've seen what you can do. You're like John Wick or that dude in The Transporter, only real life."

She smiled at the comparisons. "Okay, Brandon, why did you do it?"

"Do what?"

"Come to save me," Skye said. "I figure you must have followed us when we left at two in the morning. Damn glad you did, but I want to know why."

They stopped at a light and Brandon turned to face her. "I'm jammed up here. I don't want to be part of organized crime and I damn sure don't want to be the voice of the king pin. You think I'm scared right now? I'm scared all the time. I was starting to think I'd never get loose from these maniacs. Then I saw you. You're a real badass. I thought maybe you could make them let me go or get me away from here." The light changed and Brandon flowed with the onrushing river of cars.

"I get that. You figured if you helped me, I'd help you. But what were you going to do? It's pretty clear you can't shoot for shit and there was four of them."

"Remember, they all know me as Hetman's mouthpiece. I figured I could tell them Hetman sent word he wanted you alive. They'd have believed me."

"Yeah, if you'd got there a little sooner. That would have been a lot less messy. But I do appreciate the effort. Right now, keep going and let me know when we're three blocks from Murphy's place. And give me your phone again."

Brandon gave her the side eye and Skye considered that maybe she should have said please or something. But he handed her his cell phone and she forgot about that impulse. She needed to send a text message.

Hey. It's Skye on a borrowed phone. She gave it a slow ten count waiting for a response.

Hate me? Another pause before the responding text.
No
Drive me?
When?
45 min. I'll request thru Uber as usual. Thanx. Sorry I left you hanging. Didn't run off. Got kidnapped.
You ok?
Yes. Promise full story later.

Out the window Massachusetts Ave segued from worn downtown to a suburban area in denial strung with grand structures, many of which at first glance could be mansions, churches or apartment buildings. Large, mature trees hid many of them, and others stood behind tall wrought iron fences. It wasn't really an armed camp. It just felt that way. Brandon pulled over in front of one of the spearhead-topped fences.

"Murphy's place is two blocks up. Big, ostentatious stucco affair."

Ostentatious? People *use* that word? "Where the hell did you go to school?" Skye asked, getting out of the car more slowly than she would have liked. She walked around it and got into the back seat on the driver's side, wincing as she knelt on the floor behind the driver's seat.

"Princeton," Brandon said. "I majored in Civil Engineering."

"Of course you did," Skye said, shaking her head. "Now cruise past the place slowly."

Skye looked over the edge of the door as they passed the house. Like its neighbors it was hidden by large trees but the circular driveway gave her two good looks at the white structure and Brandon had described it well. The front door arch and whitewashed brick accents made it look like a lost home transplanted from California or Nevada. The black Mercedes parked in front of the door also looked out of place.

"Good timing," Skye said. "They must be here to pick him up. Turn around at the corner. Hey, how do you get along with Murphy? Are y'all like friends?"

"Oh, hell no," Brandon said, making a U-turn in the intersection. "He's insufferable. Why do you think I wanted you to get me out of this?'

"Just checking," Skye said. "This ought to be easy. Pull up behind the Benzo in the drive and put all the windows down. His boys won't care about you, but he'll want to know where you been and what you're up to."

Brandon did as Skye asked, stopping half a car length behind the other car. One of the passengers got out with his hand halfway in his jacket. He stared until he recognized Brandon, then waved at him and got back in the car.

"I thought he was coming back here," Brandon said.

"They know you," Skye answered. "They probably figure Murphy had called you here for something or other. Just sit tight. And don't put your ride in park. Put it in reverse and leave your foot on the brake. You're going to want to be ready to move."

"There he is."

Murphy stepped out of his door and glanced up at the morning sun. He was dressed much as when Skye met him, in two-tone wing tips and a felt fedora. One of the Mercedes passengers got out to greet him. Then Murphy turned to Brandon's car and his face hardened into a grimace. Skye crouched low. Murphy's footsteps clicked down the cement driveway until he stood beside the car.

"Anderson," Murphy barked, the way most men would spit an obscenity. "I didn't call you. What the hell are you doing?"

Skye rose up into visibility in the back seat. "Doing? He's retiring." The gun roared twice inside the car. Her first shot pushed into Murphy's right eye. The second gouged a divot out of the side of his neck.

"Oh God," Brandon said.

Skye slapped his shoulder. "Floor it!"

Brandon's car shot backward into the street. Another oncoming car swerved to avoid hitting him.

"To the left! Go!" Skye shouted close to his ear before shifting to the other side of the car. Her own ears were ringing from the pistol's concussion and she knew his would be the same. They pulled past the other side of the circular driveway as the black Mercedes was just starting out. Skye squeezed off five shots as they drove by. The other car stopped as Brandon gained speed. His knuckles were white on the wheel and he was repeating a jagged litany.

"OhGodohGodohGodohGod."

"Shut the hell up," Skye said. "Take that first right and get us on Rock Creek Parkway as fast as you can. We need to get back to downtown."

Skye figured Brandon was driving as fast as he thought safe, but it was good enough. Her last few shots had made Murphy's team hesitate. They didn't pull out of the driveway until after Brandon had turned the corner. No way they'd find the Camry, even if they wanted to follow. And she was counting on the fact that the boys at Murphy's place were just foot soldiers. They didn't really know what to do and had no guidance. Thugs don't get a handbook telling them what to do if their boss gets his ticket punched. She looked at Brandon in the rearview mirror and saw that he was staring at her.

"Look at you," Brandon said. "You're grinning like a kid at Six Flags. You enjoyed that. Killing people is fun to you."

"Killing people is business," she told the mirror. "But to dispatch a dude who wanted to kill me? A guy who threatened me and talked to me like I wasn't shit? Sending that arrogant dick to hell was a pleasure. What's your beef? You didn't like him."

"Not the point," Brandon said. But he didn't seem eager to say what he thought the point was, so after a minute of silence Skye directed him get off the parkway near the Kennedy Center and into a nearby parking garage. Once he was parked Skye sent another text. A few seconds later the black Honda Accord pulled up behind them. Skye pulled herself out of Brandon's car. She stood holding onto the car's roof for a moment to press the pain down to where she could handle it.

"Empty the glove compartment and take everything out of the car you want," she said. "You won't be coming back for it."

"What?" Brandon said, stepping out of his car. "Do you know what these things cost? I'm not just going to abandon my car here."

Skye's eyes narrowed. "Nigga, you crazy? That whole pissed off gang knows what your car looks like. And you can bet they got eyes everywhere. You better get your ass in that Honda so we can get the hell out of here."

Skye was moving as fast as she could toward Mo's car when Brandon said, "Don't call me that."

Skye pulled the front passenger door open before turning back to him. "What?"

"Don't call me the N word. I've spent half my life trying to stop white boys from saying it. I'm not listening to it from my Black brothers and sisters either."

Shaking her head, Skye eased herself awkwardly into the seat, grimacing with clenched teeth until she was settled and leaning back.

"You alright girl?" Mo asked.

"Listen, Mo, I'm really sorry I didn't get back to you last time. It wasn't on purpose…"

Mo held up a palm. "I thought you was dead. I didn't know what to do. I sat there for damn near an hour before I gave up and went on home. I was scared somebody got to you. Looks like you got lots of enemies."

Brandon slid into the back seat carrying only an iPod, his registration and insurance cards. Mo put his car in gear and headed for the exit. Once they were back in daylight he hooked a thumb toward the back seat.

"Another stray?"

Skye swiveled left, grunting as she leaned on her injured thigh. "Morris, this is Brandon. Brandon saved my life last night. Morris here gets me where I need to go. Been doing that for a couple years now."

"Saved your life?" Mo asked. "Well then, guess I better be nice to him."

The ride across town was short, but when Skye slumped against the door to ease the pressure on her left leg, she couldn't keep her eyes open. Mo turned the Cameo tune down to just over a whisper. She was smiling and bobbing her head to it when she slipped into sleep.

She jerked awake when the door moved away from her. Mo had opened it from the outside and was offering her a hand.

"We're here, Skye. Do the boy stay here or do I need to deliver him someplace else?"

Skye took Mo's hand and pulled herself up onto her feet. Brandon was standing behind Mo, silent. Waiting for her to make the call, she guessed.

"For now, he's going to stay here. He's a target now, worse than me."

Skye squeezed Mo's hand and mumbled, "Later on, okay?" Mo nodded. She smiled. He didn't. Skye turned and guided Brandon to her building, leaning on his arm most of the way. As they reached the front door, she stopped to catch her breath.

"You still got your phone?"

"Sure," Brandon offered his phone to her.

"You're going to have to ditch it. They can trace you through it."

"Not this phone," Brandon said. "Hetman gave all his senior men a phone identical to this one and gave me one too. All the GPS stuff has been removed, so none of us can be tracked by our phones."

"Damn, this guy's smart. Of course it's working against him this time."

She stepped and hopped up the two flights of stairs to her front door. The circular lock presented six buttons that had to be pushed in the correct order to open. She pushed inside and headed straight for the bathroom, leaving

Brandon to close the door behind himself. She pulled a bottle from one of the drawers and swallowed two Percocet pills. Then she moved to the refrigerator and poured a tall tumbler of orange juice, which she drank down without taking a breath. Only then did she remember that she had company. She went to her bedroom door and turned to face the man standing in the middle of her living room with a bewildered look on his face.

"Okay Brandon, here's the deal. I'm exhausted and my leg hurts like a son of a bitch. I'm going in here to get some sleep. You're safe here, but if you leave you're on your own. You're welcome to stay as long as you act right."

"Which means?"

"Help yourself to anything in the kitchen," Skye said. "But if you touch anything anywhere else in my place, I'll kill you. If you come in my bedroom, I'll kill you. If you tell anyone where you are, I'll kill you. You understand all that?"

Brandon swallowed and nodded. Skye went into her room and closed the door. It chafed that she was still wearing the shirt Ian had put on her when they made her strip. She tossed the dead man's shirt into a corner, followed by the borrowed scrub bottoms that had been her pants for the last couple of hours. Then she crawled between the sheets, naked, and pulled the heavy comforter on top of her. She curled into a ball lying on her right side. Her last waking thought was that she had clearly kicked one hell of a hornet's nest, and that fatigue, pain and medication might have caused her to invite one of the hornets into her home.

Chapter 21

The way it happened made no sense. The door was unlocked so she walked right in. He was alone, parked on a torn brown leather chair just to the left of one of the windows that faced the street. He looked at her the way you might expect a man to look at an alien that walked into his place. And there she was, holding the rusty revolver in both hands.

He was a hard-looking man, very black with short nappy hair and one gold tooth. He lurched to his feet, rusty like the smooth piece of metal in her hands. His place smelled like sandalwood incense and vomit. Light came from one lamp on the table by the chair, the table covered with small plastic envelopes full of white powder. The murder weapons that killed her brother, in plain sight.

Her heart was all she could hear, pounding so fast she feared it might burst from her chest. The man grinned as he walked toward her, his eyebrows rising with recognition.

"You that boy's little sister, ain't you?" he said. "Come up in here, all brave and shit, with that stupid piece of shit the boy used to carry around. It don't work, you know. But you got potential, shorty. I think I'll turn you out so you can make me some money. After I teach you how to act."

He was eight feet away when she squeezed the trigger. The hammer rose and fell with a loud click. His grin got bigger. She pulled the trigger again. Again the cylinder turned and the hammer slammed down with a click.

He had to be two feet taller than she was. He was looking over her, reaching for her, only six feet away when she squeezed again. This time an explosive sound slapped her ears and the gun nearly leaped out of her hands. Acrid smoke burned her eyes and nose, and a small hole appeared in the man's belly just about halfway between his chin and his belt. He lurched backward, mouth open in surprise. That quickly changed to a grimace of anger.

"You little bitch," he spit. She brought the short barrel back on line and tried again. Again the gun roared. This time the hole appeared in his chest. She was surprised that nothing came shooting out of the holes. Even more surprising was that he was still standing, almost as if his body didn't know he was shot. After staggering back a couple more steps he reached toward her with his right hand.

Skye threw the gun at him. It smacked against his left cheek and he staggered back a few more steps.

"I'm gonna kill you, you little…" His hip hit the windowsill. Skye stepped toward him, slowly at first then more quickly. As she sped up her fear turned to rage and then to something else. A cold determination to do the job she had assigned herself.

No words. Lips pressed together. Her small palms slammed into his chest on either side of the bullet wound. She heard the glass behind him shatter and then he was gone. She didn't look out the window but she heard the impact in the distance, four stories down. No, she had to look, had to verify that the job was done. She stepped forward, placed her hands on the windowsill and leaned forward.

With a short scream, Skye sat bolt upright, hands gripping the sheet below her. She was panting hard, glistening with sweat, eyes clenched hard to chase the images away. Why was that first time so much harder now than it was when she did it?

As she got control of her breathing Skye let her eyes open. They flew wide and she gave a second short scream. Brandon stood in the doorway staring at her. Was that fear on his face? Or maybe worry. Or he might just be curious. Or was he just ogling her tits?

"What?" she snapped.

"You screamed," Brandon said. "It sounded like you were… I wanted to make sure you were okay. But then I remembered what you said about coming in the room and… Are you okay?"

The space between them seemed infinite. Skye felt uncharacteristically alone. She was alone all the time, but right then she *felt* alone. She raised her right hand and beckoned Brandon forward. His steps were tentative, but he walked to the side of the bed. Watching her eyes he spread his hands to his sides, physically asking what he could do. Skye read his body language and in response raised both her arms inviting him in.

Brandon took a deep breath, then knelt beside the bed and took her into his arms. She hugged him tightly, feeling warmer than she had in a long, long time. She couldn't remember the last time she wanted a hug, but his embrace soothed her. After a long moment she released him, and he leaned back as if he knew somehow that she had all she needed.

"So, want to get some lunch?" she asked, pulling the comforter up to cover her chest. "I'm kind of hungry."

"Had lunch," Brandon said, flashing a warm smile. "You'd probably want dinner."

"Dinner? What time is it?"

He glanced at his watch. "Closing in on 7:30."

"Damn. I must have been beat. I'll order something for us. What do you think? Pizza? Or Chinese?"

"I like lo mein," he said. "Want my phone? I know they took yours."

"They took that one," Skye said. She pulled her nightstand drawer open and selected one of the four burner phones. "How about you go pull out some plates and silverware. And there's wine in the fridge. You could pour us a couple glasses."

Twenty minutes later Skye was showered and sat in her fluffy robe on one side of the island behind a plate of General Tso's chicken and shrimp fried rice. Facing her, Brandon handled his lo mein using chopsticks. Skye was too lazy to bother and thought that forks were just easier to work with.

"Could I ask you something?" Brandon asked, holding an egg roll but not biting yet.

"Sure," Skye said. "No promise I'll answer."

He swallowed to empty his mouth, then said, "The night we met. I was told you dropped my name to get into the casino. I'm wondering where you heard it." Then he bit into the egg roll.

"That's what you want to know? Okay. I was in the room when you called Judge Goldsmith. He told me he got orders from you, but you were just the messenger."

Brandon nodded and considered while he ate. Skye could see there was a real question in there and was curious, almost eager to know what was on this man's mind. Finally Brandon looked up and pointed his chopsticks at her.

"What about Chen? Was that a personal thing, were you paid to kill him or what?"

Skye laughed and sipped her merlot. "There it is. You want to know why. Well, I don't do the personal thing. It's not fun, it's business. I was hired by one of your kidnap victims to dispatch the people responsible for his son's death."

"That's what you do?"

"That's what I do," Skye said. "Like an exterminator, I eliminate vermin for a fee. In this case the client did his research and handed me five names."

"Wow," Brandon said between bites. After a pause he asked, "So, how are you doing? Was Chen at the start or near the end?"

"Chen was number two," Skye said. "It started with the punk who actually killed the child."

Brandon nodded. "The MS-13 guy who murdered that little boy? Yeah, that was the first killing I found out about. That freaked me out."

"He was just a stupid gang banger. He did the boy on Chen's orders, so Chen was on the list. My client basically wanted the direct line of shot callers to disappear. Murphy was the third target. So, I guess I'm doing okay but each target has been harder than the last one. I didn't expect this kind of risk. Murphy came close to stopping me. I'm going to have to be careful with this next guy. I hear he's Yakuza and them boys don't play." Skye smiled at Brandon, surprised at how easy it was to talk to him about all this.

"Kobayashi?" Brandon asked. His eyes fell, as if something on his plate was suddenly very interesting. "Fujio Kobayashi is one guy you really don't want to deal with. That is one scary dude."

"Yeah," Skye said, lifting the last forkful of her food. "You probably thought Murphy was scary."

"I did," Brandon admitted, "Until I met Kobayashi. Before he became a boss, he was an assassin. I heard he always killed with his hands. He's like, a martial arts prodigy or something. Super observant too. And a voice like… I don't know… like the grave."

"Sounds like a fun date," Skye said, dropping her plate into the dish washer. "Once I find him, maybe we'll see how good he is."

"Finding him isn't a problem," Brandon said. "He's in Japan right now, making arrangements for stronger ties between the Yakuza and Hetman. Supposed to be flying back in day after tomorrow."

Skye's jaw dropped open for just a moment. "Wait. You know this dude's itinerary?"

Brandon stood to follow Skye's example with his own plate. "I make, or made, a lot of the travel arrangements for Hetman's senior staff. I know a lot about the operation. Not so much the actual crime part but the rest."

For an awkward second Skye and Brandon stood in front of the dishwasher, not knowing what to do next. Then Skye picked up her wine glass and went to her favorite comfortable chair. Brandon sat back down at the kitchen island, turned to face his hostess.

"So… do you want Hetman too?"

"Hell, yes," Skye said, leaning forward. "He's number five. You know where he is?"

"Well, no. But I might be able to find him."

"Can't you just call him up on that phone Hetman gave you? Or just call the big boss himself and ask him where his Japanese killer is."

She saw fear race across Brandon's face. "Oh no! He calls me, I don't call him. Only his top Lieutenants can call him, the top guy from each gang he's working with. He made that real clear. Unless I think he's personally in danger. There's a preset to dial him. But if it's from me he won't answer, he'll just disappear. Then you'd never find him."

Skye sighed and sat back, again adjusting to take pressure off her bullet wound. "You know, you ain't no G, furthest thing from it. Not a thug, no kind of street cred. How'd you get tied up with this Hetman dude anyway?"

"He found me," Brandon said, carrying the bottle over to refill Skye's glass. "I was in a dead-end government job.

He said he needed somebody who understood organizational systems. Well, that's my thing. I get how things work, how things fit together. He needed to build an organization, and his research told him I'd be perfect to help him."

"So, what? He sent you to recruit the bad guys?"

"Honestly, yes," Brandon said, refilling his own glass and taking a drink. "He said I was the perfect combination of well spoken, nonthreatening and believable. And I had no criminal background. So he sent me to all these big time criminals with his plan to build a criminal organization, but he didn't want any of them to know who he was. I was always surprised that they went along with that part. But he was sure right about one thing. They all knew I was speaking for someone else. Nobody ever thought it was me."

"You're kidding," Skye said, her voice dripping with sarcasm. "But these other organizations, they already doing fine. So what makes this guy the new Al Capone?"

Brandon drank more wine and seemed to relax a bit. "I can tell you he's a genius when it comes to communications. And handling money. And he had a business model you can't argue with. Like this whole kidnapping thing. He says it's just a matter of picking the right victim. I don't know how he gets the inside info he does, but he's real good at picking them."

"That don't take no genius," Skye said. "Somebody who's got lots of dollars and somebody they care about enough to give it up."

"No," Brandon said. "They got to have enough that it won't hurt to give up what you're asking for. And they got to be the kind of person who won't even think about calling the police. And the kidnap victim should be easy to get at. But these guys didn't really get it. The very first kidnapping, he sent me to Chen and paid him a hundred grand to do it. That got the ball rolling."

"Kind of sounds like you admire this guy, but he ain't perfect. He fucked up when he killed my client's kid."

"I don't know," Brandon said. "Somehow word of that got around. After that, nobody even thought about saying no. They know this team is serious about their threats."

"Yeah," Skye said with a smirk, "But now he's got me on his ass, and I already poked a big hole in his team."

Brandon stared down at the carpet. "He said we had to kill one victim so the rest would know we were a serious threat. That was the day I started wanting to get free of him. But I could see no way. This isn't a job you just resign from. I know too much. But then, after I saw what you did to Chen I thought maybe you were the key to a way out."

"I'll tell you what, Brandon," Skye said, standing and stretching her left leg. "You find this Hetman guy and I will put him down for good. Then you'll be free. Meanwhile I got shit to do tomorrow but if you don't finger Hetman by the time his Yakuza man lands at the airport, I'll have things in place to take him out."

Chapter 22

Jayla was having a hard time evaluating the smile on Skye's face. She was confident that she had not seen it before. It was less guarded than usual, more open, but with a hint of confusion, almost as if she felt good but wasn't sure why.

She had arrived today in a bright green sweat suit with the yellow tennis shoes. Her hair was natural, shorter than Jayla thought it ought to be, her face scrubbed clean of makeup and her nails were unvarnished. This was as close to the baseline woman as she had ever seen.

"So you left him in your apartment?"

"Yeah." Skye looked her therapist in the eye. "That's the funny part, isn't it? I feel like I can trust him."

"You told me your place is two bedrooms," Jayla said, jotting a quick note. "But the other room is your workshop, where you work on weapons and so forth. So I take it that this Brandon stayed…"

"Don't get it twisted," Skye said, waving both index fingers. "He ain't that cute, and just cause there's a dick in the house don't mean I got to squat on it. There's a futon in the workshop. Told him to fold it down when he got sleepy. I was getting achy after we talked so I took a couple pills and went in and passed out."

"And when you got up this morning?"

"Brother was still sleeping," Skye said. "I needed to get in a good workout so went down to the gym. A lot of stretching, yoga, deep breathing stuff to try to get my left leg closer to normal. Then I had a nice run, five miles in

Rock Creek Park. Man, the sun was beautiful this morning. I ended the run back at the gym. By the time I got showered and dressed it was time to head here to see you."

"I'm very glad you did. You had some significant experiences since last we spoke." Jayla noted that Skye sat with her hands folded now, occasionally pointing her two first fingers at her. She was not playing with a coin or tossing one of her knives around.

"Yeah, well, when you stare death in the face like that it can really mess with your head. I figured you'd want to know all that for your research. The killer almost gets killed. And I ended up taking out a bunch of guys who were not part of a contract."

"All in some version of self-defense it seems," Jayla said. "But a lot of that was very up close and personal. Is that different?"

"Not really," Skye said. "When somebody comes at me it's pretty easy to go at them for real."

"But now, this Murphy fellow, that was very much a pure assassination."

"Yeah," Skye said, nodding and smiling as if she had been complimented. "Pure. Face to face, no mess, no collateral damage. Just put the animal down."

Jayla sat back and hiked her skirt just enough to be able to cross her legs. "You know, I've wondered about that side of your business. You prefer the word assassin and that's usually associated with political murders. You could get work for one of the strongmen in some third world nation and make a ton of money going after their enemies. Make a name for yourself. Actually affect history. I mean, think of the impact you'd have working for Kim Jong-Un. Or even more, killing Kim Jong-Un. Surely you've thought about it."

For a moment Skye's normal hard look returned. "Thought you got me better than that by now. The true assassin wants nothing to do with the monsters of history and their death cults. Wouldn't matter if it was Hitler, Stalin, Khmer Rouge, Shining Path, whatever. Or it's saints for that matter. The assassin doesn't mistake himself for a prophet. No sermons, no glossy brochures no propaganda."

"Even if you could be the next Carlos?"

"That Venezuelan fool Carlos the Jackal self-destructed," Skye said with a chuckle. "He marked himself for failure the day he decided to be a celebrity. We're meant to be invisible. I don't imagine myself to be the hand of God, but when I strike, it should look and feel like that to the people on the other side."

"I see," Jayla said, catching Skye's eyes again. "But now you've made yourself visible to this fellow Brandon. He gets to see behind the curtain."

"Yeah," Skye said, her easy smile returning. "It's funny, he's kind of an insider. I mean he knows the organized crime scene. But yet he's on the outside of the real guts of the life. He ain't no gangsta, that's for sure, but he's been hanging with them. I can talk to him and he knows what I'm talking about. Like I said, I trust him."

"Yes," Jayla said. Then she leaned forward, planted her elbow on her desk and rested her chin in her hand. "And how does that make you feel?"

Skye laughed and shook her head. "Damn, you slick Doc. Always manage to sneak up on a bitch. Wow. But okay, fair question. I'll admit this much to you: it feels good. I've never let anybody know, I mean, really see what I do and how I get it done."

"Really," Jayla said. "What about your computer guy, Noah?"

"He only knows what I ask him to do, never why. Right now I got him tracking down my next assignment's movements. If he knew the reason I need that information I'm not sure what he'd say."

"And your Uber driver friend, Morris?"

"Mo's not like a confidant or something," Skye said. "He gets me to the work site and brings me home after the work is done. Never thought he'd need to know what the work is. Lately, though, I been thinking maybe I should let him in on more, especially since I showed up at his car covered with blood the other night."

Jayla smiled and slowly nodded her head. "That might be a good thing. You know, Skye, you keep too much inside, I mean really extreme stuff. It would be healthy to have someone to talk things out with. You have people in your life…"

"I hear you, Doc, but every person who knows my business is a security risk. It's easy to keep clients at arm's length. But somebody close? It's different."

"This I can understand," Jayla said. "With clients you can keep it all business, and no client is likely to question why you'd do what you do, or how you feel about it the way a real friend would. Are you prepared to have that kind of conversation with Brandon?"

This time Skye gave a nervous laugh. "That nigger already asked too many questions. Funny thing is, instead of slapping him upside the head I keep answering him. What's up with that?"

"What is up with that," Jayla said. "That is a very good question for you to consider. Give that some thought. It would be nice to hear what you think at our next session."

Back at the JW Marriott, Skye rapped at Milo Williams' door with a knuckle. He opened the door and waved her inside. It was mid-afternoon and Skye saw that her client had ordered tea and pastries. She knew people called it "tea time" but she'd much rather have coffee. Still, tea was okay sometimes. She went to the table and poured herself a cup.

While selecting a Danish from a round silver tray she noticed Williams was staring at her.

"What?"

"Sorry," Milo said. "I'm unaccustomed to seeing you dressed so casually."

She sat and crossed her legs. "I don't need to look cute every time I come here. I just need to look different so a casual observer won't notice the same bitch is visiting you."

Milo nodded, moved to face her on the other side of the tea service tray and selected a cherry-laced treat. "Since you're here I assume there's news."

"Yep. Things are moving at a pretty good clip. I mean, this bunch is a lot more dangerous than I expected, but I'm getting the job done. Wanted you to know I just excised the third dude on your list."

"Truly?" Milo's eyes lit up. "That is amazing progress. I thought this would take weeks. Here, let me take care of the administrative matter." He pulled out his phone and started tapping buttons. People always stare at their phones when they're using them, Skye thought, except when actually speaking into them.

Milo said, "There you go. Another hundred thousand dollars just moved into your account. The next man will be worth a hundred twenty-five."

"Yeah, well get that shit ready, cause I already got a lead on the next dude."

"You're kidding," Milo said, sipping his tea. "Are they so easy to find?"

Skye loved a plain cheese Danish and was halfway through one. She held off speaking until she was finished chewing. "They really just arrogant," she said. "I heard from my computer whiz on my way over here. This next guy is on the road so I thought he might be tough to trace. Turns out he's travelling under his own name and travelling alone. Crazy, right? But I found out he's Yakuza, so it's arrogance I can understand. He'll land at BWI at 1:45 tomorrow afternoon. I'll meet him there and put this matter to rest."

"Really?" Milo brushed crumbs out of his beard. "You're going to do that right out in an airport? Sounds risky. A lot of witnesses, no? Not to mention lots of other people who might get hurt if you start shooting in there."

Skye swallowed the last of her Danish and licked her lips. "Who said anything about shooting? It don't always go down like that. I got a plan that probably won't put nobody else at risk. I've got to pick up some special supplies for this idea I got, but the way I'm going to pull it off, it ought to scare the shit out of Number Five."

"Oh. Do you have a lead on him?"

Skye picked up a second Danish, cherry this time, and looked over it at her host. She smiled, thinking not so much about the sugary treat in her hand as about the cash that would be hitting her account. "One corpse at a time, Milo. One corpse at a time."

Chapter 23

When she stepped out of Mo's car, Skye felt like she had gone home, although home was no longer there. Now it was a broad field of rubble, fenced off for the safety of local residents. Steam shovels and skip loaders were at work that day, and she watched hard hat workers move between them, more people standing and directing than actually working. But they were getting the job done, erasing this piece of Washington history.

In the late sixties this area near North Capitol Street was a low-income housing community called Sursum Corda. Skye was in her teens before she bothered to look up the name, which turned out to be Latin for "Lift up your hearts." At the time of construction, a group of Catholic activists had imagined an urban village for low-income families with townhouses and courtyards. Skye never knew that happy village. By the 1980s, heroin had invaded. Then came the crack cocaine epidemic. When she was growing up there, the property was a center for criminal activity. Skye had dragged herself out of that pit of drugs and despair, and finally someone had decided to tear it all down and start over.

Her goal was the trailer on the edge of the demolition activity where the on-site bosses determined how the various buildings would be safely turned into trash to be carted away. Even though this was basically Daryl's office, she knocked on the door before walking in.

"Come back later!"

Well, that was rude. It also wasn't Daryl's voice. They had been doing business for nearly a year and he was expecting her. So who was this shouting through the door and why didn't Daryl correct him?

Like most trailers, this one's windows were both narrow and frosted. Standing on the cinder block that served as a step up to the door she could hear nothing for a few seconds. Then there was a sharp sound, like a slap, followed by a lower voice.

"Kiss my ass." That was Daryl. What the hell?

The next sound was the unmistakable flesh-on-flesh sound of a punch to someone's face. Now the story was much clearer. Unfortunate timing. Maybe none of her business, but Skye was here for reasons other than nostalgia. A deep breath, and she yanked the door open. She stepped into the narrow space, scanning to take in the scene at a glance.

To her right, at the front of the trailer, Daryl sat behind a small metal desk covered with papers. He was a bulky guy, blue eyes under a blond mop, in a plaid shirt. He looked like he had worked construction all his life, which she knew to be true. The other two men in the room seemed mismatched. The one in front of the desk looked Middle Eastern, with thick, black curly hair and dense eyebrows. He wore a black suit, in contrast to his partner standing behind the desk looking down at Daryl. This one was white, with short, straight brown hair. In jeans and a polo shirt he might have belonged on a construction site. Both turned to her, but the man behind the desk spoke first.

"What you doing here?" he asked in a thick, Eastern European accent. "Get the fuck out!"

Skye stood relaxed and focused on the one familiar face. "Daryl, you okay?"

"I don't think you heard my friend here." This from the better dressed man in a very different but equally strong accent. He reached for Skye with both his large hairy hands. She grabbed his right hand with both of hers and twisted hard to her right, locking his elbow and slamming his head into the wall.

"What the hell?" she said, kicking hard into the man's stomach. "A Jew working with an Albanian? What is it, mob mix-and-match day?"

The man Skye marked as Albanian pulled a switchblade and dived for her. He was thin but wiry. Skye had no doubt of his strength. But she could rely on him underestimating hers. She crouched in the narrow space and as he stepped over his partner she leaned in. He slashed but the knife flew over her shoulder. She snapped a head butt into his stomach while she wrapped her arms around his thighs. Then she stood in a quick explosive move that slammed the thug's head into the metal ceiling. A quick twist and she had tossed him onto the floor in front of the door. Before his eyes came back into focus she was pointing her pistol at him. Her left foot was on the other man's neck who could not squirm free in such cramped quarters.

"All right, Daryl," Skye said, facing away from him but staring hard at the Albanian on the floor. "How mad am I at these guys? Two bullets? A warning? I can make them disappear, or we can send them home."

"I don't know," Daryl said. She heard him standing and moving toward her. "I think they're new around here."

The man at Skye's feet squirmed and got a hand around her other ankle. Skye shifted her pistol's aim to his head but then she felt his body shudder and heard the man make a sound somewhere between a cry and a moan. She turned enough to see Daryl's foot pulling away from the man's crotch.

"Yeah, I think it best to send a warning back to whoever was stupid enough to send them here."

"Your call," Skye said. Then to the Albanian, "Kick that knife over here dumbass, and stand up." He did as he was told, his face flushed with rage. Skye picked up the switchblade and walked toward him. Her gun was against his throat as she opened the door. Then she slipped past him, her face an inch away from his, mentally daring him to do something. Once she was a foot away from him she said, "Okay, hands up, tough guy."

Trembling with anger he put his palms toward her. She smiled and slashed his right palm. He howled and clutched the injured hand to his chest.

"Now get out," Skye said, "before you piss me off and I really hurt you." As the Albanian moved out the door, she looked at his partner. "You. Over here. Same deal."

The other man stood, brushed off his clothes, and stepped forward. His face was more passive as he raised his hands.

"Jewish Mafia?" Skye asked. He nodded. "Respect. The Albanians are a joke, you know." He nodded slowly. "Dangerous, but Pit Bull dangerous, not Doberman dangerous like you boys. Sorry you got stuck with this moron." Then they locked eyes, and she slashed his palm with a quick swipe. He balled his hands into fists and lowered them to his sides.

"Go tell whoever sent you that this particular construction site is off limits. Got it?"

"Yes."

"Good. Hit the road and think about how lucky you are I didn't blow your face off."

Skye watched the two thugs until they were off the site, then closed the door. Daryl plopped back into his chair and swiveled to pull a bottle of vodka and a small paper-wrapped package out of a small refrigerator. He poured generous portions of the clear liquid into two glasses, emptied his down his throat, and refilled it. Skye put one cheek up on his desk and sipped from the other glass.

"So what the hell was that all about?"

Daryl shook his head. "Like any construction outfit, we have an arrangement with some mafia or another, and we keep up our payments. These two jokers walk in here today and try to strongarm me for the same stuff you pay me good money for."

Skye tossed back the last of her drink. "Yeah, I hear there's a new crime boss in town. He's pulling some surprising gangs together, and I guess he's rewriting all the rules."

"Damn. Ain't nobody got time for that crap," Daryl said. "But I'm glad you got here on time. I was not prepared to face you with a story like, somebody stole the package you already paid me for. I like doing business with you, but I am not prepared to be on your bad side. So, I was stalling, hoping that when you got here, you'd straighten things out." He pushed what looked like a brick wrapped in brown paper across the desk toward Skye.

"Hey, I got to protect my supply chain," Skye said, pushing the package into an inside jacket pocket.

"Yeah, well I appreciate it, and it definitely gets you a discount the next time you need some loud supplies."

Back in the car with her small package, Skye told Mo she had one more stop to make. He laughed out loud when she told him where they were going, but she figured he knew better than to make any smartass remark. He kept his reaction to two words. "I figured."

Ross Elementary School stood right there on R Street, not far from the girl's home although farther into the city. A simple, three-story brick affair, it fit in well with the neighborhood. Beside it stood a neat little playground. Aside from the pulverized rubber ground covering and the very safe plastic slide, benches and so forth, it was not unlike the playground at Skye's old grade school. Walking up to the school, she smiled at the sign on the black, wrought iron fence surrounding it. "Embraced for who you are," it said, "and Empowered to be even more." Then came their mission statement: "Every child is known, Every teacher is invested, Every family is valued." Lofty goals, she thought. At her school it would have been something like, "Every kid fighting for his life."

Surprised at the lack of security, she stepped into the playground and dropped onto a plastic bench that wound around a large tree. Shielded from the afternoon sun she leaned back, folded her arms, stretched out her legs and crossed her ankles. One thing sniper training teaches you is how to wait.

She didn't have to wait long. The typically annoying bell sounded and seconds later the mob crashed the doors. One thing had not changed. Kids can't wait to get out of school for the day. But these were not the kids Skye went to school with. First of all, half of them were white. Then she noticed they were all dressed the same. Well, not quite. Polo shirts or blouses but they were all either white or navy blue. Pants or skirts, all navy blue or khaki. A uniform of sorts. Nobody in jeans or tee shirts. She wondered how she would have reacted to that when she was ten or eleven, trying to find her identity.

The dress code made target acquisition a little harder but not in reverse and Carla did not disappoint. She glanced at Skye, then took a longer look. Then she flashed a broad smile and joined the stream of kids moving into the playground. Skye was still, happy to be ignored by the other adults, a mix of adults, nannies and sitters. Carla stood in front of Skye, navy skirt swaying in the gentle breeze, hands clasped behind her back, under her backpack.

"Glad I get to see you again, anonymous African-American lady. We're moving away at the end of next week."

Laughing and shaking her head, Skye managed to say, "Kid, you crack me up. They call me Skye. Just don't tell your folks, okay?"

"Don't worry. I'm a good security risk."

Then Carla stood quiet, just looking at her visitor, until Skye said, "Cop a squat, kid."

"You checking up on me?"

"Nah, you safe now," Skye said. "Came by cause I just wanted to talk a bit. Kind of wanted to ask you something."

Carla sat beside Skye and leaned back, her backpack resting against the tree. Carla stared at Skye. Skye stared forward at the street. After a moment, Carla turned to also look toward the street, their gazes parallel. Carla laced her fingers together in her lap, and her feet began to swing forward and back.

Skye said, "You're a really smart kid. You already know how to be still. What are you, twelve?"

"Eleven. Sitting still is how you find out stuff. People think they like quiet but really they hate it. So if you wait, they tell you stuff."

Skye nodded. "So, a few days ago, some big, scary guys snatched you up off the street and took you to that place across town."

"Yeah. Just drove up and pushed me in a van. I screamed. A lot. Nobody came after me. It was weird."

"Not really," Skye said. "People see what they want to see. Nobody wants to believe they saw a kid getting kidnapped. So they tell themselves it was your parents and you were being a bad kid. Or maybe you were hurt, and your folks were rushing you to the hospital. They think they're good people but what they really want to do is mind their own damn business."

This time Carla nodded.

"So anyway, they grabbed you. Took you to a strange place. I'm betting they didn't say shit to you about what they was going to do. So, I'm saying," Skye turned to the little girl beside her, "Most kids your age would have been scared shitless. Most grown folks would have been scared shitless. How come you wasn't just terrified?"

Carla's feet kept swinging but her lips pouted forward, then withdrew into a hard look that Skye recognized. "Miss Skye, I'm the smartest kid in the sixth grade. At least I got the best grades. All the teachers like me. And I like the library better than I like sports."

"You a fucking nerd."

Carla shrugged. "I guess. Anyway, what I figured out is, you don't back down to a bully. That just gets you picked on worse. What you do is, you get mad back, you show them how picking on you makes them the loser. Bullies don't know how to handle that. Besides, they were going to do whatever they were going to do. I couldn't stop them. But why should I let them have the fun of seeing me scared. So I just decided not to be scared."

This kid has the seeds of a hero herself, Skye thought. Or she's a budding sociopath.

"Besides, I'm smarter than them. If I had to, I'd find a way to get away. But I didn't have to because besides all that…"

"What else?"

"Well, you," Carla said with a big smile, locking eyes with Skye. "My Mom and Dad taught me that as long as you're being good, somebody will help you. I knew my Dad would come get me. Or the police, or somebody. Like you."

Skye didn't know if she was amused, or happy or scared that this little girl carried that level of faith. Maybe all three. They sat in silence for a few minutes. What was it about this little girl that made her feel like she didn't want to let go? Totally different environment from what Skye grew up in, and loving parents, but still Carla felt awfully familiar. And her parents were doing a good job but they weren't preparing her for what life would want to do to her. Or for what she would want to do to the world.

"Moving next week? Do you know where?"

"Richmond," Carla said, and her face dropped. "Whole new school, whole new bunch of kids to deal with."

"You'll be fine," Skye said. "You ain't scared of nothing, and you the smartest kid in the room. You'll be fine."

"Sure," Carla said. Then, as if responding to some unheard signal, they both stood up. Carla looked up at Skye again. She looked you in the eye, this girl. Skye liked that. Then Carla held her right hand out.

"Thank you again for saving me Miss Skye. I may not have too many adventures in my life, but I've got rooftop escape checked off on my list."

"You're welcome, but drop the Miss shit, all right? Just Skye."

"Cool," Carla said, giving a surprisingly solid handshake. "I never had a grownup friend before."

Skye nodded, feeling an unexpected warmth, and turned to go. After two steps, she turned back.

"Not a lot of adventures, eh? Tell me, you ever fire a gun? Like on a practice range or something?"

"Nah, nothing like that."

"Well, you know, Richmond ain't that far away," Skye said with a wink. "You might see me again."

By the time Skye was pushing the buttons to get back into her apartment her stomach was telling her it was dinner time. She was mentally choosing which nearby restaurant she was in the mood for when the aroma of frying onions and peppers caught her attention. She hauled the new suitcase and bag of supplies into her apartment wondering what her house guest was up to.

Brandon stood at the stove stirring a saucepan. A large pot steamed at the back of the stove. He looked at her with hooded eyes and went back to stirring. A quick glance around confirmed that he had not touched anything outside the kitchen.

"What's up, Brandon?" she asked, passing him to drop her new possessions in her work room. She smiled when she noticed that Brandon had made the futon bed. He was turning out to be a good house guest.

"Pretty quiet day," he replied. "Didn't know when you'd be back so I figured to go on with dinner. But there's plenty for two."

"Plenty of…?" Skye asked, returning to the island and easing up onto one of the stools.

"Spaghetti," he said, still stirring the sauce.

"And you're frying onions?"

"Caramelizing," he said. "I found an onion, a green pepper and some mushrooms in your refrigerator. Didn't find garlic but what I've got should make this sauce from a jar edible."

Skye didn't want to mention that she always just poured that sauce from the jar onto her spaghetti and shoved the plate into the microwave for a couple of minutes. But his way sounded better. At least it sure smelled better. The aroma made her little place feel warmer somehow.

"Well, very nice of you to cook."

"Just trying to be a good guest," Brandon said, finally turning to give her a small smile. "Hungry?"

"Oh, yeah," Skye said. "I've been running all day. Had people to talk to and supplies to gather for the job coming up. Where'd you go today?"

"Go?" Now Brandon cut off the gas burner and finally turned to face Skye. "I didn't go anywhere. How could I go anywhere?"

"Not like you're locked in," Skye said, getting back to her feet and reaching into a cabinet for a fresh bottle of red.

"No, but I didn't want to be locked out. You didn't give me the combination to your lock. And I sure wasn't going to leave your door unlocked with your apartment empty. So yeah, I could have gone out, but I couldn't get back in."

Skye blushed a little, pouring two glasses of wine. "Sorry, didn't think. Well, no reason to keep it from you. One, three, five, two, four. Odds, then evens. And you won't be stuck here too long anyway. As soon as I finish this little assignment you can be on your way. If you want, I'll get you set up with a new identity."

"That shouldn't be necessary," Brandon said, beginning to drop spaghetti noodles onto a plate. "I'll be just another nobody in any other city. You planning on taking a trip soon? I see you got a suitcase…"

"Oh, that's for tomorrow. My computer whiz friend was able to see airport security video. I got no idea how he does it. But he was able to see what kind of luggage Kobayashi is travelling with. I was able to find one just like it. Close enough at least to let me pull a substitution when he lands."

"I suppose the new case will be full of explosives or something," Brandon said, ladling his thick sauce onto a plate of spaghetti.

"Well that's the theory," Skye said. "A little bit of misdirection."

Brandon sat facing her and sipped his wine. "It's kind of interesting watching your preparations."

Skye twirled up a small forkful of spaghetti and pushing it into her mouth. "Well I usually want to do things in a very professional… whoa! Damn, boy. You can cook!"

After dinner they cleaned up together. and Skye returned to her workshop. Brandon followed her and sat down on his futon bed. Skye brought a full wine glass with her and sat it on a workbench. Then she opened the bag she had carried in and pulled out the paper-wrapped package, about half the size of a standard brick. Brandon looked over her shoulder as she slowly unwrapped the orange contents.

"Some sort of putty?" he asked.

"Actually, it's Semtex," she said. "Commonly used in demolitions these days."

"Is that a brand name?"

Skye shook her head at his naivete. "Yeah, it's a brand of plastic explosive. It's made out of RDX and PETN. I'm betting you never heard of either one."

Brandon fell silent for a minute. Then he slowly got to his feet and said, "I'll leave you to your work then."

Skye leaned back and stretched, feeling her body's batteries running down. She was pleased that her weapons were cleaned, and all her gear for the next day's task was tested and ready. She had been her own boss from the beginning of her peculiar life, an independent contractor who had to be responsible for her own actions. This, she thought, had been a good day's work. Then she checked the clock on the worktable and saw that more than three hours had passed since she sat down. She had all but forgotten that she wasn't alone in the apartment and, for his part, Brandon had not disturbed her.

She was feeling a little tired, but also happy with herself and feeling a bit less than usual like keeping her own company. Well, she deserved some reward for her good work today.

In the living area some blonde on CNN droned on about the state of the country. The news rarely impacted Skye.

She no longer had any interest in politics, foreign wars or any natural disaster outside of the D-M-V.

She remembered when the big picture was her focus. She used to sit in front of the screen every night with Papa. It was part of her training. He would prompt her to discuss foreign military operations from a tactical standpoint, terrorist activity from a cost/benefit perspective, and any crime news with a view toward cause and effect. She had tried hard to absorb his world view, but there were times she just did not understand.

"Papa, why are there so many bad people in the world?"

"Well, Skye, I'm not so sure there are so many," Papa said. "Maybe it's just that the bad people do more stuff, so they end up on the news."

"Why doesn't somebody just get rid of them all?"

Papa laughed. "A lot of people are trying, Skye. Bad guys can be like roaches, hard to stamp out. Sometimes they're real hard to find. And sometimes, the good guys just don't agree on who the bad guys are."

"Well then, how do you tell if they're the bad guys?"

Papa got real serious then. "Skye, it's really pretty easy. If a person is trying to help somebody, that's the good guys. If a person is trying to hurt somebody, they're the bad guys."

"Well, don't we all do both?"

"Well, child, sometimes bad people do things that are so bad no amount of good will make up for it. But it's not always easy to tell. That's why you need judgement. Because before you get rid of the bad guy, you need to be sure they deserve it. That's rule number one."

Back then all that international grief seemed important, but it was hard to figure out. These days Skye stayed focused on her own little local world where the good guys and bad guys could be more easily spotted. She had lost interest in trying to figure out the world much beyond the

Beltway. Clearly that wasn't the case for Brandon, but it looked like he had passed his input saturation point. He had dozed off on her love seat, breathing in a soft purr that fell short of actual snoring. Another point in this fellow's favor. Good looks, fit enough, smarter than most, and he didn't snore. He checked all the boxes and got extra points for being able to cook. Bonus points for doing so without being asked. He deserved a reward.

She deserved a reward too. It had been a while.

"Brandon," she called. No response to his name. She nudged his shoulder. He snuggled down deeper into the love seat. She reached down and clamped his nostrils shut, pulling her hand away as he jerked awake, panting, eyes darting in all directions.

"Bedtime," Skye said, maintaining her default bored facial expression.

"Oh, sorry," Brandon said, shaking his head. "Didn't want to invade the workshop room until you were finished with whatever you were doing. I guess tomorrow will be a busy day."

"Yeah," Skye said. "But you don't have to go in there tonight." She saw confusion on Brandon's face and rolled her eyes. Did she have to hit him over the head with it? "In here. Come to bed with me. Jesus."

"With you?"

"Yes, genius." Skye sighed. "You been pretty good through all this, and I figure we can both use a little relaxation. Unless you don't want to. You boo'ed up or something?"

Brandon shook his head. "No no. I don't have even a casual girlfriend, let alone a… a boo."

"Then what's the matter?" Skye turned her head enough to give him the side eye. "Don't you like girls?"

"What? No, of course I do. And you're very… um, wow. I just didn't think… I mean, you and I aren't…"

"Well we could be," Skye said, turning and walking into her bedroom, "if you move your ass and get undressed and crawl under that comforter."

Chapter 24

Skye bit back a grunt as she threw the high crescent kick. Her form was good, but her left thigh still gave her grief. She had started with some yoga and gone through her usual karate kata fairly smoothly but in the field she would have to only kick with her right foot for a while. She heard a deep breath being taken and turned to see Brandon over her shoulder. He was standing in the workshop doorway. She didn't think he had been there long enough to see more than one kick.

"Morning, sleepyhead," she said, turning to face him. She knew the black tights and leotard showed her figure to best advantage and appreciated his grateful smile. He had pulled his pants on but nothing else, and she had to admit he had nothing to be ashamed of either. He was trim. Not overly muscular, but his stomach was flat, and a low body fat content meant good definition. And she liked them with no chest hair. Yeah, he was all right.

"Good morning." Brandon also wore a relaxed smile, although there was still a hint of shyness in his voice.

"Thought I was going to have to come in after you," Skye said. "I showered, made coffee, grabbed a bagel, and been loosening up in here for damn near an hour."

Brandon chuckled. "I guess you wore me out. Last night was…"

"Yeah, pretty nice."

"Magical," Brandon said, completing his sentence as he had originally planned.

Skye waved his comment away. "It not for this bullet wound I could have showed you some…"

"Stop that," Brandon said, stepping closer. "It was amazing. You are something else." He raised his arms to pull her in close, but she stepped around him and out of the room.

"Nigga please. I'm sure a fine brother like you gets all the pussy you can handle. It ain't like it was your first time. You got some skills, and we was pretty good together."

"Why you got to do that?" Brandon asked, following her out of the room and back into the bedroom. "Make it sound cheap when it was… well, it wasn't cheap. And please don't call me that."

"Oh yeah, you don't like that word," Skye said in a sarcastic tone. She was fishing in her closet for the right skirt and a loose shirt she would need later and debating whether she should say something nice to him for making the bed when he got up. In the middle of planning her own day she turned from the closet to face him.

"Hey, Brandon. I was going down to the range this morning to get some practice in. I hadn't thought of it before but, hey, want to tag along?"

"You mean like a shooting range?"

No, a driving range, asshole, she thought, but bit back the snarky response. Then she wondered why she didn't say it. Out loud she said, "Yeah, it's a skill that needs a lot of practice, you know?"

At that Brandon smiled warmly. "Well, sure. A chance to watch you shooting at something that won't be shooting back? I think I'd kind of dig that."

Fifteen minutes later the pair was trotting down the stairs from her stoop to the street and turned left. Skye carried a small blue case and had pulled on her favorite denim jacket over the leotard and added black jeans and boots. Brandon stayed on her street side, which Skye thought was cute. At the corner they turned left again.

"So this range is within walking distance?" Brandon asked.

"You kidding? No such thing as legal shooting in The District, unless of course you're a cop or something. I'm in a shooting club down in Fairfax."

"Fairfax, Virginia?" he asked. "Then why are we walking?"

"I just don't like to have Mo puling up in front of my place all the time."

As if on cue, the black Honda Accord pulled to the curb just ahead of them. Skye smiled and pulled ahead of Brandon to tap on the driver window. "Good morning, Mo. How's the family?"

Mo turned to look her up and down. "You walking a little better. You sure you want to do this today? Maybe need to rest your… whatever got hurt." Mo was wearing his skeptical face today.

"I'm good, brother," she said, yanking the back door open and bouncing inside. It was exaggerated, and she hoped he didn't see her wince with pain when she landed. Brandon joined her on the other side. The two men mumbled "morning" at each other. Mo pulled away from the curb and Skye wondered if his expression was about her injury or her company.

They rolled across the narrow Key Bridge (only out of towners would say "Francis Scott Key Bridge") and soon locked into the traffic moving west on Rte 66. This was usually the time for light, casual chat with Mo but this morning he was quiet and she couldn't think of much to say. Her eyes wandered out the window at the roadside wall of trees, then the rearview mirror, then over to Brandon's eyes. She was drawn to them but didn't want to just stare at him for the next hour. Besides, every time she looked at him she saw that he was watching her. Not staring. Just watching her, as if there was nothing in the world more enjoyable to do.

"Hey, you haven't asked me much," Brandon finally said in soft tones.

"I ain't nosy," she said, then mentally cursed herself, sure that he would hear, *I'm not interested in you.*

"But I'm hoping whatever you wanted to know it's okay for me to want to know."

"Sure," she said, staring at her boots. "What do you want to know that you didn't..." She cut herself off, glancing at Mo. She was thinking, ... *that you didn't find out last night?*

"Well, you asked me where I went to school, so I thought I could ask you the same."

Do I look like a college girl to you? She thought. Aloud she said, "Um, the school of hard knocks I guess. I finished high school right there in the district and that was the end of that." She smiled at him. He smiled back. But he was still staring at her. Waiting. The weight of the silence pressed her to say more.

"Well Papa, he believed more in life experience," she said. "We travelled a lot."

"Just your father? No mom?"

"Yeah. Well, adoptive father actually. My real parents didn't... they weren't... well, they wasn't parents." She knew she was fumbling for words, but Brandon didn't interrupt or try to guess what she was trying to say. He let her finish. She was surprised by how much she liked that about him.

"So, you grew up in the system," Brandon said, his eyes dropping in projected sadness.

"Oh no." Skye grabbed his hand and her face brightened. "Just Papa. Papa and me. He took me everywhere, I mean, places I didn't even know was there.

And he knew people, all kinds of people. So I met a lot of guys who were like experts in different stuff. I guess you could say I studied with a whole lot of subject matter experts, all over the world. "

"Well that explains it, then." Brandon squeezed her hand. "You don't talk like a university grad, but you're very... worldly I guess is the word."

Skye never thought of herself as a person who would blush but for a second she felt a warmth rushing up her neck toward her face. She turned to check out the wall of trees along the side of the highway. A quick glance at the rearview mirror showed her Mo's knowing smile. He was silently laughing at her. Damn him.

And Brandon was looking out his window, but he still had hold of her hand.

Brandon released her and sat up straight as they rolled past a huge, low complex on their left. He stared past Skye and squeezed her hand again to get her attention.

"Hey, I think that's NRA headquarters. Glad we're passing it. Those people are..."

Skye's chuckle cut him off. "Hey, don't confuse guns with politics. And whatever you're thinking right now, you need to lose it or keep it in when we get where we really going."

"You purposely hang out with these NRA types?"

"Not much choice, hon. There ain't no such thing as a "urban" shooting range."

Shortly they pulled off the highway for the more suburban surroundings of the Prince William Parkway. Among the clean, bright shopping centers and strip malls Brandon pointed out a sign to Elite Shooting Sports.

"That where we're going?"

Mo snorted a half-laugh. Skye said, "That place? Nah. You'd be at home there, though. Real "genteel" and upper class. But they only got a indoor range. I need a place where I can move around some. Shooting while you're standing still, that ain't real life."

They left the parkway and rolled through an upscale housing development but after the next turn the buildings got farther and farther apart with an odd mix of more modest homes and mini-mansions with swimming pools and the occasional man-made pond. Skye grinned at Brandon's discomfort.

"Yep, this here's The South," she said. "You look like I felt the first time Papa brought me out here. I was like seventeen. I had never been outside The District then. Guess I thought the whole world looked like that, or else the suburbs like I sometimes saw on TV."

Then Brandon was thrown against Skye as Mo yanked them off the main road and down a narrow track cut through a dense forest. Skye's smile grew as they pulled up to a modest looking building at the end of the road. The small parking area was filled by an eclectic collection of vehicles: pickup trucks and SUVs dominated but several luxury cars were tucked in between them.

Skye hopped out of the car with her little case, said "see you on the firing line" and marched toward the building. Brandon watched from the car as she walked between two men standing near the door. Both were big, husky white men in ball caps and camo clothing. One wore a sidearm in a holster. The other held a shotgun. Both smiled, greeted Skye by name, and nodded in deference.

Mo climbed out and stretched. After a moment, Brandon left the car and walked around to the driver's side.

"I take it you've made that drive before."

"I bring her out here every month," Mo said. "Not my thing but, everybody's got to have a hobby, right?" He meandered off and Brandon followed. They walked around to an open space of packed earth and sparse, short-cut grass. There was no place to sit but a small crowd was milling around, all white, almost all men, all in ball caps except for a couple of cowboy hats.

Brandon's first surprise was that every man he passed said "Hey" or "Morning." His second was the range itself. He had expected a series of stalls like he'd seen on television. Instead there was a wooden bench facing a tall wooden fence, with shorter, chest-high fences on either side of it. Out in front of the first short fence, three brown paper targets stood behind what looked like the cutout of a car. Past the other short fence stood seven targets. Three of them, brown, were half hidden behind three other white targets. One stood alone. Then farther out, right in the middle, stood one steel target.

"So this is how they shoot, eh?" Brandon said.

"Not everybody," Mo replied. "They set this up special for Skye. And they do it different every time. "

"They set all this up just for her?"

"This place belongs to something called the Izaak Walton League," Mo said. "I looked it up. It's a conservation kind of organization. She's never said, but I'm thinking Skye donates a boat load of money to them for this."

Brandon looked at the crowd again, noticing how many of them were armed. "I'm surprised they allow it, with all these guys waiting to shoot."

"They ain't in no hurry," Mo said. "They here to watch her."

Before Brandon could ask more, he saw Skye marching toward the bench. Her mouth was set in a grim line and her eyes said she saw but somehow didn't see him. She was in the same black jeans, top and boots, but she had abandoned the denim jacket and added a black ball cap. Amber colored glasses covered her eyes and what looked like headphones covered her ears. And she wore a holster, low slung like a western gun slinger. The gun in it was bigger than any he'd seen her with before. And six magazines hung around the belt.

The fellow walking behind her wore a shirt that reminded Brandon of a Nascar driver, with various brand names on the back. He was a lot more relaxed than she, nodding and smiling at the rest of the folks around. He stopped behind the bench. Skye stopped behind the first short fence, slowly scanned the whole target area, then dropped onto the bench and picked up what looked like a newspaper.

"Hey, you family?" someone asked in a deep drawl. Brandon spun to find himself eye-to-eye with a tow-haired man who was his personal definition of redneck. The man's grin showed a couple of missing teeth, but it seemed genuine.

"Just a friend," Brandon said, trying to relax enough to smile back.

"Bucky," the man said, switching his beer can to his left hand and thrusting his big, callused right toward Brandon. He seemed unaware of Brandon's discomfort. Not seeing any alternative, Brandon took the hand, shook it, and introduced himself.

"Ain't seen you hereabouts before," Bucky said. "But if you here with Skye you all right. And if you ain't seen her shoot before, you in for a treat."

"Well, I have seen her shoot," Brandon said, "But not like this."

"Oh, she vicious with a race gun on a fast course too," Bucky said, making the obvious but wrong assumption, "But she's hot on the single stack too, shooting major power factor like the boys. Likes to mix it up."

"I see," Brandon said, but of course he didn't. Still, this Bucky seemed to know what was going on. "Is this the way you folks usually practice? Or…"

"Oh, hell no, brother. They set this shit up special for her. We give her a challenge every month. That girl there is about the best I've seen outside the pro circuit. If she'd just compete, she'd be a champion. Been watching her for years and after maybe the first couple months, got to where she just always hits what she's aiming at. Scary good."

Brandon couldn't help himself from asking: "Watching her for years?"

Bucky turned that grin on him again and took a big swig from his morning beer. "Hell, son, I was here the first time old man Maddox brought her out. She was a tiny little thing, couldn't have been more than seventeen. He was a ball buster, a serious hard ass, but wasn't nobody could teach you better than him. Out here he always talked to her like she was one of his SEAL recruits. And the girl, well she worked hard at it, like she was on a mission or something. Besides which, she had a gift. I mean it, a goddam gift. Like her and guns just belonged together. So he was training her to be a USPSA Grandmaster from the get."

Brandon walked around behind Skye, maintaining the distance everyone else kept. She appeared to be totally relaxed, as if she was really reading the newspaper. Bucky moved with him, as if he was the unofficial welcoming committee.

"Does she always use such a big gun?"

Bucky gave a loud, rough laugh. "You must have only seen her with a nine. That's the usual thing for ladies in competition. The men get the 1911. More power, less rounds. But don't worry, she handles the 45 ACP just fine. You'll see. Reloading's harder. One reason she likes this. Eight-round mag'll kill you if you miss. But she don't. You'll see." Then Bucky stopped and stared at Brandon as if he could see one more question behind Brandon's eyes.

"Okay, I got to ask." Then Brandon's voice dropped lower. "Why are some of the targets brown and some white?"

At that Bucky scratched the back of his neck and adopted a look of deep thought. "Well, damn. It's supposed to look like a hostage setup, you know. The white targets are the ones you ain't supposed to hit. But I never thought of it in terms of, you know, color."

The man standing behind Skye slowly raised his right arm, holding a small blue box. All eyes were on Skye, although everyone seemed intent on continuing their conversations. Skye turned a page of the newspaper.

Brandon jumped when the loud honking sound exploded from the little blue box. Skye sprang from the bench, diving left, and the pistol seemed to magically appear in her right hand. From behind the low fence she swung right to fire, two-handed. A loud ping let everyone know she had hit the metal target. Then she pivoted left to fire at the targets "crouching" behind the wooden car. Six more shots inside of two seconds and those three targets were done. The hair of Brandon's neck stood up as he imagined three men where the targets were.

Skye dashed right, the magazine dropping from the gun butt just in time for her to ram another into place. Then she was behind the other low fence, quick-firing until the slide locked back, showing the pistol empty. The range officer, staring at a stopwatch, announced her time.

"Eight seven niner."

Seconds, Brandon thought. Eight targets in less than nine seconds. And the white targets untouched. A smattering of applause sprang up. Skye turned and gave a small wave, then turned to the range officer.

"Can you set them up again? I love the park bench stage."

She nodded to Mo with a smile and a wink as he wandered over to stand beside Brandon.

"Ain't that something?" Mo asked. "She's the real deal, and all these good old boys know it." He stopped when Bucky leaned in.

"Heading back out to the truck. You boys want a beer?"

The ride back to what Skye thought of as civilization was quieter. She lay back against the corner of the seat, eyes closed, palms open on her thighs, totally relaxed after barely a half hour of shooting. Her hands and arms still sang with the warm vibration of recoil. She had always enjoyed the thrill of practical shooting, the ten second adrenaline rush, the push toward perfection. Even liked the respect the other shooters showed her, the same respect they showed Papa when he used to come out. Of course, they always respected combat vets no matter what, but for her it was all about respect for her skill.

This time she also admitted to herself that she enjoyed the chance to impress Brandon. The look on his face after she would shoot a stage was priceless and with her safety glasses on she'd bet he never even knew she was checking him out.

They rolled through Checkers on the way for an early lunch. Skye was halfway through her burger when she tapped Mo on the shoulder.

"You still good with an all day?"

"I already said," Mo replied. "And I kind of expected a detour or two soon as I saw you wasn't alone."

She smiled her thank you into the rearview mirror, patted his shoulder again and turned to Brandon.

"Hey, you got any money? I mean cash?"

"Sure," he said, reaching for his wallet. "What do you need?"

"Not for me, ni…" she stopped herself, then shook her head at herself for changing her speech pattern for him. "Look, I want to get a look at this next mark as he rolls into town, so Mo's going to take me out to BWI for a little personal recon. I was thinking while I'm gone, he could run you to Macy's or J&G or somewhere so you could pick up a couple changes of clothes."

Baltimore Washington International Airport wasn't really close to Baltimore or Washington but sat between them where someone must have thought it would be convenient to both. The building was U-shaped, wrapped around the parking garage, with five concourses stretching out from the U. Each of the major airlines had their own area on one of the concourses, but international flights all came in and out of the same area.

On the lower level, The Green Bean Café was just about the first thing travelers would see once they were released by the customs agents. Skye relaxed at one of the tables in front of the counter, nursing a coffee and cheese Danish. It took her just a couple minutes to identify which luggage carousel Kobayashi's bag would be on. She also spotted the two Japanese men there to meet him. Dark suits with sharp creases, slicked-back hair, Ray-Ban shades and bulges under their jackets that no one else would notice. These guys were on the alert for a threat, but as long as she stared up at the white girder lattice that covered the ceiling she'd stay under their radar.

She didn't have a photo, but she knew Kobayashi the instant he came into view. He was the fifth person through the door. He was tall for a Japanese man, an inch over six feet and even in a finely tailored suit she could see that he was rock solid and trim. His walk was nothing short of imperial, his head held high. She was struck by the black, slicked-back hair and Ray-Bans. His men patterned themselves after him. His shoes glistened. A Breitling hung on his left wrist. Not the most expensive watch, but if you live an active life, probably the best.

Kobayashi greeted one of the waiting assistants in Japanese while the other went to grab his luggage. Skye appraised the situation and decided that conditions were just not right to take out the target. But it was good to get a good look at him. He read dangerous, but in a calm, heartless way, not the flashy, arrogant vibe Murphy had given off. She'd have to move more carefully with this one.

Luggage gathered, she watched them move smoothly toward the transportation doors. One guard walked in front of Kobayashi, slightly to his left. The other followed, a little to the right. No doubt a car waited for them outside. It was time to move into action. Skye stood, grabbed the suitcase she had brought for effect and ran after them like a woman who was about to miss her flight.

The rear guard turned as she approached, her feet loud on the tile floor. She panted harder than necessary, staring down at a piece of paper in her hand. She thumped into the man as if she had not seen him there, muttered "Sorry" without actually looking at him, and rushed on past them. No one of the three had over-reacted, but she could feel their eyes on her as she raced on. They probably just registered her as a random rude American. She wondered how much trouble the man she bumped into would be in when someone finally noticed the listening device she had dropped into his jacket pocket.

Chapter 25

Fujio Kobayashi stepped out of the armored limousine and looked up at the brick and stone building on M Street. This was in no way a suitable place to carry out business. He would move to a more dignified, less vulnerable location as soon as he could arrange it.

His men escorted him inside and to the elevator. On the way he passed three white men who evidently were meant to supply security. They were sloppy and too relaxed, off balance and too comfortable in their surroundings. They would be replaced right after he found a new, better location.

Kobayashi entered the elevator and when its doors opened at the upper floor his two men stepped out, one to either side. Kobayashi stepped out, removed his sunglasses and did a slow pan from left to right. There were eight men in the room. One at the bar and one behind it. The rest at tables on the right. Four were playing cards. All were idly chattering. As Kobayashi's gaze touched them each fell silent. Now they were waiting.

"I am Fujio Kobayashi," he said in a deep, breathy voice. "I am currently in charge of the human trafficking operation, which duties I execute through my deep connections with the Yakuza. I am here because this organization is in crisis. You are under attack, although one would not know this from your defensive posture. Left to my own judgment I would leave you all to be eliminated by whomever is attacking you, then start over with new and better personnel. However, I have sworn loyalty to my daimyo, Mr. Hetman, and he has directed me to come here and take over the gambling concern and the kidnapping operation which was the foundation on which he built this organization."

One of the card players, a big, beefy freckled redhead said, "So you're here to take over for Murphy, who got sent here to take over from Chen. Is that it?"

Kobayashi turned to him and, rather than answer the rhetorical question, said, "You seem to speak for the group. Tell me your name and tell me what happened to Murphy."

The redhead lurched to his feet. He was shirtless with a double shoulder holster rig strapped on over his wifebeater undershirt. "I'm Nick Ahearn. They call me Nicky. Murphy got popped in a drive-by. Somebody pulled into his driveway and put a bullet in his skull."

"Is this second hand, or were you present?"

"I was there," Nicky said. "I was in the car to pick Murphy up."

"And you let him be killed."

"Shit happens," the redhead replied. "He walked right up to the car like it was somebody he knew. Before we knew it, he was on the ground and the car was tear-assing down the road."

"You were worthless to him," Kobayashi said through his teeth. "And you are worthless to me. You and your pitiful countrymen."

Nicky took two steps forward, showing his teeth as well, his chest swelling. "Watch your mouth, you little slant. I don't know if you're trying to sound like Batman or one of them WWE clowns, but you don't scare me."

"Indeed," Kobayashi said, moving his legs slightly apart. "Are you a killer, Nicky?"

"I got six on my record back in the old country."

Kobayashi nodded, his eyes hooded. "Would you like to kill me?"

"What?"

"I've insulted you," Kobayashi said, stepping slowly to his right. "Would you like to kill me? If so, do it now. Kill me. Perhaps Mr. Hetman will send another worthless Irishman to take my place. Come. They will not interfere," he pointed to his two followers who still stood relaxed.

"You think I won't?" Nicky shouted.

"I think you will try," Kobayashi answered in the same soft, deep voice.

The action lasted less than four seconds. Nicky's hands snapped up under his arms to draw his twin revolvers. As he thrust the guns forward at arms' length Kobayashi darted left. Both guns roared but their target was already rolling toward the shooter. Two bullets flew over Kobayashi and then somehow he was standing in front of Nicky, between his fists too close to shoot.

Kobayashi's right hand snapped into Nicky's right shoulder, then his left rammed a knuckle into Nicky's left elbow. The redhead's arms dropped useless at his sides, pistols sliding from nerveless fingers. Then the heel of Kobayashi's palm slammed up into Nicky's nose. The big Irishman shuddered for an instant, then canted backward like a felled tree. The back of his head cracked against the edge of the table on his way down, but Nicky didn't know. He was already gone.

No one else had moved. Kobayashi stood flexing his fingers, not breathing any harder than he had been five minutes before. Now that he had established a basis for their respect, he wondered who would speak for the group. He hoped it would be the man Hetman had designated.

"Which of you is Brandon Anderson? I was told you would brief me on the operation, and that you would be my contact with my Daimyo going forward."

After almost ten seconds of silence one of the other card players said, "Anderson's not here. Nobody's seen him in the last three days. Not since the night before Murphy got hit. We was thinking whoever got Murphy and Chen got him too."

Kobayashi raised his left hand to smooth his eyebrows with a thumb and middle finger. It was, for him, a great show of emotion. "So, Mr. Hetman's spokesman is missing? You have received no instructions from him since before Murphy was killed? This is more serious than I realized." He pointed at the bartender, then slowly turned to take in the entire room. "You all need to be on high alert. Evidently the attackers are focused on this organization and no one is safe. With Murphy dead, who is in charge here?"

The men all looked around at each other. The card player who had spoken before said, "Nobody, really."

Kobayashi's astonishment was clear. "Are you saying this Irish mobster had no second in command?"

"Murphy did pick a second in command," the same man said, "but that guy disappeared the same night as Anderson and a couple of others. Murphy didn't have time to pick somebody else, so…"

"I understand." Kobayashi pointed at one of his guards, the man on the left. "This is Benjiro. He will remain here and begin to get your defenses organized. You would be wise to do whatever he tells you to do. He speaks for me, and I would be most displeased if he is not afforded the respect that befits his station." He stared down at Nicky for a second, just to make sure everyone present understood him. He walked over to the bar and stared at the bartender. Here at least was a man who returned his gaze.

"Where should I dine?" Kobayashi asked.

"I understand good beef is hard to get in Japan," the bartender replied. "You should go to Morton's while you're here. Or else Ruth's Chris Steakhouse. And hey, should I get sake in here? Or soju?"

"Order Awamori, the drink from Okinawa," Kobayashi replied. "What happened to your arm?"

The bartender continued to lock eyes with Kobayashi. "I was here the night Chen got killed. I grabbed my shotgun but the killer was faster than me."

Kobayashi nodded and smiled. "You made an effort, and you are honest about your failure. You may stay after these others are gone. I will now go to have a meal and see if the beef in one of these places you named is superior. Afterward, I have arranged for a suite in the Fairmont Hotel. You can reach me there if you have questions or further trouble. Once I am settled in there I will brief Mr. Hetman of what I have learned here and of my plans for reorganization. I will return in the morning and we will begin the hard work of turning this into a more effective organization."

Across town, Skye was already on her feet, gathering her new suitcase and a small shoulder bag filled with useful tools. She hustled out of her workshop and into her bedroom. Brandon was hanging his new clothes at one end of the closet. Skye elbowed him aside, flipping through hangers for the right uniform.

"Hey, you taking off again?" Brandon asked.

"Was just listening in to our Japanese friend. I think he fought with, or maybe even killed, one of the boys who was supposed to be guarding Murphy."

"What? For failing to protect him against you? This guy is really strict."

Strict? Do people actually use that word?

"Well as it turns out he's staying at the Fairmont, just a few blocks from here. I need to get there ahead of him. Then I'll eliminate him."

"So you have to go right now?" Brandon asked while she sat on the bed and pulled on a pair of white shoes, the kind nurses often wear. She shrugged.

"Assassin's law number twenty-one. When you see a chance, get to it fast."

Chapter 26

The Fairmont, ten stories of elegance, spanned a city block in Washington's West End, less than a mile from the area generally considered Georgetown. It was an impressive edifice, even to a man as worldly and well-travelled as Kobayashi. After a steak dinner worthy of all the praise he had heard about Morton's, he strode into the hotel followed closely by his loyal retainer, Riku, carrying his one suitcase. The hotel lobby was more like a courtyard, modern but comfortable, with several conversation areas set up. Armless blue chairs faced sofa-like benches with small round tables between them. Riku handled check-in and led his boss to an elevator.

They rode up to the eighth floor, always Kobayashi's choice. Eight was his number, a lucky number associated with increasing wealth. The walls were all a soft, relaxing blue. The hall was vacant except for a lone Black woman pushing an overloaded luggage cart toward them. Riku looked at Kobayashi but for him the woman did not set off any alarms. She was alone, there was no place for any support people to hide, and her hands were full pushing the cart.

The woman wore black tights, a short skirt and a denim jacket that was just a little too big for her. He saw frustration on her face as she passed him. Perhaps this was not her luggage. Maybe she was someone's assistant. It was far too much luggage for a lone traveler, and it was stacked on the cart in a haphazard manner. Harmless and not unattractive. At least her efforts revealed strong, trim legs and a firm backside. And those looked like good quality shoes, the kind hospital workers and servants would wear. Probably for running around for some insensitive boss.

As the woman passed Riku she seemed to lose control of the cart. "No no no no!" she said as it wavered, twisted and finally tipped over. "Shit!" she said, dropping to her knees. Kobayashi stopped to witness this sad spectacle. The woman seemed to be near tears. American women were so weak and the Black ones seemed bred for subservience. With a wave of his hand he indicated that Riku should help her.

Riku choked back a sigh and began to pick up suitcases, trying to position them on the cart in a way that would avoid another spill. The woman beamed at him, grabbing at the bags in a clumsy way. Had she never done this before? He smiled at Riku's increasingly irritated efforts to get the suitcases on the cart in an orderly manner.

"Thank you. Thank you so much," she said, even while she seemed to thwart Riku's efforts to do this simple task properly. But then Kobayashi saw something that did cause his internal alarms to go off.

The suitcase she was fumbling with now looked very much like his. In fact, it was identical in every way. While he watched, she moved to Riku's side and began to ease his own suitcase onto the cart. Was this woman actually trying to switch suitcases on him? He had to admit it was a well-played maneuver, and he respected expert work on any level. He figured she must have already hit several of the hotel's customers. The suitcases she left behind were probably filled with rags or trash. Americans are so unobservant he knew this would have worked on almost anyone else in the hotel. Too bad for this little hustler he was not anyone else.

Without a sound Kobayashi moved forward and gripped the girl's right arm from behind her. She looked over her shoulder, startled, her mouth dropping open.

"That was an impressive display, especially for an American girl," Kobayashi said in his graveyard voice, "but I'm afraid I need the contents of my suitcase."

"Let me go," the girl said in a whiney voice, trying to yank her arm out of his grasp.

"Don't be stupid," Kobayashi said. "I don't want to hurt you…"

"Don't worry," the girl said, shooting a stamp kick back into his knee. Surprised, Kobayashi barely shifted his weight in time to avoid a dislocation.

"I see you need a lesson in manners," he said, swinging her body toward the wall. But instead of her face meeting wallpaper she kicked up so her left foot hit the wall, then her right. She seemed to be walking upward. Then she twisted so that she flipped through the air and landed on Kobayashi's back. Now her right arm was around his neck, her left reaching under his left arm trying to establish a solid choke hold.

This girl's technique was unorthodox, but he could see the signs of good training. He might have enjoyed sparring with her, but this was a serious attack and he had to respond in kind. He gripped the forearm that was trying to press his throat and snapped his head back hard into her face. She grunted as he felt her nose flex under the blow. Her grip loosened. He crouched low and flipped her forward. She rolled and landed face down, but only for a second or two. She came up on one knee and turned to face her opponent. Riku, on her right, stepped in to deliver a blow. Before Kobayashi could call him off, the girl's right swung out with a knife hand blow to Riku's neck. She struck exactly the right nerve cluster, and Riku crumpled unconscious on the carpet.

Kobayashi moved into a guarded combat stance, smiling for the first time since he landed in the United States.

"You are she," Kobayashi said as the girl also assumed a combat stance. You are the one who killed the Triad representative, Chen."

"That's right. Call me Skye."

"You are clearly a professional so, not revenge or vigilantism, but a contract. Yes?"

"Uh-huh. And you're next on the list."

"You are very good," Kobayashi said. "But not that good."

"Think so? Let's see."

With a shout Skye exploded toward her taller opponent, then leaped left. Her left foot hit the wall, driving a kick toward his head. He blocked with a forearm but was still driven back. When she landed, she crouched low, spinning into a leg sweep that caught his left foot but he managed to shift his weight so as not to fall. Then she was up, driving knuckles into his solar plexus. He blocked her following punch to his face and her snap kick before managing a kick of his own that drew a grunt as it grazed her ribs. She fell back panting. Kobayashi advanced, but cautiously.

Behind him, a woman cried out "What the hell?"

A glance over his shoulder told him that a middle-aged couple was standing in the hall watching the conflict. The woman pulled out her cell phone and was pushing buttons. When she held it up he realized she was not calling the police but setting up to record video.

Skye snarled, "To be continued" through her teeth. She back-pedaled until she reached the stairs and darted through the door.

A low moan drew Kobayashi's attention to Riku, who had managed to rise to his hands and knees. Kobayashi moved close to his assistant, who muttered "I am shamed" in Japanese.

"No," Kobayashi replied in their native language. "You were felled by an assassin of considerable skill. Yakuza level. There is no shame. She surprised even me. I believe she meant to kill me, perhaps with a bomb in the suitcase she tried to switch with mine. When her plan failed, she was prepared to do the job with her hands. Again, she failed. But she was good."

Standing, Kobayashi moved to his room door. Over his shoulder he called, "Bring my suitcase, and the duplicate. Leave the rest of the mess for someone else to clean up."

Once in the room Kobayashi sat on the bed and thought through the recent events. This woman, this Skye, was a clear and present threat to the organization that Hetman had assembled. Considering Hetman's security awareness, this was unexpected. Kobayashi knew he was one of only five men who had actually met Hetman, so he wondered how an outside assassin had gotten so close to the top tier of their criminal enterprise. Had Chen or Murphy understood the level of the threat? Probably not until it was too late for them to alert anyone. He reasoned that she must have inside information, or a very broad and effective system of spies. Either way, Hetman had to be made aware of her. They must form a plan to search for her and destroying her.

He pulled his cell phone out of his inside jacket pocket. He only carried the one Hetman had given him. He looked down at the screen and pushed the single preset button, the one that would connect him with his lord, his daimyo.

Skye crouched in the stairwell just inside the door, her back pressed against the wall. She replayed the recent scene in her mind's eye. By now Kobayashi would have figured out that hand to hand combat with him was only a backup plan. He would have reasoned that the luggage switch was the main plan. He would have connected her to all the trouble Hetman's team had faced in the last few days. And he would want to reach out to his boss with a warning. If she understood him well enough…

The concussion was more than she expected, and just loud enough to hear in the stairwell. As soon as it shook the building, she was jogging down toward street level. Once Brandon had told her that he and Hetman's top lieutenants were all issued the same telephone she had no trouble convincing her new lover to surrender his. The real challenge was switching phones with Kobayashi when she was wrapped around his back.

She had added a shaped charge with good shielding, so that even if there were others in the room, they would be safe when Kobayashi died. Almost all the force of the explosion, set off by pushing the preset for Hetman, was directed toward the phone user, effectively turning his head into scattered bloody fragments. His hand may have also been destroyed but the blast would only carry a few inches in that direction.

She was walking calmly through the hotel lobby before an alarm was sounded. She saw a desk clerk chatting with someone and wondered if it was one of the other people on that floor, calling to complain about a loud noise. Then she was out in the crisp night air, breathing deeply but feeling the soreness from Kobayashi's kick. Could she have taken him in a fair fight? Maybe, maybe not. Luckily, that was never her intent.

Two blocks into her casual stroll home, Skye saw the lights and the traffic of Pennsylvania Avenue. Above her the sky was unusually clear. She could even make out a few stars. She was feeling good after dispatching the fourth name on her list. That kind of success was liberating, and she didn't really feel like being indoors. But she needed to make a stop.

When Skye opened her apartment door Brandon jumped to his feet. He stared at her as if he expected her to be dripping blood or maybe carrying a gore-soaked machete. She went to the refrigerator and poured herself a tall orange juice.

"Well, how did it go?" Brandon asked, as if she had been on a sales call, or a date with a new man.

"Mission accomplished!" she said with a smile. "One more name off my list." She raised her glass in a toast and drained half of its contents.

"Great," Brandon said. "And you look no worse for wear. So, now what?"

"Now?" Skye walked over to stand very close to him. "Now you get me to my last target." She pulled a cell phone out of her inside jacket pocket and poked it at him. With some reluctance he accepted it.

"I don't get it," Brandon said. "When you took my phone you said you needed it for this, er, assignment. Now you're giving it back?"

"Not your phone," she said, wandering away restlessly. "I needed yours because his had the same presets. That's Kobayashi's phone. I loaded yours with a sweet surprise and switched phones on him while he was distracted."

"Uh-huh." Brandon slowly put the phone down on the island as if he thought death clung to it. "So this is, what? A trophy?"

"Don't be stupid," Skye said. "That's how you finally get to help me. You said you can't call Hetman. And he don't seem too eager to call you. But he sent one of his top guys down here to straighten shit out. Now that guy's out of the picture." She said the last with a broad grin.

"So? How does that affect me?"

"Damn, you slow," Skye said. "It only makes sense he gone expect Kobayashi to report in when he gets settled. When he don't hear from his Japanese fixer he gone want to know what the hell happened. So he'll call." She made a dramatic gesture toward the phone. "He'll call, you'll answer."

"Me?"

"Of course," Skye said, rolling her eyes. "You answer. You tell Hetman somebody got to Kobayashi. You went to his hotel room and gathered his stuff. That's how you got his phone, right? And you got some other stuff, records, notes, all Kobayashi's shit but you don't want to hold it. You ask him where he is so you can bring it to him. But instead of you showing up, I go in and close his account. Simple, right?"

Brandon's eyes shifted left and right. "Yeah. Simple. Except I'm not a very good liar."

"You ain't got to be," Skye said, gripping his shoulders in both hands. "All you got to do is say what I said, and sound scared. You won't have any trouble sounding scared on the phone with this guy, will you?"

"Oh no," Brandon said. "Won't be any acting there. He scares the crap out of me."

"Yeah, I figured."

"So with my help, you might be able to get close to the big bad," Brandon said, 'And get on with your holy quest." He looked at her with what could have been a smirk.

"Quest? I look like a knight to you? I ain't on no quest. I'm just out here trying to do what I was put here to do. You know, what I was hired to do to do."

"I think you got it right the first time."

His grin was warm and childlike. More to the point, it was real. Skye pulled him down to give him a kiss. She originally planned a light peck but it got deep and hot. She did like this boy, and he turned out to be a lot of fun in the sack. To her surprise she found herself wanting to repeat the experience. But she actually had too much nervous energy after the day's success. She wanted to shake some of it before she ravaged her new toy.

"Listen, I'm feeling a little antsy," she said, breaking the kiss but looking deep into his eyes. "Going to go walk for a while. Be naked when I get back and you just might get lucky again."

The moon had risen but hung low in the sky, almost as if it was afraid to show its pock marked face. Skye was wandering in no particular direction but found herself drawn by the brightest lights. A couple of blocks of aimless wandering brought her to Pennsylvania Avenue again.

At the corner she stared off to her right. Milo Williams' hotel, the JW Marriott, was only a couple of miles down this wide thoroughfare. She wouldn't encounter too many on the sidewalk at this time of night. On an unexpected impulse she began to jog down the street toward the White House. She thought she'd loop around it, jog up to Milo's room and give him a face to face report. Then she would watch him move her next hundred twenty-five thousand into her account.

She fell into a comfortable rhythm as she moved down the wide sidewalk toward the center of power in her city of power. She was stretching her leg muscles and smiled at each of the other joggers she passed. Even after dark it seemed there were always people running here. On her left side her ribs started to complain as she passed the small park ironically named for seminal television reporter Edward R. Murrow, back in a time when the truth was revered in this city.

A block later she passed H Street and Pennsylvania narrowed as she pushed through the long green block between the White House and Lafayette Square. She waved at the statue of General Rochambeau as she entered, and again at the statue of General Lafayette, placed there at an even earlier time when courage was also revered in this city.

Five blocks later she was panting as the front of the JW Marriott came into view. She paused for a moment, hands on knees, to recapture her breath and idly wonder why they chose griffins as their symbol on the front of the edifice, before pushing through one of the revolving doors. The wide, ornate lobby seemed unusually empty this evening. Hotel workers' eyes followed her to the elevators. During the silent ride upward she thought about what a welcome surprise she would be to her current client.

But as the doors slid open her brow furrowed. Something didn't feel quite right. She couldn't put her finger on it, but that was the nature of instincts. Anyone who saw her walking down the hall would see a relaxed, happy girl checking the door numbers, looking for the right room. Inside, Skye was on full alert, every nerve aware, invisible feelers out probing for any sign of danger.

At Milo's door she knocked twice, then twice more. She heard movement inside, the sound of a man coming to answer the door. She was just about to relax when the next door, the one she had just passed, opened. What looked like a football linebacker in a gray suit stepped out of the room. He held his Glock automatic close to his side, pointed at her. His passive, bored expression told her he didn't care if he shot her or not. Then Milo's door opened to reveal a stranger matching the linebacker type in the hall.

"Come on inside," he said. "I think we need to have us a little chat."

Chapter 27

Skye put a shocked look on her face, eyes and mouth wide open, before slowly stepping into the room. She raised her hands to shoulder level. The gunman backed off as she advanced, maintaining a comfortable space between them. Once she was three paces in, she heard the other gunman come inside and close the door.

The room was neat as if housekeeping had just left. No surprise, really. Milo would not have resisted pros like these guys appeared to be. Not Murphy's boys or Yakuza but their training was obvious. But how much did they know?

"What the hell, fellows?" Skye said. "If this Williams guy was into something shady, I don't know nothing about it. My man sent me up here to give him a good time, but I get paid to party not to have guns pointed at me. So how about I just head on home? If you let me go I won't say nothing to nobody."

"Nice try," the man facing her said, "but you're not fooling anybody. And anyway, the boss thinks you got information he wants. You just chill and you won't get hurt."

The man behind her grabbed her left arm and was pulling it back. She might not get another chance at freedom. She reached over with her right, gripped his sleeve and pulled forward. She dropped into a deep crouch, pushing her hip up into him, flipping the man over her. He landed hard on his back. His partner seemed unsure what to do so Skye dived forward before he could decide. A forward roll brought her within striking distance. One quick kick sent the standing man's gun flying across the room. Then she snapped forward, her right fist slamming into him just above his crotch. He grimaced and dropped to his knees. Skye followed up with a heel of palm strike to his chin. He flopped backward, and she hopped to her feet before his head hit the floor.

Behind her she could hear the first attacker diving for her again. Her right palm pushed her left fist as her body spun to her left, driving her elbow into his solar plexus. As the air burst out of him Skye wrapped her left arm around his leg. She leaped to her feet, bringing the big man's foot to her waist level. He hung suspended in space for a second before his body crashed down to the floor.

"Please stop," a familiar voice said. "And you guys get up. You're embarrassing me."

Behind her and to her left, Orson Rissik sat at the table where Skye had taken meals in that room. She glared at him, surprise and annoyance wrestling for control of her face.

"What the hell? Are these boys cops?"

"Two of my detectives," Rissik said. "Who, I think, will be taking a little more hand to hand training and maybe review their procedures for taking a suspect into custody."

Skye took a couple of deep breaths, stepping away from the men slowly regaining their feet and their weapons. It made her scalp itch to be talking to a policeman again so soon. She had no way to know what Williams might have told them or why he wasn't there. She focused on Rissik, working to ignore the other two.

"What's your business with Milo Williams?" she asked.

"No, that's my question," Rissik said. "You're no call girl, so what brings you here?"

"He's a friend," she said. "You got him in custody?"

Rissik grinned. "A friend, eh? Well, my research told me your friend might be one of the victims of this new crime cartel. Some reports of a missing son. So I thought I'd interview him. Men with big money don't move too quietly so it wasn't hard to learn where he was staying. But when I got here, he was gone, but he hadn't checked out. So I asked my men to wait here with me, thinking he might return tonight. After a few hours I was starting to think maybe someone snatched him up. I wasn't expecting anybody else. But then you showed up."

"What, you didn't recognize me?"

Rissik grinned again. Skye liked it better when he stayed with his usual dour expression.

"Oh, I recognized you," he said, sipping from his water. "I just wanted to see how these men would handle you."

"Now you know," Skye said, glancing at the two red-faced detectives. "You also know I'm not some kidnapper, and I don't know where Milo is. So, am I free to go?"

Rissik raised a hand to his chin. "I think not. Yeah, I know. I doubt I could stop you from leaving without shooting you. But I think you and I need to talk."

Skye moved a little closer to Rissik, cutting her eyes toward his two men who were standing close to the door.

"We kind of had our talk," she said in a low tone. "That was kind of a one-off. I'm not planning on becoming a friend of the force." Again, she eyed the two detectives by the door. Their eyes returned her contempt.

Rissik stood and stepped closer. Skye stared up into his eyes but didn't back down. For a moment they seemed like the only two people in the room. "I didn't think so," he said, "but we seem to have ourselves a situation here. As far as I know you're the only person in the city who knows the missing Mr. Williams. I fear he may have met with foul play. And here you are in his hotel room resisting arrest. I think that makes you our only suspect. I'm afraid I'll have to take you in for questioning. I hope you'll come voluntarily."

Skye's eyes flared, but before she could say anything, Rissik added, "Please."

She didn't really know this man, but she had a limited amount of trust and even a little respect. It was clear there was more going on. And anyway, she could always escape if she had to.

"You want to take me in?" she asked.

"Yes, I'm afraid so," Rissik said. "Just until we straighten this mess out."

Skye needed to throw one more test. "You. Not these two apes."

"Me. My car. They'll just escort us downstairs. Procedure. Now, hands please." Rissik produced a pair of handcuffs from the back of his waistband under his jacket. Biting back her strongest instincts, Skye held her hands forward, allowing Rissik to lock the cuffs around her wrists. He put his hand on her shoulder and guided her to the door. The two detectives, who Skye had mentally dubbed the "Men in Gray," parted to let them pass, then followed them to the elevator. They rode down to the ground floor without a word. Rissik walked Skye through the lobby and outside to his car. He opened the door and with one hand on her head, eased Skye down into his back seat. Then he turned and waved to his subordinates.

"Hey, fellows. Listen, I got this. You're dismissed for the night. I'll get this one checked into detention, then I'm going to call it a day."

The two detectives mumbled their goodnights to their boss and moved off to another vehicle. Rissik started his own and pulled away from the curb. After two blocks of silence, he pulled over again. Without turning his head, he tossed the small handcuff key over his shoulder.

"I'm guessing you could get out of those things by yourself, but this will be easier. Why don't you come up and sit in the front so we can talk more easily?"

Skye quickly shucked the cuffs. As she stepped out of the car, she realized what an expression of trust this was. She could easily just disappear into the night and get lost in downtown Washington. Instead, she opened the door and dropped into the seat beside Rissik. She detected a small smile on his face as he pulled out again.

He seemed focused on getting through the lights to I-395. Skye crossed her arms, leaned against the door and waited. Once they were on the highway Rissik broke the silence.

"I know what you said with the detectives in the room but, *do* you know where Williams is?"

"No clue," Skye said. "Really, that's no shit. I expected him to be there when I got there."

"He's not a target for you, is he?"

Skye shook her head. "No he ain't. And I got no reason to lie to you about that."

Rissik nodded. "No you don't. I got nothing on you. Nothing to tie you to Williams' disappearance, or to a handful of messy deaths that have rocked this city in the last couple of days. But I've been checking my sources and my research tells me that someone is biting into this new criminal cartel pretty badly."

"Is that a bad thing?" Skye asked. "A murder is a murder and like that?"

A gentle rain started to patter down, kicking in the Honda's intermittent wipers. Rissik kept his eyes forward, watching the traffic. Skye watched his face closely and decided this man must be a great poker player. It seemed he had decided not to respond to her question. Instead he asked one of his own.

"As an observant citizen of this city, would you expect this wave of bloodshed to continue?"

"Yep," she said, "but not for very long."

"Anything I can do to stop it?"

"Nope. And you and a lot of your men would get hurt if you tried."

Rissik heaved a heavy sigh and shook his head at something Skye couldn't guess. He gripped the wheel with both hands and squared his shoulders. She imagined this was his posture when he had made a decision.

"Okay, I'd like to share a theory with you. You tell me if I go wrong, okay?" Without waiting for a response, he continued. "I've got unconfirmed reports that Milo Williams had a son who was kidnapped and subsequently killed in The District. Travel records indicate that Williams only arrived here last week, just days before the criminal organization recently formed by Hetman came under attack. My theory is that Williams wanted to do something about his son's death. Bringing his considerable financial resources to bear he was able to learn quite a bit about the kidnappers. And he saw no legal recourse that was likely to succeed. You with me so far?"

"How did you…?"

"I'm a detective," Rissik said. "Does my theory make sense so far?"

Skye gripped the door handle. "Yeah, I guess it does. So?"

"So here's what I figure. Williams does some research into underworld figures and hires someone who can get him revenge for his son's death. He probably pays this person a great deal of money and provides them with intel about the killers who took his son from him. And I figure this person has been doing a damned good job at earning their pay. How am I doing so far?"

In her mind, Skye was screaming *Holy shit!* Verbally, she managed to say, "That all makes sense, I guess."

A self-satisfied smile flashed across Rissik's face, almost too fast to see. "Okay, so that brings us to tonight. I go looking to question Williams, to confirm my theory. But he's gone from his hotel. Not checked out but gone. Doesn't seem to have any family or friends in the area. And if I'm right and he's here on a mission, he's not likely to leave town until that mission is completed. And I now have reason to believe the bloodshed will continue for a while."

"Yeah, doesn't make sense he'd just split without telling… somebody."

Rissik shook his head again, stifling a chuckle. "Certainly the person he paid a lot of money to wouldn't spirit him away, and even if they did, they'd have no reason to go back to his hotel. I know the police don't have him. He's not in any local morgue or hospital. So, what does that leave?"

Skye shrugged her shoulders. "Hey, you're the detective."

"The only possibility I see left is that the people he's after somehow figured out he's after them." Rissik turned his eyes toward Skye for a second. "They must have found him and snatched him up."

"You think Hetman's boys took him out?"

"Maybe, but I don't think so," Rissik said, pressing down on the accelerator to pass a tractor trailer in the middle lane. The rain picked up a bit, but his driving didn't change. "I don't think they'd want to just kill him. They'd want to find out who he hired to do all this damage, so they can find that person and kill them."

Then Rissik fell silent. Skye sat back as his words sank in. Everything he said made sense. If he was right, she would be a target soon, if she wasn't already. She was accustomed to being the hunter, a ghost who strikes out of nowhere. She knew how easy it was to come up on someone unexpectedly and end their life.

She stared out the window as they travelled down a too-familiar road, bored by the passing of the generic night scene. When she looked at her driver he seemed relaxed but focused. She could easily kill him and escape, but he trusted that she wouldn't. For some reason, just the awareness of that trust stopped her from considering it.

Rissik let five minutes pass before breaking the silence. "I'm always curious about new people I meet who might be players on my field. So I did some digging. When I talk to my contacts and informants about a professional who might be able to put the touch on the untouchables, the name Skye kept coming up. No last name, unless of course that is a last name. One person told me it was a black girl, but nobody could confirm that. Again, no hard evidence attaching to any particular death, all rumor and innuendo. And fear. People are afraid of this girl."

After a few more seconds of silence Skye felt pressured to respond. "Interesting," she said.

"One wonders if the absence of Milo Williams might mean this bloodbath is over."

"Bloodbath?" Skye said. "I don't know if I'd call it…" She saw Rissik smile again and got that feeling she often got in Jayla's office. She returned his smile with respect and continued in a calmer voice. "If your theory were correct, one might assume that this person Williams hired would feel obligated to complete whatever job they was hired to do."

Rissik gave a grim nod. "Would it be reasonable to assume that this current wave of violence would end if this Hetman was gone."

They were rolling onto the grounds of the Fairfax County government complex. Skye stared hard at Rissik.

Was this a threat? A challenge? Aloud she just said, "I think that would be a reasonable assumption."

Rissik held further talk until he had parked in front of a building whose front lights stayed on all night. He turned so that the office lights gave his face a pale glow.

"How close to Hetman are you?"

Well, here it was. She either trusted him or she didn't. He already knew a great deal and had not used any of it against her. Yet. He was, after all, a cop. But at that moment, in that oddly cooling light, he seemed to be more.

"You want him gone, don't you?"

"I'm just asking if he's going to be."

"Look, I got a line on him," she said. "A solid contact. I might get close enough in a couple days. Then, this job can end."

"What about Williams?"

"His absence got nothing to do with the contract," Skye said. "My name is on the line here. The sixth law of assassins: tend your reputation like a rare, fragile flower."

Rissik nodded, and took a deep breath, the way a man does when he's about to take a running jump off a cliff without getting a chance to test the depth of the water below.

"You can't just go by Skye," he said. "You must have to do actual business sometime. Bank accounts, the lease on a place to live, phone contracts. I figure you got an alias or two or maybe more."

"Yeah, I'll cop to that much."

"With ID?"

"Of course," she said.

"Any of them in the system?"

"Yeah. What's your point?"

Rissik turned his face down but his eyes looked up at her. This, she figured, was his conspiratorial look. "What if

I took you inside and did the paperwork to hold you as a material witness? Officially detained you here?"

"You want to lock me up?"

"Well, only on paper," Rissik said. "The word could get out pretty fast. It might stop people from looking for you for a couple days. Or get them looking for you in the wrong place."

Skye's eyes narrowed. "You're offering me an alibi?"

"I'm thinking if somebody thinks they're a target, they might let their guard down a little."

"How long you think you can hold a ghost?"

"I can buy you three days," Rissik said. "Tomorrow's Friday. Nobody wants to do anything official; paperwork is lax. But, and here's the hard part, you would have to be back here Monday morning for me to interrogate you, after which you'd be released."

"And if I'm not?"

Rissik smirked. "Then I am well and truly screwed."

Was that true? Was this cop putting his career in her hands? She turned the idea over in her mind, looking at it from every angle. She could see the risk to Rissik, but the whole plan seemed to work to her benefit. When she came out of her head she noticed Rissik sitting there, as still and silent as the sphinx, evidently waiting for her agreement. Unable to see a reason to do otherwise she picked up the handcuffs and handed them back to him.

"You might want to put these back in place, for effect. Now, do you want to arrest Skye King or Cloudy St. James?"

"Is one of them your real name?"

She smiled. "Both of them is."

The process at the Fairfax County building took the better part of an hour. The staff working after hours was bored and uninterested. They let Rissik do almost everything himself, even fingerprinting her. All records would match Cloudy St. James, a minor hustler with three arrests but no convictions on her record. Her entire history was fabricated of course, but no one would dig too deeply, and nothing would connect her to Skye's reality. Rissik informed whoever was in the office that he was taking her to the Detention Center and would sign her in to the West Building which holds minimum security inmates under direct supervision.

In fact, she had walked away from the building and strolled in the light, refreshing rain for a while. Papa Maddox had called this infantry weather, even though he was Navy to the bone. Somehow it brought back her month in Sheffield. It was always gray and rainy there. Papa had left her at the hotel while he went off on a job, as always he was an advisor or a consultant in some foreign land. But before he left he introduced her to her latest tutor.

"Skye, this is my good friend Willie. He'll watch over you while I'm gone. You are in his care and you are to obey him as you would me."

"Instruction?" she asked. It was always exciting to see what her next learning adventure would be.

"He'll be teaching you about knives."

When Papa was gone, the sandy haired man with the angular face looked her up and down and nodded.

"Maddox tells me you've got fast hands and you're a quick study," Willie said in a strong Cockney accent. "Says you're nineteen but talks to you like a kid. Well, I won't be treating you like some wee bairn. I've got a good practice area set up for us and we'll go at it every day until you're right knackered. See, I won't be disappointing the Colonel. By the time we're done you'll be the best with a blade." Then he winked. "Well, second best, next to me."

"Eager to get started, Uncle Willie," she said. It was perhaps the one thing she kept from her childhood. She had been taught to call her mother's male friends "Uncle."

Lessons had started slowly, with knife fighting technique in the morning and knife throwing at night. But over that month he took her from wooden knives to practicing with live blades. He showed her how to hold the weapon, how to strike and where to strike. She found throwing to be more fun. She could soon hit the target at any distance out to sixteen feet with a spin, and she mastered the close up no spin throw as well. Impressed by her progress after the first week, Willie showed her how to throw underhand, sideways, behind her back and even when pushed off balance.

The rain picked up, but the chill felt good. Rain has its own smell, she knew, and most people never noticed it. Wet and cold were just things to push through, and success was its own reward.

In England her Uncle Willie offered more tangible rewards. He showed her London. He took her to shows. They spent a day exploring the National Maritime Museum in Greenwich with its six hundred strong collection of swords, and another at the Sheffield Industrial Museums where more than a thousand blades were collected.

She soaked it all up, but the practical applications were the most important lessons. When Willie thought she had mastered large and small knives, he showed her the uses of Japanese throwing stars, machetes and the specialized Gurkha Kukri blades. She remembered how these various techniques echoes each other, and yet were distinct. By the time Papa Maddox returned her hands and arms were worn to exhaustion, but he was not disappointed.

Raindrops dancing on the asphalt gave it a mirror sheen, turning the black surface white, almost imitating a desert mirage. That shifted her memory to her training in Israel, because for all his excellent instruction, Uncle Willie had never asked her the pivotal questions. It was Uncle Irv, when they first stood face to face on the sand outside Tel Aviv, who had looked her in the eye and challenged her with it.

"You're a hard woman already," he had said, "but are you really prepared to kill a man?"

The question had taken her by surprise, but it pulled everything she had learned together in her mind and somehow attached it to the loss of her brother. That, she decided, was when that switch was thrown. She smiled at him with new understanding.

"Isn't that the point of all I've done the past couple of years? Of course I am."

He held his hands wide. "Then show me."

She did. She showed him her intent with some ferocity. And then he showed her how to do it right.

A car had passed, a bit too quickly, and splashed water up on her. With a start, Skye realized she had been aimlessly walking for a couple of miles. She stopped beneath a streetlamp to make a call, stopping herself before the first dialing was completed. Ultimately, she called an Uber to take her home but not her usual. She didn't want to drag Mo out of bed so she sat behind a stranger riding back to the District. She got out five blocks from home and splashed back to her flat. The stairs felt higher than usual and she realized that fatigue was starting to set in.

Chapter 28

When her eyes opened, Skye felt restricted. She was staring at her own bedroom wall and the clock radio on her side table told her it was 7:35am. She was on her right side, curled up on her foam mattress, under her own heavy comforter. As far as waking up was concerned all was normal except for two details: She was still dressed, and there was an arm around her. Brandon lay behind her, spoon style. His tan left arm held her, his hand gripping her left forearm which was pressed against her breasts. She felt constrained by her jeans and tee shirt. The arm was oddly comforting. She lay still for a moment, feeling warm and safe. She closed her eyes again and pushed her mental replay button.

When she opened the door last night, Brandon had jerked awake, almost falling off the love seat where again he had been snoozing through the news. He was a quick study though. He had already figured out not to ask a bunch of questions when she came in the door. "Are you okay?" was as far as he went.

She had pulled off her denim jacket and tossed it over the kitchen island. She had pulled off her running shoes and socks and left them in the middle of the floor. Her hair was soaked but that was okay. She pulled it off in the bathroom and stowed it with the rest of her wig collection. She planned to return to the living room to update her house guest but never made it past the bed. It just looked so comfortable and if she just lay down for a few minutes…

She must have slept pretty soundly. Somehow Brandon had gotten the comforter out from under her, covered her with it, and tucked in behind her to sleep. Even through her own tee shirt she could feel his undershirt. Freeing her left hand she reach behind to confirm that, yep, the boy still had his jeans on as well. That raised a smile.

Gently pushing Brandon's arm away, Skye eased herself up into a seated position. She ran quickly over all the events of the previous twenty-four hours and decided that on balance, life was pretty damned good. As she stretched her arms wide Brandon stirred, then sat up beside her. He had a pirate's smile she decided, the arrogant look she had seen on men's faces before on the next morning, but only after they had gotten laid. There was a lot about this man that kept surprising her.

"Morning, sleepy head," he said, kissing her lightly. "Hungry?"

Skye grinned. Who asks you that first thing in the morning? Any other fool would be trying to make her lay back down.

"You crack me up," she said.

"Is that yes or no?"

"Look, in the last twenty-four hours I have blown a man's face off, beat up two cops, walked a few blocks in the rain and slept in my clothes. Right now what I need is a shower."

Skye scrubbed herself vigorously under a torrent of water turned as hot as she could stand it. She peeled away the bandage on her left thigh, noting with her fingers the line that she knew would become a scar. She shrugged. She couldn't see it, so it didn't matter. Clean and invigorated, she brushed her hair out, moisturized her face and rubbed store brand baby oil all over her body. Her mother had told her it was the only way to avoid dry skin. Of course, Mama had also told her that men liked fucking a woman better when she was drunk, so Skye was selective about the parental wisdom she accepted.

An enticing aroma prompted her to pull on her white terrycloth robe and matching fuzzy slippers. She went out to sit at the island, watching Brandon's shoulders and back muscles move as he did something in a pan on the stove. There he stood in her kitchen in jeans and a wife beater and it occurred to her that he should have a robe and slippers to wear in the morning. But would he even be there long enough to need a bathrobe? Did she want him to be? Was it even up to her?

Then he slid the pan's contents onto a plate and turned to hand it to her. She mumbled thanks as he gathered his own plate and two cups of coffee. She picked up her fork and looked down at the surprise. Would his omelet be as good as the ones she made herself?

"Well, dig in while it's hot," Brandon said, settling in beside her. "It's about the only thing I can handle for breakfast."

His smile was so warm she had to return it. Then they raised their forks in unison and shoved the first bite of eggs into their mouths. Skye had a standard compliment prepared before her real reaction pushed it away.

"Hey. That's, that's really good," she said. She chewed a couple more times. "Mushrooms? I never think to add mushrooms. And something else."

"You had some pretty good cheddar here but I prefer the extra sharp," Brandon said. "Just seems to go with eggs."

"It's delicious," Skye said. "You are now the official breakfast maker in this apartment."

Brandon seemed to relax further, and they continued to eat in relative silence, maintaining eye contact most of the time. When he got up to clear the dishes Brandon asked, "So what's the plan for today? The phone hasn't rung. I haven't heard from Mr. Hetman. I'm guessing you have other business to take care of beyond this one, er… contract?"

"Yeah, you can call it that," Skye said, wandering over to the narrow desk that held her laptop. "And actually, no. I tend to work one job at a time. So for a while my time is my own. If we don't hear from your boss in a couple days I'll need to pull a plan B out of my ass."

Brandon chuckled.

"Really?" Skye asked. "What's funny?"

He covered his mouth for a moment. "Sorry. Sometimes your somewhat colorful speech pattern catches me off guard."

"Glad I entertain you," she said in a dry tone. "As for the day, I was thinking we might go out and fill in your wardrobe a bit. I only saw you twice before I dragged your ass in here but from what I seen your wardrobe stays intact. I'm betting your closet in your old place is jammed full. Right?"

"Guilty as charged."

"Well we need to get you a few more outfits." While she spoke, she punched keys on her computer. She confirmed the hundred twenty-five thousand dollars for punching Kobayashi's ticket had been deposited in her account. She took that as evidence that Williams was alive someplace and prepared to drop the final hundred seventy-five on her when she took Hetman on his final dance. Then she picked up her current cell phone and asked Morris to meet them two blocks north.

It was a short and quiet drive across town. The city still glistened from last night's soaking, and clouds hovered low as if they had more to share but were debating whether or not to release it or move on to another target. When Mo pulled over to drop them off at the CityCenter, Skye told Brandon to go ahead. They had both ridden in the back seat, but after they got out Skye hopped into the front and asked Mo to circle the block once.

"What's up Skye?" Mo asked, hanging a right onto New York Ave.

"Just wanted a quick read," Skye said. "What do you think of him?"

"What?" Mo asked, crawling to avoid hitting pedestrians who crossed the street as if there was not a car in sight. "What difference does it make what I think? Look, girl, I ain't your daddy. I just drive."

Skye slapped his thigh with the back of her hand. "You may as well be my daddy. And you the only one's seen him."

"I met him," Mo said, navigating the sharp right down Seventh Ave. "But I don't know shit about him. He's polite. He sounds educated. Wears real good shoes, but a cheap ass watch. But can you trust him? Is he loyal? Is he a stand-up nigger? I don't know nothing that matters."

Mo slipped under a yellow light, avoided creasing a slow woman's hip, and got back to where he had dropped Brandon. Skye popped her door but didn't open it yet.

"Is that the shit that matters? Okay, thanks, Mo." Bowing to an unfamiliar impulse, Skye leaned forward and kissed Mo's cheek. Then she was slamming the car door and running for the shops.

CityCenter DC is a commercial development just off New York Ave west of the White House. A blatant attempt to revitalize a crumbling downtown, the sprawling complex covered five city blocks trying to be all things to all people, at least all the people with money. Two office buildings, two buildings of condos and two more of apartment complexes were all tied together by a small park and maybe thirty upscale stores and restaurants. Anchored at one corner by the glass-walled Conrad Washington Hotel, the space called CityCenter DC was practically a neighborhood to itself. Skye met Brandon under a square arch between buildings. Its sides and ceiling bore a mural of the universe. Brandon had been leaning against a planet.

"Well that must have been some conversation," Brandon said as Skye approached. "Is Mo a business associate? Part of your, er, profession?"

Skye walked past him, waving to him to follow. "He helps out but he's not really part of what I do. Come on. Let's find a men's store and get you some stuff that fits your style."

So much glass and steel. So many unfamiliar names. Wandering past display windows, Skye was trying not to stare around too much. She didn't want to give away that it was her first time there. Brandon didn't seem to care. He walked patiently beside her, eyeing store displays. After wandering for fifteen minutes or so Skye spotted sport coats in one window and pulled Brandon into a store called Loro Piana. A salesman immediately arced toward them, a shark sensing blood in the water.

"Good morning," he said in a vaguely British accent. He had both the build and the cheekbones of a fashion model, olive skin and a hundred-dollar haircut. Skye nodded at him and wandered to a display of shirts. She pulled at the collar of a polo shirt with one hand and tugged at Brandon's sleeve with the other.

"What do you think?"

His face said what she held in her mind: who the hell was Moncler and what made a polo shirt with his name on it worth two hundred and fifty dollars? But she held a good poker face. She pulled the black card out of her pocket and handed it to Brandon, making sure the salesman saw it.

"Baby, I want to check out some stuff over in the Gucci shop," she said. "Why don't you pick out three or four casual outfits here? I'll be back in a few to see what you liked."

Brandon looked unsure but Skye pulled him down by his shirt to give him a soft kiss. A smile, a wink, and she was out the door.

Skye came out on H Street and walked to the corner. The clouds had backed off and now it was a sweet sunshiny day. She had no reason to hurry. She turned right and moved up the narrower 10th Street. Her destination was two blocks away, past rectangular plots holding trees and greenery embedded in the wide sidewalk, and across Palmer Alley which seemed oddly named to her since it was twice as wide as 10th Street. She guessed it was an alley because of the barriers preventing anything but foot or bicycle traffic.

It was a nice walk that allowed her to think. What was she doing? Why did it make her feel good to buy this man expensive clothes? And what had prompted her current mission? She had gone to Gucci mostly because it was one store name she recognized, and she knew what she was looking for. One thing Mo said had bothered her. Brandon should not be wearing what looked like a cheap watch.

Again she ignored the eager and helpful staff, scanning displays for something that would reach out to her. She had no idea what she was looking for until her eyes fell on a watch she'd never seen before. The face held no numbers, just a big gold bee. The background under the insect picture was green with a red stripe down the middle. The nylon band followed those colors, making the watch and band seem like one.

A golden bee. B, for Brandon? Yeah, it seemed perfect. Now she called a salesman over, pointed at her choice and handed over another credit card. Was $900 a lot for a man's watch? This wasn't the place to ask. Hers had set her back about a hundred bucks and kept time fine. But hey, this was a gift. A gift for the man who saved her life. Besides, right now she was liquid. She had already made three hundred twenty-five large on this assignment, and Brandon was shopping with Hetman's money right then. And with Brandon's help she would finish the job soon, even if Milo didn't resurface to deliver the final hundred and seventy-five thousand dollars.

There were only four or five other people in the store. While she waited for her package, she scanned them idly. One young fellow glanced away when she looked at him. Like her, he was dressed casually and didn't really look like he belonged there. Maybe he was on an errand to buy a gift for someone else. He was pale. His nose had been broken. Red hair poked out under the back of his cap. She didn't recognize him, but she knew his type.

Accepting her small package, Skye stepped back out into the bright sunshine, again strolling down the sidewalk, retracing her earlier steps. The entire path back was a wall of glass, usually with mannequins behind it. It was natural for her to look at each one, but she wasn't window shopping. She noted that the redhead had left Gucci's just a few seconds behind her. Hands in his pockets, he was following her. Sure, it could be a coincidence. Lots of people were out walking that day. Or he might just be enjoying the view of her behind. Or he might be the clumsiest tail ever.

When she reached the corner and crossed 10th Street, the man behind her crossed mid-block. That eliminated Skye's last drop of doubt. He was definitely following her. Now it was harder to keep her pace slow. He was average height and build but looked like he might be a strong runner. She still thought she could lose him, but this time she had someone else to think of.

When Skye walked back into Loro Piana the same sales associate rushed toward her. She saw Brandon in the waiting area holding a shopping bag and what looked like a disposable suit bag. His eyes perked up when he spotted her, but he didn't move other than to shrug his shoulders and smile. She didn't know what was going on and didn't have time to play games so she cut the salesman off before he could speak.

"Is there a problem here, smiley? Didn't that card…?"

"Oh there is no issue with your credit card, ma'am," he rushed to say. "No no, all is fine. It's just that … I worked with Mr. Anderson to choose a charming collection that perfectly suits his frame, his coloring and his personal style. You will be quite pleased when you see him in any of these pieces."

"But?"

"Well, Mr. Anderson was reluctant to complete the transaction without your express permission. I'll be happy to show you each…"

Skye waved him off. "Ring the shit up," she said, "and toss this little bag in with that stuff." Then she walked over to Brandon, cursing the plate glass world they stood in now. There was no hope of concealment. They were as much on display as the merchandise and she could feel her follower's eyes on her from outside the store. When she reached Brandon, she took his arm and tugged his face down toward hers. The kiss was quick, then she hugged him, so her mouth was beside his ear.

"I'm going to need you to take all this shit back to the crib," she whispered. "I got some unexpected business to deal with." She broke the embrace and stood back a pace.

"We good?" Brandon asked.

Skye shook her head, already backing away. "Just stay frosty. I'll catch up to you later on after I take care of this thing."

With that she stepped back outside, smiling and acting as if everything was normal. She spotted her tail right away. He was across the street, talking on his cell phone, pretending he wasn't watching the door for her reappearance. Probably giving her location to other trackers. Or maybe getting instructions from his boss. Kill her right away, or bring her in for torture? She needed to shake this fool but running did not promise success.

Skye wandered back down H Street, looking for an idea. Hop in a cab? He'd just do the same. She could make a break for the metro station but again, he could follow her onto any train. She would need to stop him from following.

The shop on the corner, taking up two store fronts, was called CH for the designer, Carolina Herrera. Clothes and some nice purses in the window assured her this was a women's only place. Again, she saw few people inside. Then an idea made her smile.

Skye slowed her pace and stepped inside the store. Over her shoulder she saw her shadow race to cross the street. He was holding the right side of his jacket close to his body. Concealing a weapon? Did this fumbling amateur nurse fantasies of taking her out himself?

It seemed more crowded and cluttered in CH than the men's shop she just left. This place was overflowing with a huge variety of clothing and accessories. Skye wandered through the racks as if she had all the time in the world. She hoped the man following her still believed he had not been spotted. She made a point of not reacting when she saw him watching through the shop's front window. She even engaged with the sales girl, a narrow blonde who may or may not have made it out of her teens.

She spent almost ten minutes shopping, selecting a couple of pairs of slacks, three tops, some tights and a jacket she might wear. Her watcher moved up and down the sidewalk but never lost sight of her. When a matronly white woman and her pimple-faced daughter entered Skye sent the sales girl off to help them. Then she took her bundle of clothes into a dressing room.

Skye laid her clothes on the padded bench and stood against one side of the little room. Lighting was dim, blunting the impact of the bright yellow walls. The air was filtered and lightly perfumed, she guessed to make customers less claustrophobic. The gain of privacy and a small enclosed space was counter-balanced by losing sight of the man watching her. She had to picture him in her mind's eye. Her best guess was that Kobayashi's team, previously Murphy's team, had issued an all points bulletin on her. Maybe Rissik was right and they knew who she was. Her bogus arrest would alibi her if law enforcement and courts ever got involved. But she thought this redhead had been in the room when Murphy threatened her and had just happened to be in the right place at the right time to spot her that day.

He probably just wanted to prove himself to his new boss. How long would he pace the sidewalk before impatience got the better of him? How long until he realized how helpless the killer woman might be at that moment. He could literally catch her with her pants down. He'd be a hero if he took her out. Hetman might even have put a price on her head, so the redhead could be in line for a reward. The temptation should eventually overwhelm him.

He would have to come into the shop, as if he was looking for his girl. If he described her the sales girl would tell him which changing room Skye was in. She had to hope he wouldn't just stand in the store and start blasting away at the little room. Maybe he'd give the sales girl a story about surprising his gal. Or not, depending on how clever the boy was. But if so, a nod and a wink would be all he needed. Skye didn't imagine antics in the changing room to be too unusual. And wouldn't the smart move be to get up close, kill her, then run out of the store covering his face? Actually, the smart move would be to call for help and wait for her to leave the store, but she didn't think he was that smart.

Skye stood, calm and relaxed. Seven minutes passed. Eight. She was just beginning to doubt her read of the situation when the wooden door opened and the redhead stepped in holding a pistol inside his jacket. Standing on his right, Skye snatched at his gun with her left hand while she slammed the middle knuckle of her right into his solar plexus. She dropped the gun on top of the clothes and slammed the stunned man against the opposite wall. She crossed her arms, grabbed his jacket lapels and pulled her hands apart while she thrust her face very close to his.

"You're out of your league, dumbass," she whispered. Confusion showed on the redhead's face. He could breathe fine, but his arms were too weak to push her off and his legs were starting to tremble. Skye's grip on his jacket was pulling both sides of the collar hard against his neck, restricting veins and arteries that supplied blood to his brain. Cutting off that blood flow would have him unconscious in a couple of minutes.

Skye maintained the pressure and followed his body as it slid to the floor. She left him seated against the wall, shoved his gun into the back of her waistband and showed no hurry as she left the changing room with all the stuff she had gone in with. The salesgirl gave Skye a conspiratorial smile as she moved toward the door. Skye gave her a wink.

"It might take him a couple minutes to recover from that," Skye said, smiling and waving on her way out. "Brian will take care of the bill. I earned this stuff."

Once on the sidewalk her smile dropped. She kept on the move at a moderate place, not knowing for sure if she was followed or not. Hetman might have more professional trackers in his team, and there was no way to know who the stupid redhead had called.

Chapter 29

A bank of jealous clouds had rolled in, cutting off the brilliant sunshine that had dominated the morning. Skye continued her shopping tour, stepping into and out of every third or fourth door. By now Brandon should be at her place, but she didn't dare go home. If she did have eyes on her, leading them to her home base would be a disaster. But outside she was exposed and vulnerable, and she had no place to go.

Her chances of losing a tail were better in office buildings. At least she thought so. She headed west on H Street, dodging hurried pedestrians moving through tunnel-vision paths toward their destinations. Women in business clothes and inappropriate heels marched along with men in business suits and sneakers, all moving as if they could not see anyone else but somehow not colliding. If the building had an elevator she took it up a few floors, then walked down the stairs.

Still, she had no idea where she could land long enough to form a plan without being spotted by some watcher, if there were any. Her focus was simply to keep moving forward, knowing that a moving target was harder to hit. Her location seemed random until she looked up at a street sign and found herself on Connecticut Avenue. She was close to the only place she ever considered a safe haven.

To an observer she would still appear to enter each building randomly. She was confident at least that no one followed her into the building but just in case she left the elevator four stories above her actual destination and took the stairs down. When she pushed through the familiar office door she faced an unfamiliar obstacle. Because she almost always went there after normal business hours she had only met the receptionist once. She was a big woman, very dark with a broad nose and small, sharp teeth. Dreadlocks piled on her head made her look taller than she was, but in any case, she looked like she could defend the inner door if called upon to do so. Skye slapped both palms on her desk.

"I need to see Ms. Johnson."

This woman looked like someone's mama, or maybe she was Tyler Perry in disguise. Her mouth twisted into an unmistakable look of "I am not impressed." She waited five seconds before responding, as if to make sure Skye understood her level of unimportance.

"Your name?"

Damn! What name had she given Jayla when they set up her appointments? Ahh, yes. "Masterson. Skye Masterson."

"Right," the receptionist said. "Well, Ms. Johnson is with a patient right now. Please have a seat and I'll see when she can speak with you."

"This is kind of an emergency," Skye said.

"Of course," the receptionist said with the slightest edge in her voice. "Ms. Johnson's current appointment will end in twelve minutes. I'll ask her if she will see you afterward. Please have a seat."

"This is important," Skye said, leaning in closer. The receptionist did not blink.

"Please have a seat."

After one long, deep breath Skye wandered over to the waiting area and plopped down into a chair. She stared out the window at the bland cityscape. She glanced at the collection of news magazines she thought must be required by law in every doctor's office. Then she noticed a very high-tech coffee machine at a station at the other end of the room. That might help. At least holding a hot paper cup would give her hands something to do instead of juggling a knife.

Returning to her seat she considered that she would have to be patient. This issue was not the receptionist's fault. She probably saw a lot of people who thought they were in life-and-death crises. It was really kind of ironic. Under normal circumstances it would be to Skye's advantage for everyone to see her as just another…

Patient? Was that what she was? From the beginning she had thought of herself as Jayla's customer. A client, like the people who came to Skye to have a job done. Skye reminded herself that she was not just talking to a counselor. As a psychiatrist, Jayla was a doctor of sorts. Skye went to these sessions to have a sounding board who could help her make sense of her life. But was she in fact getting treatment? In the moment she decided it didn't matter. She was temporarily safe from the threat posed by Hetman's mob and that was what mattered.

Time passed with agonizing slowness until the inner door opened and a well-dressed mature looking man came out. The buzz of an intercom was followed by hushed conversation. When it ended the receptionist turned toward Skye, her face still devoid of emotion.

"Ms. Johnson will see you now."

Jayla didn't know what to expect when Skye walked into her office, closed the door and began pacing the length of the room. She had never seen Skye in such a state of agitation. She was glad this time she was behind her desk.

"So what's going on, Skye?" Jayla asked, sipping from a bottle of water. "You're not one for unannounced appointments."

"Being followed, Doc," Skye said, not yet looking at Jayla. "Needed a safe place to land. Don't worry, they might know what building I'm in but not what office and there's no way to connect me to you, so you're safe."

"I never thought otherwise," Jayla said. "And I'm glad I'm able to help." Skye stopped at the window, staring down at the street below. After allowing a moment of quiet, Jayla said, "Is this situation the result of your current assignment? Did you ever catch up to the fourth man on your list?"

"Oh yeah," Skye said with a chilling laugh. "He is definitely out of the game. I blew that fool away."

"Sounds like a successful day," Jayla said. "But clearly you are not in the frame of mind I usually see you in after a success like that."

Skye turned and resumed her pacing. "Yeah, well I've never had a target's people come after me. Plus, I was out with Brandon so he was at risk too."

Jayla perked up at that comment more than the news of Skye murdering another man. She picked up her notebook while her eyes tracked Skye's movements back and forth in front of her.

"I have a free hour right now. Want to go ahead and have a session?"

"Not that much to talk about," Skye said. "A phone bomb. One less Yakuza boss."

Chilled as usual by how sanguine Skye was about killing, Jayla smiled and continued in a soft voice. "Honestly, I'm more interested in your thoughts about being the hunted instead of the hunter. I imagine you're feeling what your victims usually feel."

Skye stopped, turning to Jayla. "Victims?"

"Sorry," Jayla said, cursing herself for the obvious misstep. "Poor choice of words. But the people you are assigned to pursue…"

"Never know they're marked for elimination," Skye said. She finally settled onto the edge of the chaise, legs braced to move at any time. "In most cases they never even know they're about to die. A well-placed bullet or properly timed explosive doesn't give you time to think, 'holy shit, I'm dying now.' You're just there one minute, gone the next."

Jayla was writing furiously now, absorbing a new revelation, but she maintained her cool professional voice. "So, it matters that your targets don't suffer."

Skye's smile softened. "Look, there's guys who make their living hurting people. You know, to scare people into paying their debts or doing what they're told. Sometimes they hurt one dude to let others know what happens if they fuck up, you know? But that ain't me. My job is to liquidate specific individuals."

Jayla nodded. This was all very valuable for her work-in-progress on the inner workings of the professional assassin, but she wanted to steer the conversation back toward something that may be more helpful to her patient. She took a long drink from her water bottle and leaned forward on her desk with a conspiratorial smile.

"I was thinking, you commented that when you realized you were being followed you thought about Brandon being at risk. That mattered to you?"

"Well, yeah,' Skye said. "He saved my life, remember. Besides, he's taking a big risk siding with me over Hetman's mob. I guess I feel like I got an obligation to keep him safe. Like he's under my protection." Jayla held the smile and lowered her eyes a bit. Skye's eyes wandered the room during five seconds of silence before she added, "And I kind of like him."

Jayla stretched her smile wider and tilted her head a little to one side. "You slept with him, didn't you?" Skye nodded, returning Jayla's smile. "And how did that go?"

Skye gave a broad laugh and said, "Girl, I turned that nigga out."

Jayla shared the laugh, putting down her notebook for a moment. "Yes, yes, I'm sure you got skills, girl. But how was it for you?"

"Oh, he was up to the job," Skye said. "I think it had been a minute since he got some so shit happened pretty quick. But the second time around he showed me what he could do and, yeah, he got it going on. Checked all the boxes, rang all the bells."

Jayla could not pass this up. She leaned back in her chair, interlaced her fingers and held eye contact with Skye. "So, how did that make you feel?"

Skye gritted her teeth, clenched her fists, lowered her head and shook it back and forth. "God damn it! You always catch me. But Doc, this ain't what I wanted to talk about today."

"I can see that," Jayla said in a calm, soothing voice. "But it's important. You reacted to this man's, er, attentions. There had to be an emotional response."

"I don't need to go there."

"Well, yeah you do. This is our contract. This is our deal."

"Yeah, I know," Skye said after a heavy sigh. "But some things, you know. Besides, he was good and all, but it ain't all about that."

"Alright," Jayla said, softening again. "Tell me what it's really all about."

Skye sat with hands on her knees, looking down as if she had lost something in the carpet and was determined to find it. When she spoke, Jayla heard the unfamiliar tones of fear.

"The nights," Skye said. "It's the nights. Sometimes they get…"

Jayla allowed ten long seconds of silence, then decided to fill in the blank just to get Skye unstuck.

"Long?"

Skye nodded.

"He helped?"

"He held me," Skye said. "They don't do that. He did." Jayla wasn't sure, but she thought she may have seen a tear drop to her carpet.

"Skye, this is pivotal. This may be a breakthrough. A first important step toward repair." Skye's face snapped up and Jayla knew she had made a serious misstep. "What I mean is…"

"You saying there's something wrong with me?" Skye asked, her face flushed with rage. "You think I'm crazy or something?" Skye lunged forward with a speed that made Jayla gasp. The killer leaned forward over her psychiatrist's desk making Jayla lean all the way back in her chair.

"I am not crazy," Skye said through clenched teeth. Her left palm was flat on the desk but Jayla wondered if she even knew she had snatched up a letter opener with her right.

Fear pushed adrenaline through Jayla's body and squeezed perspiration out onto her forehead and under her arms. Feeling clammy, she struggled to maintain her composure. She knew it was important for her patient that she not back down. Respiration up and pulse pounding, she still managed to maintain eye contact and speak without shaking.

"Skye, think. You're both a highly intelligent and a highly perceptive woman. On some level you have to know there's something broken in there. Your need to kill people…"

"I don't need to kill people!" Skye snapped, stabbing a finger at Jayla. "It's just, there's people out there that need killing."

Skye stepped back a pace and Jayla knew her patient had just revealed something that neither of them had heard before. Skye actually looked a little embarrassed. She looked at her right hand with some surprise and put the letter opener down. Jayla forced her soothing smile back into place.

"Skye, damaged is not crazy," Jayla said. "But if you recognize the damage, then you can get to the place where you give yourself permission to heal. This work you do, it may be like a form of self-medicating."

Skye's brows dipped and her mouth opened a little, showing confusion. Jayla was sensing a little progress after all their months of sessions and was trying to choose the best way to proceed when she heard the opening bars of the old Queen song, "Killer Queen." Skye pulled a phone out of her hip pocket and held it to her ear. It was a cheaper model, Jayla thought, maybe the kind you throw away when you're done with it. She strained hard to hear both sides of the conversation.

"Where are you?" It was a frantic man's voice. "I was getting worried. It's been…"

"Are you at the apartment?" Skye asked. She pressed the phone harder against her head and the other voice became unintelligible, so Jayla focused on Skye's face and body language.

"No, you stay in that apartment," Skye was saying. "You're not safe on the street. There's plenty of food and anything else you need. (pause) Come on, Brandon, you know how dangerous these people are. The smart move is just to stick to the plan. Has that damned phone rung yet? Yeah, but I'm sure it will. He's going to need to make contact with Kobayashi. This guy can't stand to be in the dark for long. You know what to say. (pause) I'm in a safe place and you don't need to know where that is. Because it's complicated and none of your business. Okay. Yes. No, I'll stay here until you get that call." There was one more long pause which brought a smile to Skye's face. "Well, me too. All right, take care of yourself."

When she put her phone away Skye looked at Jayla as if daring her to ask a question. Jayla decided to take that dare but she didn't think she was asking the question Skye expected.

"Tell me again why you're here?"

"I told you, Hetman's goons are on the street looking for my black ass. If they had eyes on me, they know I'm in the building but no way they know which office I'm in."

"You couldn't defend yourself if you went home?" Jayla asked.

"You know better than that, Doc," Skye said. "But no way in hell I'm leading them to my home. Besides, not so sure I could defend Brandon."

Jayla interlaced her fingers, tilting an eye toward Skye and in a very soft voice said, "You care about him."

"What?" Skye hopped to her feet again. "No. Well, I don't know. Maybe. What if I do?"

Jayla smiled. "Then you might find out there's something even more fulfilling than completing a contract."

A light flashed on the intercom on Jayla's desk. She pushed a button in response.

"My next appointment is here," Jayla said. "I'm afraid we can't stretch the time the way
we normally can when you come after normal work hours."

"It's okay," Skye said. "I didn't want to talk any more anyway. There are a couple of shops on the ground floor. I'll just hang out there this afternoon. Okay for me to come back after five?"

"Sure," Jayla said. "We can figure something out then. After all, you have to have someplace to go."

Chapter 30

For Skye, the world was a rough circle bounded by Interstate 495, the Capitol Beltway. This was not really its own city. In addition to the District of Columbia it included a chunk of Northern Virginia and a slice of Maryland. In her world you could hear a dozen languages in a five-block walk, people did business using cards ten times as often as cash, and small businesses were ethnically segregated. Regardless of the neighborhood, 7-11s were run by Pakistanis, nail salons employed Korean women, and small eating venues were run by Greeks. The cuisine might be what you'd expect in a deli, it could call itself a diner, it might be a pizza and spaghetti place or specialize in Mexican food. Nonetheless the guy behind the counter, like the guy she was ordering from right then, was Greek.

Skye accepted her two slices of New York style pizza and soft drink and handed over a credit card. She managed to settle into a chair behind a corner table just ahead of the lunch rush. A long line quickly formed, mostly men and women in office attire. Most of them would work in the building, and the Greek guy and his two girl helpers would know what most of them wanted before they reached the counter. Most of them would accept their usual and either return to their desks to eat or take their station at their usual table in the diner and inhale their lunch. Some days Skye saw the appeal of predictability in life.

She did not like being cornered like this, but she needed to minimize her exposure. She had caught many a target unaware in a place just like this and left them bleeding out without anyone noticing her. She had no intention of being on the other side of such a meeting. But she admitted to herself that she had not recognized the danger chasing her until too late. She had left home with just the little .38 at her back and the dagger in her boot. She was ill equipped for a pitched battle. All she could do was to remain vigilant, enjoy her pizza and root beer and scurry back upstairs.

And then what? She felt an unaccustomed temptation to call Brandon. To check on him, she told herself, but quickly admitted that she really just wanted to hear his voice. How odd. And foolish. But what if she misread Hetman? What if he had somehow figured out that Milo Williams was the source of his troubles and snatched Milo? What if someone in the hotel told him what happened to Kobayashi? He might have figured out that his boy Brandon Anderson was a traitor. If he was that smart, he would never call Kobayashi's phone. He could simply put an ever-growing price on Skye's head until one of the hundreds of petty thugs and gang members inside the beltway spotted her and decided to cash in.

She had finished one slice of pizza and was sucking on her straw when she saw death walking toward her. In this case death wore a dark colored suit with a white shirt and red tie. His thin, emotionless Japanese face was familiar to her. Would he even get the Hit Man reference if she made it?

She held her second slice in her left hand while she slid her revolver out from under her jacket and held it on her right thigh under the table. The newcomer stood stiff and erect, the calm eye of the chaotic storm swirling around him. He scanned the room slowly before focusing on Skye. When he made eye contact, he kept his hands low but showed her his palms and walked toward her table. He stood by the opposite chair for a second and when she didn't speak, he pulled the chair out and sat. He kept his hands palm down on the table. The equivalent of waving a white flag of truce, Skye assumed.

"We meet again," he said.

"Yeah, I remember you," Skye replied. "You were with Kobayashi when we fought in the hotel."

"I am Riku," The man said with a small head bow. "And you are called Skye. You felled me with one blow. My master Kobayashi-san described you as an assassin of considerable skill."

"He was a hell of a fighter," Skye said, "but I didn't need to beat him in that hallway. And now he's visiting with his ancestors. So, we got beef, you and me?"

Riku blinked and Skye could almost see a translator working behind his eyes, scanning her words and reinterpreting them. After three or four seconds he smiled as understanding hit.

"Your actions were impressive. Kobayashi-san reacted to what appeared to be assault by a samurai warrior, but your attack was more that of a ninja. Deception, misdirection, well played. I can only offer respect. We have no… beef."

Skye fought not to roll her eyes. "What then? You here to deliver a message?"

"I was assigned to watch for you, as so many of us were throughout this city. Your location is now known by most of the criminal establishment in this city. There is a considerable bounty."

"You do know I could snatch your larynx out of your throat right now, right?"

Riku's face was absolutely passive. "Yes, but you won't. This place is too public, and if you were arrested – really arrested - you would be in even greater danger from Hetman's cartel. Many in the Fairfax County Detention Center are searching for you now."

"And you're telling me this why?" Skye asked.

"This Hetman. He does not command my loyalty. I am Yakuza. Those of us who arrived here with Kobayashi-san will return to Japan in the morning. I came to speak to you before we leave because you acted honorably. I understand that you are a professional assassin, and that Kobayashi-san was an assignment for you. You could have easily killed me as well. You chose not to."

"The ninth law of Assassins," Skye said. "Don't kill everyone in the room. Life's not a free fire zone."

Riku nodded as if he had heard this before. "I personally thank you for your professionalism. Beyond this, I am here to tell you three things. First, I have not shared my knowledge of the results of your actions in the Fairmont Hotel. Hetman has no direct knowledge of Kobayashi-san's death."

"I guess I owe you now," Skye said. "Thanks."

Again, Riku gave a small bow. "Also, the Yakuza are officially closing out our business arrangement with the Hetman organization. This alliance is too costly and lacks proper leadership. Even a strong, smart leader needs a solid chain of command if his soldiers are to be successful. My team and I will leave for Japan in the morning. And finally, I am instructed to assure you that there is no unfinished business between the Yakuza and you. I'm asked to obtain assurances that this is not a one-sided decision."

"You kidding?" Skye said. "My mama didn't raise no fools. I'm sure as hell not going after any Yakuza people. You guys are dangerous as hell."

"Then, you would be comfortable putting your gun away?"

Skye snickered and returned her small pistol to the back of her waistband. "Yeah, guess I can trust all that Japanese honor shit. You had some balls walking in here and stepping to me like that. I sure don't want no shit with your gang."

Riku stood, bowed one last time, turned and disappeared into the lunchtime crowd. Skye finished her now-cold pizza and less than five minutes after Riku left she was on her way up the stairs to Jayla's office.

Chapter 31

Skye had come home all smiles that day. It hadn't been perfect, but those days didn't exist at Dunbar High School. That same boy had tried to put his hand up her skirt again and the teacher didn't say a word so she had to change seats. Then after school that Puerto Rican slut had got all up in her face and she had had to beat the girl's ass. But that was life at Dunbar. Mama had told her it was once a college prep school for good black students. But all that changed in the 1950s when segregated schools were outlawed. Good news in most places, but in Washington it meant all the schools became neighborhood schools, so then they could only accept students from the ghetto neighborhood the school sat in. By the time Skye got there it was a typical ghetto school full of unmotivated, unruly and disruptive students.

But she had had that conversation with the counselor. She had been praised for her good grades and her determination to succeed. They talked about grants, scholarships, and how, if she managed just one more year of great performance, they'd find a way to get her into college. They planned college prep classes for her senior year, even if she'd have to go to school then travel to another school a couple days a week.

So when she walked into her apartment she had some good news for Mama. Of course she didn't see her right away. Mama usually napped in the afternoon. Skye didn't know what she did the rest of the day but Mama almost never cooked. Which was okay. Skye could take care of them both.

Skye went into her bedroom, shrugged off her backpack and returned to the kitchen. She moved quietly, pulling out an iron pan and Crisco. She found a couple of pieces of chicken in the refrigerator. Not quite enough for dinner. But if she made some rice it would be okay. She pulled out the pitcher and poured what turned out to be the last of the Orange Kool-Aid into a glass. She dumped a new pack into the pitcher but then remembered they were out of sugar. Mama held the welfare money but she'd let go of a couple food stamps Skye could run down to the grocery. She tapped on Mama's door to rouse her gently. At least Skye never had to worry about finding a man when she got home. Mama was married to the bottle and didn't have space in her life for a man.

"Mama?" She was surprised to hear no soft snoring. She tapped again. Nothing. She eased the door open and padded inside. The bed was unmade, as always. Tanqueray stood guard on one side of the bed, Johnny Walker on the other. But between them, just crumpled sheets. Nothing else seemed out of the ordinary except Mama's closet door was ajar. Skye went over to close it but for some reason her hand pulled the knob instead of pushing. The darkness inside was a void, empty save for two or three hangers holding nothing.

"Mama?"

A cold fist closed around Skye's heart, and for a moment she thought the earth would open up and swallow her. She HOPED the earth would open up and swallow her. There was such a traffic jam of tears rushing forward that none of them could get out. Her mouth opened and a silent cry squeaked out. In that moment she prayed for The Lord to take her, then asked him why he hated her, what had she done, why....?

And then the moment passed. She closed the closet door, nodded to herself, and said,
"Well. I guess there's plenty for dinner after all."

Sleep rolled off Skye like a thick woolen blanket, leaving her cold and unprotected. The first thin rays of sunshine were slicing into the room, strained through the slats of wooden blinds, or perhaps focused by them. Those rays brought no heat, just piercing light.

Skye swung her feet to the floor and took a couple of deep breaths. Her first thought was to wonder if she should one day tell Jayla about the dreams. Then she wondered if Brandon had gotten through the night in her bed. Her next thought was that she never wanted to be indebted to anyone the way she now was to Jayla.

The chaise was uncomfortable enough when she was being analyzed. It was even worse for sleeping on. And it had been even less comfortable to bring herself to ask Jayla if she could crash in her office overnight. Understanding the danger Skye might be in if she left the building, Jayla had agreed. She had ordered Thai food, sat with Skye to share dinner, and gone home around seven. Skye then paced, did a yoga routine, read a couple chapters of a book on psychoanalysis she found in the office, and generally burned time until ten or so when she was finally tired enough to go to sleep.

Dawn had brought renewed energy and anger at the man who had turned every petty thief and aspiring gunman in the city into a search and destroy drone after her head. But she still had no plan to end that situation. She could not stay hidden in a downtown office building forever. Nor did she see a benefit in going back out on the street and killing pursuer after pursuer until one of them got lucky. But a third choice wasn't presenting itself.

She had slept in her clothes for what she hoped was the last time, and now she needed to do something about that. She could get food in the lobby, but first she needed to handle personal hygiene. She knew there was a health club in the building. That seemed like a good place to start. She grabbed the bag she had left Carolina Herrera's with and headed for the stairs.

The smiling attendant was too chipper for six in the morning, but Skye accepted a towel and swallowed the snarky comments bouncing around her brain. Since she was there, she decided to make use of the facility. In the locker room she switched to the tights she picked up at CH, wondering about the clown who had followed her into the changing room. Did the store make him actually pay for her new clothes?

She had no lock, but no one else had come in yet so she expected her things to be pretty safe in the closed locker. As she stowed her stuff she held her phone for a second. Should she call Brandon? Say good morning? No, he might still be sleeping. Let him rest. She'd check in on him later.

For the next forty-five minutes she worked on a variety of machines designed to strengthen your back, chest, shoulders and arms. Two or three other people wandered in, dressed for business. They changed in the locker rooms and returned to work out, but no one looked at or spoke to anyone else. They each stayed in their own mental and emotional space, as was the culture there.

Having worked up a good sweat, Skye returned to the locker room, stripped, and stood under a stream of water so hot most people couldn't tolerate it. She scrubbed hard with one of the gym towels, then dried off with another. Without a comb or brush she ran her fingers through her hair to detangle it a bit.

Back at the locker she pulled her jeans back on. She abandoned the panties but had to wear the socks again to protect her feet. Fully dressed she grabbed her jacket and picked up her phone again. Then she saw that she had a voice mail. She tapped the button to listen as she walked out of the locker room and into the hall. Hearing the voice made her smile.

"Hello, Skye. It's Brandon. Sorry I missed you. But since I don't know where you are or what you're doing I can only guess you're someplace where answering your cell phone would be bad. Anyway, I'm calling not just to say good morning, but to give you some news. You know, I thought you were crazy, but you were right. Kobayashi's company phone just rang, and it was Mr. Hetman. He was pretty rude, wanted to know why he hadn't heard from Kobayashi and wanted a full report on how he was pulling the organization back together."

Skye, rushing down the stairs, slowed her pace to listen more closely.

"Well, I played it just like you said to. Told him how I was first on the scene when the Japanese killer got smoked, how I cleaned out the room and took all his personal stuff, including the phone. How I was afraid to go back to the gang because people were getting killed right and left. And of course, asked him where he was and if we could meet so I could get further instructions. He sounded rattled, but guess what? He went for it. Told me to meet him out at the point in East Potomac Park."

"Good man!" Skye said aloud. "We got him."

Then Brandon said, "Since you're not here I called an Uber and I'm on my way there now."

Wait. What? No!

"I'm sure I can find out where he's staying so you can catch him and, well, you know. Take care of him."

"No no no!" Skye had reached the lobby and was punching buttons on the phone, desperation eating at her. This was not the plan. She was to meet Hetman in

Brandon's place. This fool had no idea the kind of danger he was stepping into. She listened to the phone ring five times before going to voicemail. Shit! Why wasn't he answering? There was no verbal prompt to leave a message, but the tone was enough.

"Brandon! Brandon, God damn it do NOT go to meet Hetman. He's too dangerous. He'll have overwatch and backup, and they might decide to take you out as part of their tying up loose ends. Call me when you hear this."

Skye fell back against the wall next to the stairway door she had just come through. Did he leave the phone behind? Was he already with Hetman and didn't want to answer? How could she protect him now? Where was East Potomac Park from there, and how fast could she get there? The thoughts flew through her mind like bats trying to find their way out of a cave. But she knew what she needed to do next. She pushed an autodial button.

"Mo? It's Skye. I'm up on Connecticut Avenue. How fast can you get here?"

Chapter 32

Skye always figured East Potomac Park existed because some bureaucrat at the start of the 20th Century decided there already wasn't enough green left in The District. The man-made island sits in the Potomac River where you can see the Jefferson Monument from one side. Less than a half mile away, the other side of the island stares at the Virginia shore. A quick look at a map Mo handed her made clear why Hetman chose it. Once you got past the attractions, the pool and golf course and so on, it was a very open space. There was no sneaking up on a fellow there, and it was too public to do anything unseen. Still, people tended to spread out enough that conversations could be totally private. The southern tip was called Hains Point, a popular picnic area that could only be approached from one direction. It was the perfect meeting place.

Skye fidgeted in the back seat while Mo drove down I-395, his speed capped only by the limits of safety. Earlier, when he pulled up in front of Jayla's building, she had run out to his car, hoping that the change of clothes might fool her watchers, at least for a little while. But as her hand settled on the car's door handle her eyes were drawn to a young Latin man across the street with a kerchief tied around his head. He was sitting in an old beater that was stripped down to its primer black paint. As soon as he saw her, he picked up his phone and started stabbing at it with a finger.

"Give me a sec," she had hollered to Mo. She sprinted across the street and looped around the back of the aging

Pontiac. The driver's window was down and his elbow rested on the door. Skye reached in to gather the front of his shirt in her left hand. She yanked hard, dragging his head out the window and pressed the point of her dagger against his throat, just under his jawline. She didn't push hard, just hard enough so he would know without doubt what it was. His wide eyes told her he understood what could happen next.

"You know who I am?" she asked in a whisper. The driver shook his head rapidly. "Good, cause I don't really want to kill you, and I don't think you want to get dead. Right?" Again, an enthusiastic nod. "Whoever you're on the phone with, you tell them to pass a message for me. Y'all can follow me around all you want. I guess somebody wants to know where I am. That's okay. But if anyone interferes with my business or gets in my way, that person is going to die. Slow and messy. You understand? I ain't got time for this shit."

"I got you," the driver said. He swallowed, and his Adam's apple flicked her knife's point.

"Good. Now get gone before I forget I didn't want to kill you." She had let him go and backed away. He had started his car, slammed it into gear and took off. Skye returned to Mo's car, staring down one BMW driver who thought she should have the right of way.

Mo drove without asking anything, blasting the Ohio Players and Slave on their way. Skye stayed silent while they worked their way through the dense morning traffic, like swimming through maple syrup. She checked her phone every couple of minutes, monitoring elapsed time. She glared at drivers they squirmed past and shot mental daggers at the people in front of them, thinking their slowness could cost a life.

Skye reflected back to that first day. That day after the landlord came and discovered that Skye was living alone.

That day she was packed and waiting for someone from social services to come and take her away. Instead, he had come. He stood in the doorway, as big as a tree and as dark as a moonless night. Was he smiling? She wasn't sure.

"You don't look like no social worker."

"Gunnery Sergeant Matthias Maddox U.S. Navy, Retired. And no. Not a social worker." He stood straight and stiff, hands behind his back. He wore a suit and tie but for some reason it looked like a uniform.

"So, what you doing here?"

"I'm here, young lady, because I've been watching that school." His eyes bored into hers and she could not look away. "I was looking for something. I found you. I know how smart you are. I know how brave you are. And I know that if you go into the foster system, even for one year, it will result in a waste of all that potential. I am here to offer you the opportunity to be more. To be something better."

That was it. He held out a hand, and somehow, she knew she should go with him.

When he took her in it was like she had disappeared from the world. Or maybe, like she had moved into another world. Much later she learned that he had driven a SEAL team until age and regulations forced him into the civilian world. He had spent half his life creating, training and refining warriors and she figured he wasn't ready to stop. Which was a good thing as far as she was concerned. It was surely what drove him to find her. She was his piece of clay, and she became a different person. He was her first teacher, the first of many. He pushed her, challenged her, drove her.

Her senior year of high school was basic training. There was an hour of physical training in the morning before class. And weekends were filled with adventures. They went to the shooting range, or a swimming pool, or scuba diving. They went climbing, or caving, or sky diving. And always there was the harsh, hard drive toward perfection.

It was a hard life, but he fed her well, kept her in new clothes and a clean house and most importantly, he paid attention. He checked her homework every night, listened to what had happened in school every day, and advised her on how to handle every situation that came along. When she started martial arts lessons, he made sure her focus was not on winning, but on proper form. He said if your form was right then winning would come as long as you never quit.

She remembered thinking that this regimented, predictable world where rewards and punishments were fair and based on your performance was a perfect existence. Then she graduated and the world shifted again. They sat at the kitchen table and Papa held her diploma in his hands like she had won the medal of honor.

"Skye, I can't express how proud I am of you," he said. "Top of your class. You took in everything that school had to offer."

"Thanks, Papa, but you taught me a hell of a lot more. Stuff that matters."

He nodded. "It all matters, Skye. But I think I've taught you just about all I can. So it's time to move on."

"Got offers from half a dozen good colleges," she said, "But I wasn't really thinking about going to any of them. Kind of thought we'd just stay here a while longer."

"Nope, not staying here," Papa had said. "You need some more advanced training. But I'm picking the best people to tutor you. I know who can teach you what you need to know next. So it's time to pack. Our first stop is the Netherlands."

At the time she had no real idea what all the training was for, but it didn't really matter to her. All that mattered was pleasing the one person on earth who cared about her. Her first flight was transatlantic, and her first view of anything outside the Mid-Atlantic states came with stepping off that plane in Amsterdam.

Schiphol Airport was modern and bright and so much cleaner than she thought an airport could be. The day was bright and sunny, and she felt as if she was seeing everything in high definition. They boarded a taxi for what turned out to be a twenty-minute ride of wonder. Skye had read about the canals in Venice but had not expected them to be so plentiful or so elaborate anywhere else. She saw row houses just like back home, but they looked much narrower. And there seemed to be more bicycles than cars, although it didn't seem to slow traffic much because there were bike paths on every street she saw.

When they reached the hotel, Skye stood on the sidewalk for a moment and turned a slow three-sixty. Papa had tapped her shoulder to get her attention.

"You'll get a chance to explore the city, I promise. My girl does need to be well rounded and seeing the world is one way you do that. That's why I decided to stay in the city center. Over that way," he pointed and her eyes followed, "The Royal Palace is maybe a mile away. About a quarter of a mile that way is the Dam Square shopping area."

A voice behind them said, "There are many sightseeing tours and boat trips, but it is easy to walk to everything you might want to see."

Papa had turned, grinning, and joined in a fierce handshake with the newcomer. Heavyset with white hair and a thick, Germanic mustache, he turned curious eyes on her.

"Skye, this is Hendrick, an old Dutch friend."

"Pleased to meet you, sir," she said.

"Ach, don't call me that," Hendrick said. "I was never so arrogant as to be an officer."

They checked in quickly and went up to what turned out to be a very comfortable room decorated in bright colors. Skye's first hotel experience was a suite, and she wandered around it, breathless at the décor, the thick carpet, and the balcony full of flowers. The two men joined her on the balcony and sat while she remained standing.

"Skye," Papa had said. "I need your attention now." She knew what that meant. She took a deep breath, let it ease out of her, and focused on her mentor. Family time was over for now. It was time for business.

"Skye, this hotel room is going to be your home for the next thirty or so days."

"*My* home?"

"Yes," Papa had said. "I'll be travelling as an advisor to the American forces in Afghanistan. I'll be helping them get rid of some men who have done bad things and proven that they should not be there. You understand?"

"Yes sir," she said, but she remembered already feeling abandoned.

"While you are here, my good friend Hendrick will take care of you. You can trust him. We go back a long way. He is a good man in all respects. He is also the best sharpshooter I've ever met. With the right rifle and ammo he can hit targets too far away to see. He knows everything there is to know about being a sniper. And he has agreed to share his knowledge and experience with you."

Skye's heart had leaped at the prospect of another opportunity to excel, another chance to prove herself to Papa. Another chance to become more valuable for whatever plan he had for her. She turned to the stranger who was now family in her mind.

"Uncle Hendrick, I'm already a pretty good shot. I'm fast and I hit the bullseye almost every time."

Hendrick's eyes had wandered from Skye to Papa Maddox and back again. "I see you are much older than your age. This old bull must be the reason. If you are all that he told me you are, I can make you the best. But do you realize what it is you are training for?"

"Sure!" Skye said. "When I'm ready, I'll be able to help Papa stop the bad guys."

When Mo pulled off the highway Skye asked him to head toward Hains Point, the picnic area near the far southeast end of the island. They rolled down Ohio Drive, which circles the perimeter of the island except for the north side. Mo bypassed the pool, the golf course and other attractions, moving to the tree dotted area. He parked in a free space on the edge of Ohio Drive, in the shade of an ancient willow.

"Stay here," Skye said. "If I'm not back in fifteen…"

"No," Mo said. "Not this time. Skye, what the hell's going on?"

"No time."

"Make time," Mo said, "Or else when you get back to here I'll be gone."

Skye stared at her driver in the rearview mirror and knew he was dead serious. She didn't want to get into this now, but she needed to be able to count on Mo and realized, maybe for the first time, that she owed it to him to let him know what she had dragged him into. She hopped out of the car and jumped into the front seat. They faced each other and she was struck by the calm in his face, just waiting for her to speak.

"Okay, look," she began. "Remember that guy you picked up with me? Brandon?"

"Yeah. Seemed like a nice fellow."

"Yeah, well he's mixed up with some bad people. Right now I believe he's meeting with a major gang leader out there at the end of the park. He thinks he's going to get information from this boss, but he's in real danger."

"This gang dude got a name?" Mo asked.

Skye nodded. "Goes by the name Hetman."

"You mean like the 'head man?" Mo asked.

"I guess. He's the real deal, a serious badass."

"I've heard of this guy. One thing about driving Uber, people talk like you're not even there. So you here to pull Brandon loose from this dude?"

"Something like that," Skye said. "But I need to scope out the situation before I approach them. If they really are down at the point they'll be out in the open."

Isn't that good?" Mo asked.

"This guy's smart. He'll have overwatch. If I just walk up to them Brandon could end up dead."

"You too," Mo said, resting a hand on one of hers. "This sounds like some serious shit. Why not just call Five-O?"

Skye grinned and shook her head. "The cops are too damn slow and too damn clumsy. You call them in, you get a blood bath. Besides, this is for me to do. My job."

Mo examined her face for a moment, then slowly drew his hand back from hers. "Go do what you got to do, girl. I'll be here when you get done."

Skye squeezed his hand in thanks and got out. On their left, a thick path of grass and trees circled the park on the outside of Ohio's two narrow one-way lanes. That swath of poplars and willows along the edge of the island held the shoreline together. Outside of that was a narrow cement walking path separated from the river by a short metal railing seemingly made of lead pipes screwed together. Just beyond the railing she could see the river, a more perfect deep blue than Skye could have imagined on her own. A couple of large vessels were docked on the far side of the channel. Between them and where Skye stood, small sail boats bobbed and skimmed across the sapphire waves.

Skye had run that narrow path several times. Today she could jog down that path to the wider cement patch at the very end where Brandon and Hetman would be – *if* she had arrived in time – but instead she went to the middle of the island and walked south across the short-cut grass toward the end.

While she walked, something Mo said tickled the back of her mind. Hetman sounded like hit man but also like head man. Maybe not a name but a word. She pulled out her phone and Googled Hetman just to see what she would get.

Walking and reading on her phone, she wound up weaving around and between picnic tables, enjoying the aroma of each family's signature barbecue sauce as she passed. It forced her to notice that on this morning, everyone she could see in the park was Black. Families were loud, joyous, with kids running and laughing the way she thought kids should always be doing. She envied them. Her mother never brought her here, she never had a father cooking out and boasting about his expertise on the grill. Maybe if she did, she wouldn't be who she was now, a wolf living among wolves. Sometimes she wished she was one of the sheep.

Brandon was one of the sheep.

And there they were. Brandon's form easy for her to recognize, facing another man, shorter than he was. They would have no reason to turn toward her, not with that beautiful view beyond them, the widening channel that reached out to the horizon to meet up with wispy cotton ball clouds.

For just a moment, lost in those clouds, Skye reflected back on the day she got the news. She had travelled the world with Papa Maddox but then she was back in her city, or at least near it, in Papa's house in PG County, Maryland. He was off on one of his consulting jobs in Beirut this time, but that was fine. She had her daily routine and her studies and would surprise him when he came home with a custom

1911 pistol she had build from parts, with a Heinie black ledge rear sight and a red fiber optic sight on the front. The barrel was crowned and magna-ported, she had added a custom trigger and even extended, faceted, and angled the magazine catch herself. He'd be home soon, and the gift would give him joy.

But when the doorbell rang, she found Uncle Hendrick at the door. She had spent a month with Hendrick in the mountains learning how to hit targets that were too far away for most riflemen to even consider. The portly Dutchman with the long mustache entered with bowed head, accepted a glass of lemonade and told her in halting sentences that Papa would not be coming back. That they were working together helping American forces suppress a drug cartel's activities. How a massive explosion had caught them by surprise. How Papa never knew what hit him and there was no time to suffer and he went out the way he would have wanted, fighting the good fight.

Her heart had frozen, and she slowly lowered herself onto the sofa and stared out the wide picture window at the vast view Papa had loved. She felt that she could see the whole world from there, but where did she belong in it?

Hendrick had pulled a chair up to her and asked, softly, "What will you do now, child?"

What indeed? Papa had given her direction but now he was gone. Her compass, her roadmap, was gone. She had fantasized about a military career, but could she take orders from leaders who were less than Papa had been? She considered law enforcement, but could she follow the rules that restricted and hampered those who wore a badge. Tears welled up and she turned to Hendrick.

"Right now, I don't know. Life without Papa…"

Hendrick gave a grim nod. "Warriors die, and other warriors mourn. This is perhaps the one thing Maddox didn't teach you. But you are a grown woman, smart and tough, and after the grief your heart will lead you to your next destination.”

“Maybe. But right now…”

“Right now, if you have no immediate plan, I could use your help.”

“What? Right now? But Papa…”

“The man who ordered that explosion yet lives,” Hendricks said. “This cannot be allowed to stand. I must take him out, but I cannot do this alone. I need one person I can trust. One who can be still and shoot and disappear. One who understands the rules of the game, which I know Papa drilled into you.”

Skye’s mind wandered around the situation, looking at it from all sides as Papa had taught her. “Mercenary work?”

“Oh no,” Hendrick said, leaning back. “Merc work requires teamwork and Maddox hardly prepared you to be a team player. And this job is not military or police assistance. This is an assassination.”

And so, her course was set. She went to Beirut with her Uncle Hendrick. She had helped him finish the last assignment Papa had taken. And when she got home, she knew what she would do.

It was Hendrick who had taught her all there was to know about the work of a sniper. And it was because of him that right then, she knew what to look for.

Cover was scarce, but she knew Hetman would not appear at a meeting without backup. She scanned slowly from right to left, her eyes reaching under tables and up into trees trying to imagine where she would be if she wanted to take out the man Hetman was talking with. Could she be wrong? Was it someone on the water, or on the far shore? There was little in the way of concealment here, but she knew there had to be a place…

Then she started walking to her left. Not far from the end, the cement path had become too cracked and broken to be safe. Now there was a fence to keep joggers from continuing. Just past that stood a bramble of vine entangled trees. Dark, dense and forbidding, it was an eyesore in the midst of the lush beauty of the park.

She approached the bramble still facing the point. Her movements were slow and relaxed, like any tourist just wandering across the grounds. Soon she was crouching beside the dark, matted nest. She could just make out the human form inside. He lay prone behind a rifle that was aimed at the point. The man was invisible, unless you were looking for him, so he had good reason to ignore anyone walking past.

Skye stood slowly and took ten paces back. This needed speed if it was to work. She knelt to untie one of her running shoes and pull the lace out of it. She stood holding the lace with both hands and glanced around. Only one five-or-six-year-old noticed her. She smiled at the little girl, winked, and sprinted forward. She dived into the ball of brush, ignoring the scratches and scrapes, focused on the impact that knocked the air out of her. She knew her unexpected landing had done the same for the sniper below her.

The smell of rotting vegetation inside the natural sniper's nest almost made her gag. She pressed her forehead against the back of the shooter's head and whipped the lace around his throat. Then she pulled hard, crossing her fists under her chin, putting all her strength into tightening her make-shift garrote.

The shooter bucked and squirmed, struggling to free himself. Her arms started to ache while she clung to the shooter's back, her legs wrapping around his to hold him in place. He clutched at her arms but couldn't get enough of a grip to matter. She heard his larynx crack as the lace cut into it. With no oxygen pumping to his brain his flailing became disorganized. Cognitive ability was gone. She was only wrestling with his survival-oriented lizard brain now.

It took a long four minutes before Skye relaxed her arms, confident that there would be no more resistance. The form below her was enclosed head to toe in a camouflage <u>ghillie suit</u>, which was itself covered by a mass of Polypropylene "Strings" that looked just like moss choked grass. It was effective camouflage indeed. She knew nothing about her most recent victim, not even if he was black or white. It was a totally anonymous killing.

And a totally anonymous death. He never saw it coming, could not have anticipated he was in danger at all. His last thought may well have been to wonder who the hell was killing him. Skye seldom thought about her own end, but she realized then that she did not want to die wondering.

Enough introspection. She muscled the corpse aside and settled into the warm impression he had made in the earth. She leaned to her side to get a look at the weapon. Sweet. It was a Barrett Model 98B, a bolt-action number, chambered for a .338 Magnum. A professional choice. She liked the idea of finishing her current contract with it. If the police didn't find it after she used it and escaped, she'd come back in a couple days and take it home.

She snugged the rifle's butt into her shoulder and found the trigger with her right index finger. Then she peered through the scope and swung the weapon toward her intended target. Brandon's handsome face came into focus first. He was talking but with an air of urgency, probably spinning some long alternate history of how three of Hetman's trusted lieutenants had been killed. He had to delete his own involvement, which might not be easy, but also would not matter in a minute or two.

With a smug smile, Skye swung the barrel an inch to the right to zero in on her next target. What she saw froze the blood in her veins. This could not be her prey. But there he was: the ruddy complexion, neatly trimmed beard, salt-and-pepper hair. Milo Williams was calmly explaining something to Brandon. How could this be? What sense did it make? And then, the oddest question occurred to her. If she squeezed the trigger now, would she get paid for it? And if not, was she still obligated to complete her mission?

There were too many questions. She needed to talk directly to Milo. But if he really was the mastermind known as Hetman, confronting him could put a target on her back. He was too wily by half. It made sense that he'd have redundant protection, but there was nowhere else on the island that a shooter could get this kind of vantage point.

Not on the island.

Skye swung the rifle to her left and began scanning the water. She spotted only one vessel on the water, a small sailboat, rolling gently on the river's swells with its side turned to the island. Damn, Hetman was smart. A man lay on the deck, embracing a rifle just like the one she was holding. He was blond and wearing Spandex. His aim was locked on the same general area Skye's weapon covered. Like the man Skye had just killed, he had no reason to think he was in danger. The poor fool knew he was a hunter, but never suspecting he could be someone's prey today.

Skye settled the rifle scope on the other killer's exposed head. She held the rifle butt tight against her cheek. She took a deep breath, then let it out. Her finger pulled back on the trigger with such s smooth and gentle touch that she didn't anticipate it when the hammer fell and the pin hit the primer. In the scope she saw the target's head pop up as if he had heard something surprising. Then he slumped down on the deck, as if exhaustion had overcome him. If not for the red mess splattered on the deck on the other side of his head, it would be easy to think he just fell asleep.

He never knew he was going to die. He was never really aware of his change of status, from alive to dead. He had simply ceased. Yeah, that was the way Skye wanted it, when her time came.

She set the rifle down, waiting for any sign of alarm. The rifle barrel wore a silencer, but she knew that name to be a gross exaggeration. Sound suppressor was more accurate. It certainly reduced and altered the sound, but there was no way to make a high-powered rifle "silent" when fired. Still, the openness of the island allowed the sound to fly in all directions, with nothing bouncing it back except the river's surface. Most people would notice a foreign sound, but it could be coming from anywhere, and as long as they didn't see a body drop to the ground they wouldn't automatically think it was gunfire. The few people she could see from her hidden perch looked around with puzzled expressions for a second, then got back to enjoying their picnic.

Skye lay still for two minutes, then slowly crawled forward until she could stand and leave the sniper's nest to its previous owner. She wondered how long it would take someone to notice him there. It seemed likely he would only be discovered when people complained of the carrion eaters who would sniff him out and move in to disassemble the corpse.

She scanned the area while she stood and brushed dead vegetation off the front of her body. She had gone unnoticed except for that same little girl who stared at her as if wondering what she'd do next. Skye smiled, winked, and raised a finger to her lips in the universal signal to be quiet. The little girl giggled and returned to her play. At that age, playing was her job. Skye still had one, and she felt she should get to it.

Skye lowered her shoulders and walked as casually as she could toward the two men. They were still talking on the cracked cement semi-circle that lay at the point where the island runs out and the Washington Channel and the Anacostia River join hands and slide into the Potomac.

Her focus was on the face of Milo Williams, the man she knew as her client, but it was Brandon who noticed her first. He turned toward her, mouth agape, eyes wide. Seeing this, Milo turned toward Skye. His reaction was far more understated. He held a gentle smile until she stopped about six feet from him.

"Skye." He nodded and waited.

"Milo." No smile, but her raised brows betrayed more curiosity than he did.

"What? No," Brandon said. "Skye this is Mr. Hetman."

Milo looked at Brandon with an amused half-smile before turning back to Skye. "You two know each other. So this, then, is a set-up of some sort. Very good. You are smarter than I gave you credit for."

She turned to Brandon. "So this is the guy you been taking orders from?"

"Yes," Brandon said. "Looks like you know him too. What the hell?"

"Exactly," Skye said. Then to Milo, "I didn't get the name until I Googled it a few minutes ago. Hetman isn't a name at all, is it? It's a title."

"Very good," Milo said with a confident smile. "I wondered if anyone would catch on. Hetman has been a title of military leadership in my part of the world for centuries. Throughout much of the history of <u>Romania</u> and Moldavia, and a hundred years ago, a hetman was the highest military officer in the Ukrainian forces. It was the perfect name for me while I gathered my twenty-first century Cossacks."

Skye let him run on until he ran out. Then she nodded and asked, "So, what's this all about? You hired me to take out members of your own crime cartel. To kill your Cossacks. Who does that?"

Milo stepped to his left, smiling with way too much confidence to Skye's way of thinking. "I will admit it's a new business model as far as I know," he said. "But I put this thing together, based on sound research. Superstar criminals like Capone and Gotti get hunted down, so I stayed anonymous. If your men are all loyal to the same organization, instead of an individual, then that loyalty can be redirected from one man to another. Uniting disparate gangs was an experiment, and it was quite successful. This criminal enterprise has netted me several million dollars in a short space of time."

"Okay, so you're Moriarty, the New Napoleon of Crime. But why kill your own golden goose?"

"Well, I'll tell you…" Milo focused on the distant sniper's nest and gripped his belt with his right hand. A signal?

Now Skye allowed herself to smile. "Your boy in the bushes over there? He's grabbing a dirt nap. So, you were saying? Why put a contract out on your own guys? A couple of them were damned good, by the way."

Milo took a breath, but hardly missed a beat. "Oh, I was planning to avoid the errors organized crime leaders have made in the past. You see, every crime committed has a byproduct. Each time you make a new enemy. The victim, or a loved one, or a family member. Eventually they add up and someone comes after you. One could quit, of course, but the structure left behind is a big basket of evidence pointing to the original mastermind."

"So you hire a pro to take the organization apart," Skye said.

"Yes," Milo said. A sharp breeze came up off the river. It ruffled Skye's hair and flipped Milo's jacket just enough for her to notice the bulge of a shoulder holster.

"And what next? You just take the cash and retire into obscurity?"

Milo stepped to his left, closer to Brandon, who backed away a little. "Don't be silly," Milo said. "I can refine this model and repeat it in a dozen cities across the country."

He finally got to what she had been waiting for. His eyes flashed out to the sailboat drifting nearby and again, he gripped his belt. She allowed a couple seconds just to watch the look of triumph on his face turn to disappointment.

"Yeah, your man on the sailboat? I sent him to judgment too. You get points for smarts though. Truth is, this plan would have kept you safe if Brandon or some random moron tried to come for you. You just didn't count on me. You're pretty damn smart, but you can't set a death trap for a bitch that does this for a living."

Milo blinked and she could almost see him reconfiguring the situation in his mind. He would talk first, she decided. Then he would go for it. She circled to her left, moving just enough that only the open river was behind her, not the kids playing in the park.

"You do understand that I won't pay you to kill me. Right?"

"Maybe I should make an exception in your case," Skye said. "I'm guessing you never intended to make that last payment. You must have figured you could ghost on me. But you know, it's not good for my rep to leave a job unfinished. People will talk…"

The wind flipped Milo's tie. Skye saw the shore in the distance behind him. She was still on the fence. Was deceiving her and making a contract under false pretenses a capital offense?

"Or, we can make a deal for the future," Milo said. "I'm going to gather the gangs in Chicago the same way. You could clean up there after a year or so."

"Yeah, like I'd trust you after this. I don't see how anybody could. What kind of a dick kills his own son to get a gang going?"

"What?"

It was Brandon, louder than either of the others had been. He turned to Milo, stepping between the crime boss and Skye for just a second. She pulled her revolver from the back of her belt but held it against her thigh. She expected Milo to draw on her. As soon as she spotted his weapon in his hand, she could end his time on earth, toss her gun into the Potomac, grab Brandon and disappear.

But Milo did not aim at her. He shoved the muzzle of his gun into Brandon's ribs.

Damn! Shit just got real, Skye thought.

"Don't be stupid," he said. "I don't even have a kid. I invented a son and, as a well known recluse, no one ever wondered why they didn't see him."

"But somebody got kidnapped." Skye said

"I just grabbed some little snot off the street and fed him to that MS-13 nitwit to establish my street cred. After that, when I put the word out, I knew nobody would refuse to pay ransom."

"You're even more disgusting than I thought," Brandon said.

"Like I care what you think of me," Milo said, pushing Brandon toward the picnic area. "But at least you know I'm not afraid to kill. So, you and I will just step over to my car now."

Skye laughed, following. "Before you can open a car door I'll bust a cap in both your asses. What makes you think I care about this asshole?"

"Seriously?" Milo said. "Anybody who can see your face can see that you care about him. You let me drive away, he lives."

Milo side stepped through the Hains Point picnic area toward the parking lot. Most of the people ignored him, focused on their families, their food on the grill, or the intense checker game they were in the middle of. Those few who noticed what was happening turned away, pointedly minding their business. This was clearly a personal issue they didn't want to get involved in. These were not the kind of people who call 9-1-1. These were people who would let their neighbors handle their own business and would expect the same respect in return.

While most would rejoice in a bright, sunny day like this one, Skye hated the need to squint and wished she had sunglasses or at least a ball cap with a brim. She wove between picnic tables, maintaining a constant five-yard distance from Milo. She hardly noticed when the grass under her feet turned to asphalt. Then they were walking between cars in the parking lot. Milo stopped behind a white BMW and grinned.

"Now you're going to watch me get in my car and drive away, with this gun in your boyfriend's ribs."

"He's not…" Skye moved two feet closer. "I wasn't sure, you know. I might have let you go if you hadn't threatened him. Now? You got to go."

"Sorry girl," Milo said. "It's not my time."

Then Skye blinked but held her face still. That was Mo walking up behind Milo. He must have gotten out of his car to see what was keeping her so long. From where he was she thought he could see her gun, and probably Milo's. Mo was looking from side to side as if searching for help, but actually she suspected he was trying to decide what to do next. She wanted to shout to Mo to get back in his car. He didn't need to see this.

Then he seemed to decide. His fist clenched. He took a deep breath and shouted the one word he must have thought would shake Milo up.

"Police!"

Milo spun toward Mo, gun raised. Skye fired a tenth of a second later. Her bullet smacked into the side of Milo's neck, pushing a good deal of flesh and a serious spray of blood out the other side. Milo spun back, already dead but reflex pressing him to defend himself. Halfway back to facing Skye his finger clenched and his gun discharged. The muzzle of Milo's pistol was less than an inch from Brandon's chest when the nine-millimeter pellet spun through the barrel, cracked through Brandon's sternum and dived into his heart. Brandon's expression was surprise, not pain, as both men collapsed.

"No!" Skye shouted, rushing forward. She slid to her knees beside Brandon, scooping up his head and cradling it in her lap. She knew some basic first aid but there was no point trying to use it. She could feel that Brandon's spirit or soul or whatever it was that was his living essence had already moved on, leaving an empty shell. Her hands were shaking for some reason, her pulse racing like it never had when she ended a life. And for an instant she was unaware of her surroundings. She zoomed back into sharp focus when she heard Mo screaming at her.

"Skye, for God's sake come on!"

Skye turned to see that Mo had pulled his car up right beside her. She spun, expecting a crowd of onlookers, but only three or four people were close enough to be watching. They must have heard the shots. But the "Mind your own business" ethos in Washington was stronger than most residents' curiosity. And so, she might just escape without being identified, if she could take the bulk of the evidence with her.

Her mind went into high gear, despite unexpected hand tremors and her heart having just learned the drum line to Earth, Wind and Fire's Boogie Wonderland. None of the last half hour was in her plans but she was adapting. She knew that even when you're writing the sheet music, life is a tune you often have to play by ear. Mentally thumbing through a variety of optional scenarios she saw a path to a relatively clean finish. It started with yanking the back door of Mo's Honda open. But she didn't jump in. Instead she bent at her knees and grabbed Milo under his shoulders.

"Come on, you bastard," she muttered through clenched teeth as she pulled him up off the ground. First sitting on the back seat, then sliding over, she hauled Milo's corpse into the car. The blood pulsing from his neck was already down to a trickle, but she knew she'd have to get Mo's car detailed anyway. She popped the other side door and slid out. Then she pulled Milo into a sitting position, slammed that side door closed and ran around to the other side. Now for the hard part.

Skye knelt beside Brandon and looked into his startled eyes, already clouding over. She bent to hug him to her, then straightened up. Out the corner of her eye she saw Mo suddenly standing beside her.

"Here, let me help…"

"No," she snapped, louder than intended. "Get back in the car. I got this."

Skye's eyes and stomach clenched as she pulled herself to her feet, spun, and shoved Brandon into the car. She fell forward onto him for a second, but then pushed him upright and moved his legs over. She shoved a hand into her jacket pocket and picked up Milo's gun with that hand, then hip-checked Brandon to get seated beside him and pulled the door shut.

"Get us out of here," she screamed to Mo. "Head for Virginia. Do you need the address of the Fairfax County government complex?"

"I can pull it up on the GPS," Mo said, "But Jesus, Skye you can't sit back there with those…"

"No time to stop and switch seats," she said, dropping her face into her hands. "Just drive."

In her corner of the backseat Skye tossed Milo's pistol onto the floor by his feet. Then she pulled out her own pistol. She used her shirt to wipe it all over, making sure not even any partial prints could remain. Then she took a deep breath and reached for Brandon's right hand. She wrapped his hand around the grip and carefully pressed the pad of his index finger against the trigger. She didn't understand why her face was wet. That wasn't helping anything. Anyway, now she just needed his left hand for prints on the cylinder from loading the revolver. That would be enough. She pulled on his other arm.

Fuck!

He was wearing his new watch.

Skye's face collapsed in on itself. The cogs and flywheels of her brain all jammed. She dropped his arm, suddenly gasping for breath. All of a sudden nothing made sense, and it felt like the whole world was spinning down a dark, narrow drain. She turned her face into the corner where the seat met the door and moaned deep inside herself.

Chapter 33

It took Orson Rissik a moment to size up the mature African American man who appeared in his office. The gray tips on his sideburns were the only indication that he was past fifty, but in Rissik's experience Black men aged more slowly than their white counterparts. His posture and manners marked him as old school, proud but courteous. You see that in hotel workers, waiters, chauffeurs. His clothes said lower middle class but pushing upward. A church goer, Rissik guessed, whose wife and children lived better than he did, wore better clothes, were well taken care of at Christmas. A man to respect.

After his ten-second appraisal, Rissik stood and extended a hand. "Good afternoon, sir. Orson Rissik. How may I help you?"

The visitor seemed startled but recovered quickly and took Rissik's hand in a strong grip. "Morris Gardner. You're Detective Orson Rissik?"

He had already identified himself, there was a name plate on his desk, and the man had been directed to him by someone. So, this man felt he could not take the slightest risk of talking to the wrong person.

"I am indeed," Rissik said. "Now, how can I help you?"

"You know Skye?" Mo asked.

"Is this the woman I recently arrested as Cloudy St. James?"

"Yes," Mo said. "She told me you'd know her by that name."

Rissik smiled. "I understand your need to be careful. But my sense is that you're just the messenger. Will Ms. St. James be visiting soon?"

Mo nodded. "She's waiting now in the parking garage. She asks that you join her, alone, to discuss what she believes will be the satisfactory conclusion of a major case you've been working on."

As he stepped into the parking garage, Rissik knew that his instincts could be leading him into a trap. He didn't know this messenger he was following. If it was a setup he was alone and could never employ his service weapon before someone could stand from between any two of these cars and put a bullet in his brain. He wasn't sure just why he trusted this man or the woman who apparently sent him. But he'd made a career of trusting his gut, and it was too late to turn back now.

And there she was, standing in the empty space beside a car that was the same make and model as his own. Rissik could see the backs of two male heads through the rear window. She leaned against the car but was clearly not relaxed. In his earlier meetings with this woman she had been jovial, confident and somehow charming if it made sense to apply that word to a professional killer. This time she seemed colder somehow.

The Black man stepped to the side, letting Rissik take the lead. Their steps echoed through the garage with a hollow sound, emphasizing how alone they were. Rissik stopped six feet from her and slid his hands into his pockets.

"Thanks for coming back, Ms. St. James. Was your hunting trip a success?"

Skye returned a small smile. "Call me Skye, please. And you look like you're not sure what answer you really want. But, yeah, things worked out for us. Your goal, and mine.

Completed. It's all good. Or at least, it will be if you're willing to do what I ask."

Rissik looked down and shook his head, grinning. "Yep, here it comes. And now I set both my feet on that slippery slope."

"Hey, you don't have to break the law or nothing," Skye said. "In fact, If I've got this worked out right, all you might have to do is not be a real good detective."

That raised one of Rissik's eyebrows. After thinking for a couple seconds, he gave one long, slow nod. "I see. You're saying you're going to give me a neat little package and all's well so long as I don't dig too deep. Is that it?"

Skye waved him closer. "You and me, we only had one thing in common when we met. We both wanted this Hetman character stopped from building a criminal enterprise in the DMV. Am I right?"

"To be clear, I wanted him found and arrested," Rissik said. "If I'm not mistaken you were hired by one Milo Williams to murder the man."

"Murder is a harsh word, Detective," Skye said. "And in this case, it don't even apply." With that she yanked the car's rear door open and reached in. She gripped the front of a man's shirt and pulled. The man hung there, face up, well past the point of being able to resist as Rissik could see. He was staring down into the face of a corpse and that face looked familiar.

"This here's Hetman," Skye said. "I knew him as Milo Williams. And yeah, he hired a pro to eliminate several members of his own team so it would all fall apart when he disappeared."

"I'm guessing his disappearance didn't go as planned."

"He lied to me about the plan," Skye said. "He figured he'd disappear before I found him. He figured wrong."

"So you found him, and you killed him," Rissik said.

"Whoa," Skye said, pushing Milo back into the car. "Pump the brakes, would you? You see that other guy in the back seat. He was one of Hetman's inside men. He's got ID on him, and when you check out his apartment, I'm betting you find plenty of evidence to confirm that shit."

"You killed them both."

"Slow your roll, Detective," Skye said in a harsher tone. "I did not kill them both. When your crime scene boys get in there, they'll find forensic evidence and fingerprints showing that these two had a beef and, from the looks of things, shot each other."

Rissik glanced at the sticker on Mo's windshield. "Shot each other in the back seat of an Uber?"

"First of all, his car," Skye said, pointing at Mo. "He's a Uber driver. Second of all, they didn't shoot each other in the car. Your crime scene boys will tell you there ain't nowhere near enough blood in the car."

"So what? They shot each other then called for a ride home?"

"You're killing me, Detective," Skye said, walking around to Mo. "They was dead, both of them, and this fellow, Mo here, will testify that some bitch stopped his car, shoved these two bodies and their guns in it, and told him if he wanted his family to stay healthy he'd drive them both here and ask for you."

Rissik turned to Mo. "That your story?"

"Just like she said," Mo replied. "I'm sitting there in my car and this woman stopped me and dragged these two dead guys into my back seat."

Rissik folded his arms and took two steps back. "So these two, Hetman and one of his thugs, gunned each other down in some public place."

Skye nodded. "Yep. East Potomac Park, actually. If you want to, you'll probably find a few witnesses to that. Their stories will be confused, like witnesses always are, but they'll all agree about the bitch dragging the two dead guys into the car."

"Right," Rissik said. "A neat little package. Except how do I know this guy's Hetman? I'm betting he doesn't have ID with that name on it."

He saw a cloud pass over Skye's face, but she quickly returned to full business mode. This was a hard woman, but something had surely scratched her armor this day. When she pointed into the car she looked away from it.

"The other dead guy was Hetman's right-hand man. Kept all the records and was Hetman's mouthpiece to the others so nobody else would know his face. All you got to do is follow the money. I'm sure it will eventually lead you to Milo Williams' accounts. And as you know, he was connected to bosses in a half dozen major gangs. Ought to be some sweet intel in there. This guy can get the credit for bringing a lot of scumbags down."

Skye let go of Milo and Rissik stared down into the face frozen in a rictus of fear. "Did you say Hetman's men didn't know who he was? If that's true, they won't know he's dead. Sure would be nice if I could round them up while they're in the dark. We could totally gut the organization."

Skye tilted her head to one side, looking at Rissik with her mouth open in what he interpreted as curiosity. "So tell me, how real is this deal between us? You going to take the story and close your case? Are we good?"

"How do you mean?" Rissik asked.

Skye stared hard into his eyes. "Are you coming after me, Detective?"

Her hands hung open at her sides but to Rissik it always felt like she was armed. But just the question seemed a statement of respect, and he was prepared to return it.

"Can't condone murder," Rissik said. "And I know the story is, if not a straight-out lie, then at least a hard spin on the truth. But if it hangs together, we'll run with it. And to be clear, I know that if I wanted to I could dig down to the truth and bring you in. But no, to answer your question directly, I'm not coming after you."

"So what about Cloudy St. James?"

"Well, I was holding her in relation to the Milo Williams missing persons case." Rissik looked again at the dead man hanging out of the car door. "As Mr. Williams is no longer missing, I can process the paperwork to have Ms. St. James released. The system is convoluted enough that I can manage that without anyone having to actually see her."

Rissik smiled. Skye returned it and nodded toward Mo. "In that case, you get the bonus prize. Mo here has an address for you. It's a place down on M Street in the District. Little shithole bar. It's connected to an illegal casino that doubles as a high-end whore house. Hetman's boys was running the games and running whores out of there. Upstairs you'll find the nerve center of the operation, at least the gambling, the hooking and the kidnapping part. Raid that place, and I think you'll rip the guts out of the whole Hetman setup."

"I'll pass that intel on and leave that mess to the DC boys," Rissik said, crossing his arms again and leaning back on the car's trunk. "You know, you've done a lot of good here, even if it does sound like it was mostly by accident. I'd hate to have to come up against you during a future case. Before that happens, why don't you consider coming over to the side of the angels?"

"I don't know," Skye said. "Maybe I already am? Maybe I'm an angel myself. The angel of death."

Chapter 34

Despite Jayla's protests, Skye had insisted on bringing a bottle of wine to her session. It wasn't exactly professional, but then, neither was meeting a client in her office at 8pm. Still, after three days out of contact this was when Skye wanted to come in and Jayla had agreed. So there they sat, in the dark again except for the city lights that wandered in through the window. Jayla had changed back into a navy blue power suit and matching heels. Skye wore jeans with an oversized plaid shirt that obscured her form and a puffy afro wig. Was she hiding herself?

After filling two big glasses with shiraz, Skye plopped onto the chaise. Jayla decided to take her glass to the chair that was not shielded by the desk. Skye sat facing the desk but hunched over forward. She swallowed a third of the wine in her glass and turned her head to the left to speak to Jayla.

"So, a lot has happened since the last time I was here," Skye began. "It's the kind of stuff you usually want to know about, so I figured I'd just lay it all out for you, then you can ask your usual pain-in-the-ass questions and I'll feel like I'm holding up my end of our deal."

"That will be fine," Jayla said. "It sounds as if you completed your assignment. Is that right?"

"Yeah, I eradicated the designated asshole," Skye said.

"But you're not showing your usual level of emotional fulfillment and satisfaction," Jayla said.

"Yeah, well shit got complicated." From there Skye launched into the flow of events beginning with the phone call from Brandon. Jayla was surprised at the level of detail Skye shared, far more granularity than in the past. The matter-of-fact way that Skye described killing men, both up close with her hands and at the other end of a telescopic sight, chilled Jayla. She had seen this flat affect before, but not from this patient. Still, she listened silently while Skye poured out her story and took copious detailed notes. The retelling slowed for a moment when Skye got to the part about wrestling two grown men's bodies into the back seat of a car. A change in her voice implied that one body was much heavier than the other and Jayla made a note that the difference was more likely psychological than physical. She also noted that the retelling changed there. After a stream of very detailed description, the sentence "We drove to the Virginia cop's office and gave him a story along with the two bodies," was jarring.

"So you and this Mo worked out a story to explain events and, I suppose, to forestall a criminal investigation," Jayla said. "How in the world were you able to do that? It seems unlikely that any of this was part of your original intent."

"Oh, hell no," Skye said. "But we were in it, and I had to come up with a way out of it. When you're in that spot you kind of go into automatic, problem solver mode. My training said got to come up with something quick. Assassin's law number 16. If you can't control the kill, control the aftermath. A good, thorough cleanup is what really scares the shit out of people. Besides, I couldn't leave Mo holding the bag, could I?"

Jayla offered a tentative smile. "Of course not. You would not abandon a friend, the way your parents abandoned you."

Skye's eyes flashed at her, then cooled and narrowed. "It ain't like… well, maybe he is a friend. Kind of. I count on him. And he always comes through, just like out there on that island. I owe him."

"And you always pay your debts," Jayla said. "Just as you expect others to do. But it sounds like you left Mo with the police to spin his carefully crafted story. How did you get home?"

"He's not the only Uber driver in town," Skye said. "I just called another to bring me back. I'll square it all up with Mo in a couple days when I'm sure he's not under anybody's magnifying glass. Hated to leave him there, though. And to leave Brandon behind."

"That must have been hard," Jayla said, her sympathy really a thinly disguised question.

"Yeah," Skye said, her face displaying unaccustomed surprise and confusion. "I didn't want to just leave him there in that car with that little shit that conned me. I don't even know what will happen to him."

"Him," Jayla said softly. "Not them."

"Fuck Milo," Skye said, in the same soft tones. "Talking about Brandon. Will the cops be able to find any family? If nobody claims a body do they just give it to a med school or something? And I should have grabbed that watch. Will somebody get it? I mean, I got no idea what will happen to him."

Jayla nodded, paused for a beat, and asked, "How does that make you…?"

Skye raised a palm toward her. She emptied her glass, then hung her head. Her eyes were clenched tight, but water still leaked out.

"It feels like shit. At first I was like, he can't be dead. But point-blank bullets in the heart are hard to argue with. Then I was just pissed off. At Milo, then at me for letting that shit go down like that. This. THIS!" Finally, Skye looked up to make eye contact with her therapist. "Why it got to feel like this?"

Jayla's training kept her detached from her patient's experience, even when she could relate to it. And despite the pain she saw her patient was feeling, she also saw the leading edge of a breakthrough.

"Skye, what you're feeling is the normal, healthy response of grief. When we lose someone or something we care about, we grieve."

"You ain't been listening," Skye snapped, fists clenched. "I didn't give two shits about that nigga." Then her voice dropped. "He didn't like me to call him that."

The comment startled Jayla, and she scribbled a few more notes into her book. She let a few seconds of silence fill the room. Then she took a deep breath and pushed an idea.

"Skye, I think you need some time to put all of this into perspective. Accept that this job has indeed been a bit more complicated than previous work, more emotionally complex. Maybe it's the time to consider another way of life, a different profession."

"No!" Skye said, standing. "What I need is work. I need to kill somebody. I need to get pointed at some asshole that needs killing. Point and shoot. That's when the world makes sense. That's when there ain't time to hurt."

"Please, Skye," Jayla said. "We are all changed by life events. This is how we learn. But when things don't go according to plan, we have to be careful not to learn the wrong lesson."

"You right," Skye said, jabbing a finger at Jayla. "But I got this one straight. Don't get involved with people that's connected to the target." Skye turned toward the door, an abrupt signal that the session was over.

"Skye, wait," Jayla called. "There's more to this. Consider how you will feel in the future when you think of Brandon Anderson. Trust and believe, you will think of him."

"Why should I?" Skye tossed over her shoulder as she gripped the doorknob. "The bastard's dead."

EPILOG

"Squeeze it real easy now. And hold it tight like I showed you."

Skye remembered the boom the first time she pulled a trigger. She figured her little student would always remember the crack from the rifle today. You never forget your first.

Carla looked up, saw the .22 caliber hole in the paper target and burst into a huge grin that lit up her whole face.

"I did it," the girl said, over and over again. "I did it, I really did it!"

"Yeah girl, you did." Skye stood beside the twelve-year-old. She would be a woman soon, and this afternoon would add to her self-confidence in ways her parents would never understand.

It had been tricky, finding her down in Richmond, getting her cell phone number, making contact, and arranging for her to skip school for the first time in her life. But Skye knew her parents saw her as a dangerous criminal. They would never agree to let their little girl go anywhere with her, let alone a firing range.

"Can I go again?"

"Sure," Skye said. "There are ten rounds in the magazine, and you don't have to worry about recoil with a twenty-two. Just keep the butt snug up into your shoulder."

Carla looked over the rifle's iron sights and pushed her chin forward just a little. She had the focus and had already mastered the breathing. She squeezed the trigger and put three more shots into the target in a respectable little grouping for a beginner.

"This is so fun," Carla said, sitting back. "Thank you so much for bringing me. Mom and Daddy, they think guns are bad, but this is just… just cool. I know we can't stay long but, can we do this again?"

"If we can keep this our little secret, maybe I'll come down again next month. And maybe we can try something a little bigger."

"Our little secret," Carla repeated with an impish smile. "I do like having a grownup friend. You're like a cool aunt who lets you do stuff your parents don't like."

"Hey, I ain't old enough to be no aunt." But Skye laughed.

There was so much she could teach this girl that her parents and school would never think about. And it felt good to pass on some of what she knew. And more time with Carla was something she could look forward to.

"You're going to be okay, Carla. We both will be."

AUTHOR BIO

Austin S. Camacho is the author of eight novels about Washington DC-based private eye Hannibal Jones, five in the Stark and O'Brien international adventure-thriller series, and the detective novel Beyond Blue. His short stories have been featured in several anthologies and he is featured in the Edgar nominated African American Mystery Writers: A Historical and Thematic Study by Frankie Y. Bailey. He is a past president of the Maryland Writers Association, past Vice President of the Virginia Writers Club, and one of the creators of the Creatures, Crimes & Creativity (C^3) literary conference.

To My Readers…

First, THANK YOU for going on this thrilling ride with my new action character Skye. She has a lot more exciting adventures ahead and I hope you follow her through them.

I love to hear from my readers! After you've read my novel please do send me some feedback. Your opinions and reactions will help me with shaping future novels. You can write to me at ascamacho@hotmail.com and I will always respond. You can also reach me through my website – www.ascamacho.com – see my latest news on Facebook https://www.facebook.com/austin.camacho.author and follow my random meanderings on my blog https://ascamacho.blogspot.com

The only thing better than hearing from my readers is meeting them! So, if you're a member of a book club, I would love to see you. If your group decides to read one of my books I would be most happy to attend the meeting when you talk about it. That way I can answer any questions you have and fill you in on the background of how that particular book came to be (and bring along some special gifts.)

Thanks again for reading my work, and I hope I get the chance to meet you or hear from you in the future.

Ciao, for niao,
Austin